UNTHOLOGY 3

2012

UNTHANK BOOKS

Mark Bond-Webster.
Bradenton, January 2013.

'Wisdom begins in wonder.'
Socrates.

. First published in 2012

By Unthank Books
www.unthankbooks.com

Printed in England by Lightning Source, Milton Keynes

ISBN 978-0-9572897-0-3

Edited by Robin Jones and Ashley Stokes

Cover design by Jenny Swindells

CONTENTS
UNTHOLOGY 3

Introduction

– The Editors –

This is Hardcore.

According to some marketing types, 2012 was to be The Year of the Short Story. As it always does, the money said differently, with 2012 being very much the year of apishly written softcore pornography.

In these uncertain, frightening and recessionary times (and not just in the world of publishing) it's only natural to want to switch off the daily terror and hide in a warm fantasy. It's something of a shame here that the chosen fantasy is EL James' *Fifty Shades* series where the repetitious copulation of sock puppets stands-in as a love story. *Fifty Shades* is "Double-Dip Fiction", index-linked to the flow and flight of money, its author a satellite of the bankers and financiers who willed these times into being. Just like few regulators and fiscal overseers foresaw the 2008 crash, no marketing genius or trendspotter in publishing predicted the rise of apishly written softcore pornography in 2012. This says a lot about experts. So why not make a few more unscientific analogies and gross generalisations about the connection between the financial crisis and apishly written softcore pornography. We are championing the art of fiction, after all . . . it doesn't matter.

Earnestness and shamelessness are personality traits that both the blockbuster writer and rapacious banker have in common (see master of boilerplate fiction Lee Child's recent statement that he could write most 'literary novels' in two weeks). Likewise, isn't Dan Brown embarrassed that he believed and then made a fortune by appropriating the crankish gibberings contained in *The Holy Blood and the Holy Grail*? In the style of a Dan Brown melodrama the comparison can be taken further. The architects of the financial crash, like EL James, disregard the first principles of their trade. Both are paid handsomely for something that neither is marginally proficient at. Equally for both, there seems to be no rebuke, no opprobrium and there is immunity from prosecution.

To criticize either group is to be written off as merely jealous. However important, however useful you think 'serious fiction' is; however shaming the idea that a mature person in her forties could even *admit* to having *read* the *Twilight* series, let alone sat down in all earnestness to write apishly written softcore pornographic fan fiction; however morally and culturally wrong it is that random porn-typing equates to mass success; however correct you may well be in this opinion, however much EL James should be embarrassed by the gutter-stoop nature of her ambition she has vast wealth and is therefore better. You're jealous and a snob so shut it and change: give the people what they want.

Lets not overcomplicate or overload this. Let's hope this is taken as a parody of a rant, a jokey passage, a backhanded compliment (even though it ruins the effect, sometimes you have to spell these things out.) Let's revise our opinion of EL James. Hats off to EL James and her beguiling *Fifty Shades of Grey*. Like easy credit, people have been given what they want. Like unearned wealth and status, people have been given what they want. Everyone wants an easy ride, so everyone has got what he or she wanted. Sometimes an author comes along who, however inadvertently, however flukishly exposes something hiding under the skin of the culture. As Lady Macbeth says, 'To beguile the time / Look like the time.' *Fifty Shades* looks very much like the times to us. How have the priapic, one-dimensional rich and the superficially suave experts who merely act the part and coin nothing, treated us all? Is this what we really wanted? Was this our secret dream?

Earlier this year, a notorious currency speculator and *rentier* class goon (to hell with libel, let's name names: it was Rupert 'Bladder O'Bolly' Spassky) made a casual remark to *Unthology*: 'You must give people what they want.'

We said a resolute, steadfast, 'Non!'

Welcome to *Unthology No.3*.

PS: there is some sex in it

Terra Cotta

- David Rose -

Please keep hold of the rope and move to the bell. The carpet also will guide you.

The walls, I should explain, are a pale terracotta; a story in itself.

Originally they were green, an approximation to the colour of baize, in imitation of the Royal Academy. Also an indication of our Benefactor's love of billiards. Which love, alas, precipitated the death of his wife. Clad only in a green baize kimono to attract his attention, she tripped down the marble stairs. On seeing her body, fearing both the rape of his wife and the vandalization of his billiard table, he was hit by a heart attack, giving him time only to adjust the terms of his bequest, namely the stipulation that the walls be repainted to match the ossuaries in which their remains now lie.

Enough scene-setting.

Our first painting, ladies, gentlemen (please gather round) is from the Fifteenth century, depicting an elderly man in his study, with a large wart on his nose and a small dog in his lap. His tunic is magenta, his jerkin black, his complexion - background to the wart - is florid, clashing, I'm sorry to say, with the terracotta wall. His dog, whose breed has so far eluded the scholars, blends in part with the jerkin, and

3

echoes, in others, the wart. Its ears are pricked. It misses its mistress.

Through the window to the right, we look out onto the landscape: stylized, Italianate table-top mountain, columnar cypresses, toward which winds the road along which its mistress travels. She is on a pilgrimage to the tomb of St. Silvio, besides which lies also the grave of her betrothed, stabbed to death by cutpurses for the relic he carried a sliver of apostolic sandal given him by the woman to ward off poxes after the lunar eclipse.

After impressing the grave with her knees she is now travelling home with her maid.

What is the relationship of the man to the woman? Her husband from a later betrothal? Father, father-in-law, financial adviser? We cannot tell, as she has yet to appear. Only we and the dog anticipate her presence. Or are we misreading the vacancy of those eyes of Raw Umber?

Raw Umber predominates in our next painting, along with Burnt Sienna, establishing the tonal values. A still life, ladies, of exceptional stillness, from three centuries later.

Against the even Umber background, on a rough shelf of Ochre graining, stand - if that is not too vibrant a verb - a jug of milky glazed earthenware and a bottle of absolute transparency.

In the immediate foreground right, five figs tremble, held in the gravitational pull of the loaf in the middleground left, its texture crumbling as we look, which half hides a pewter skillet almost containing a fish, a herring, its drying scales still shimmering silver with flecks of Hooker's Green.

Tempting though it is, to work the figs, fish and bread into scriptural allegory would put us on the wrong track entirely.

This is rather the setting of a Friendship Feast. Ad hoc and informal, groups of Anti-enthusiasts would meet, the host being rotated weekly, to plot trade agreements and debate the latest Enlightenment tract. The theme for this group, this evening, was to have been Newtonian optics, surmised from the empty bottle. Alas it will not take place. There is one fig missing.

The fig, we may guess, was that week's pass-fruit. As six was the usual quorum, one has yet to appear. Betrayed by a sister-in-law to a lover with debts, he has been waylaid and stoned, possibly to death, by a small enthusiastic mob. So the jug remains motionless, the last tics of the fish's tail give out, and the five figs tremble on for eternity.

But the moment cannot be abolished - it is historical fact - and though the air inside grows musty, the bottle still holds its *clarté* though empty of claret, and the Burnt Sienna now absorbs *our* light.

Clarity of air and its distortion by distance is in part the subject of our next painting, of horizontal layout: a Dutch riverscape, late Seventeenth century.

The river flows across the middle foreground, goldenly reflecting the turreted wood and flat-topped hills of the background, beneath the sweep of Ultramarine sky and Cobalt-tinged cloud.

The light, from the left, spills across the foreground bank, highlighting the humped cattle who rhyme morphically with the hills behind. Our gaze, registering first the angler in the left hand corner, travels across the carpet of sunlight, up the trunk of the oak barring our egress on the far right, back down the trunks of parasolid beeches, to rest (cunningly conspired) on the figure of the horseman who forms the real subject of our interest.

His cloaked back and horse's rump are toward us, his gaze directed over the cows toward the hills. You would just make out, were you sighted, the short sword in his right boot. It is, he hopes, a souvenir; he hopes not to use it again. But since this is year three of the Nine Years War, the chances are he will.

But maybe next time it will be to impale a Frenchman, rather than cutting free the corpse of his friend from entangling stirrup, and loosening the hardened pan for his grave.

Were he now to dismount, we would notice the limp in his left leg, caused not by grapeshot or cuirass, but by his mistress' donning his spurs and riding him in celebration of his return.

But he does not dismount, he remains in his saddle, gazing leftward in the golden light.

Our next picture is far removed from the Low Countries in time and space - a mountainscape by a Chinese, in ink and colour.

A winter journey. Sheer and sharply drawn cliffs, *literati* pines, cloud no more than a breath on the paper, pavilion roof in the valley, and a hut on the summit.

A row of figures in faded Vermilion file up the mountain ridge from right to left. There have been rumours of an icicle formation in the perfect shape of a lotus. They hope to see this, to use it in their contemplation.

Beside the hut is a stone tablet inscribed 'Reach out - touch the moon'. An ice lotus in the light of the full near moon - more than worth the hardships of the journey.

They carry lanterns and tea bowls, and potted trees, this being the month of winter sacrifices. We can make out the head of a packhorse. And the rope of twisted jute looping from figure to figure, waist to waist. We could, under magnification, see the frayed end trailing from the figure who is now last of the file.   Their contemplation of the lotus, their meditation on transience, will have an added sorrow, a sharper focus.

They are nearly at the summit.

Summits, valleys, several crevasses are prominent in our next painting, gentlemen, a study of a nude, female, naturally, since we are now in the Nineteenth century. But this is no ice maiden. Rather, a body of Southern warmth, with skin tones of Gambodge, Raw Sienna, Yellow Ochre and shadows of Rose Lake, cleverly counterpointed by the Chrome Green of the towel slipping from her shoulders.

Her back is toward us, partially turned on its axis, her gaze just engaging ours. But her mind is elsewhere.

On the fruit on the sideboard? Hard to make out in the half shadow: peaches, mangoes, maybe avocado. Plump in the polished wood bowl. Their brown tinge may just be the artist's delight in the subtlety of shade, or discolouration of the varnish, possibly no more.

Either way, the fruit is there for consumption. And by their morphic echo we are led back to the convex of a breast, rhyming in turn with the cheek above and thigh below, emphasising the ripple of flesh in its brushed solidity.

6

That solidity of flesh in turn hides from view a second bowl, of surgical steel, flecked on its rim with a sprinkle of Rose Madder and a slur of Payne's Gray.

In the background right, taking its cue from the towel, the Ultramarine curtain bellies in the breeze. And beyond, the life of the streets, trade, traffic, gossip, trees.

For life must go on.

Which is exactly what happens in our next painting, ladies, which normally you would have to step back to admire: life, joie de vivre, bustle, made busier by the brushstrokes - nervously jabbed points of colour, dots of paint unthinned. In fine, a *pointilliste* work.

Light, gentlemen, is the ostensible subject - the attempt to break down light into its constituent hues, atoms of colour, to be reconstituted on the retina of your - rather, my - eyes, in all its subtlety of gradation.

Yet so many factors come into play: the arthritis in the artist's fingers, his habitual stammer, the impecunious range of brushes. And the possible emotional turmoil of his material.

Gay Paris, ladies, in the Belle Epoque.

The Pont Neuf across the background a grey-violet band underpinning the haze and shimmer. An expanse of green blocking in the middleground, the mauves and blues of the river in the foreground left.

Atomised strollers merge and emerge with the shadow of the trees: a bowler-hatted clerk, a marine lieutenant, a cravatted *flâneur*, several women of fashion. One has a feathered hat appearing to extend to her shoulder - it turns out on inspection to be a macaw, on a chain attached to her parasol handle.

They stroll, take the air, take the sun, as is their right as right-minded citizens.

In the river, discernible beside the Indian Red *bateau à rames*, a little whirlpool, and a tracer line of bubbles.

How subtly this is handled. The nexus of Prussian Blue and Viridian suggesting the downward current, the flecks of whites and lemons of the splash. We can almost feel the rock of the empty bateau.

Then our eyes are distracted, drawn to the head of the sunbather, whose hair of Naples Yellow gives a beautifully judged tonal chime, and whose gaze - a masterstroke - directs us back to the empty bateau and the froth of bubbles.

And we move back for a final view, and the myriad points of colour coalesce into shimmering light.

Our next painting is the antithesis of the last - or its synthesis, depending on your point of view.

First we need to make a right hand turn - the rope will guide you.

We now enter the Twentieth century.

When all the complementary colours merge, the result is: white. White. Both theme and subject. A white cross on a white ground. But the daring of the composition is matched by the delicacy of execution.

The ground, of Zinc White, thinned, is brushed in lightly, in alternate directions, to form a fine-grained tilth.

Overlaying this, the cross, of Titanium White, in which the brushwork thickens, impassioned, at times impasto, ridged and trudged like village streets of snow.

Is this perhaps our clue? A stormy *soviet*, a street meeting of workers and kulaks? Or is it more personal? A crisis of conscience? A troubled love? A buried childhood?

How to decide between competing narratives? Let us return to its theme. Apotheosis of colour, teleological goal of colour - the white absolute.

Absolution, ladies, the forbidden word. Note the date, gentlemen - 1922. And a painting that only by chance survived: almost painted over in a later purge, discarded in a studio corner, rescued, ironically, by a German soldier, sold for a box of matches to an American, traded, with a pair of nylons, for who knows what, thus to an English aesthete with advanced - though by then, outmoded - tastes, and now the subject of a repatriation appeal.

All of which has left its mark on the painting, its grubby thumbprints in the corners. But from a distance, they disappear. As does the brushwork, the texture of its birth, the drag of its execution. We are returned, gentlemen, to the whiteness, the blank daring.

Reconstituted purity. Is that possible, ladies? A fresh fall of snow over the footprints? An anti-patina?

Such questions border on the mystical.

Which links it with our next work, painted twenty years earlier.

In this, a certain tonal subtlety is evident, the ground of white showing traces of palest pinks, magenta, Cadmium Yellow, Terre Verte. The subtlety is overlaid, however, by a uniform field of plus and minus signs, sketched - we can make out on close inspection - in charcoal, then painted over in Lamp Black. They could at first be seen as crosses and dashes, and at certain angles may even suggest elements of perspective. But no.

Pluses and minuses are what they are. For these lie beyond perspective, behind the surface. A glimpse of mathematical reality, of the transcendent.

There is a story, probably apocryphal, of the artist as a child, tied to a tree by his father, a teacher, while he memorised his multiplication tables, which tables in turn became his escape.

As an adolescent, he would spend hours by the sea, soothed and assaulted by the rhythm of the waves, as, notebook on lap, he would work through pairs of differential equations.

It may thus be no accident that the first series of works of his maturity should be seascapes, the waves increasingly abstract, reduced finally to short horizontals and vertical endstops.

Followed by the tree series, the branches stylised, compressed - constrained - into a rhythm of curves drained even of colour.

Having achieved the breakthrough, his whole career was the pursuit of transcendence, more rigorous than any physicist, for even energy was too gross for him. Pure thought alone was worth the painting.

How strange, then, gentlemen, that one of the first fruits of his austerity, the mathematical purity of plus and minus, should remind us of carnality. Pictured in your mind's eye, what does it conjure up? A limitless field of wooden crosses?

The calmness of mathematics, the comfort of figures - a motif and theme in our next painting.

A room, a study, is depicted identically in each quarter of the canvas.

A window gives a view through velvet drapes, of sky and cloud. In front of the window, a clothed table. Next to it, on the Chrome Green carpet, stands a cylindrical iron stove of Ivory Black, its prominent chimney pipe cutting up through the ceiling.

At the table, reading by the evening light, sits a man with a newspaper. Impeccably dressed - grey suit, stiff collar, trim moustache. A civil servant, maybe, a *chargé d'affaires?*

Were we able to read his paper we would realize his vocation. It is a financial paper, columns of stocks and shares, indices, fat stock prices - a feast of figures.

An accountant, by training and temperament. All day in his office casting, adding, carrying forward, has not sated his fascination for the dry, dancing figures. His evenings are spent likewise, such is their calmative power.

But things become more curious, gentlemen, for this is a description of the first, top left quarter.

Now imagine the same scene, but erase in your mind's eye the man's figure. Everything else remains the same. Except that the stove assumes a new prominence, though in truth no larger.

The bottom quarters, left and right, are identical with this second quarter.

What of the man?

His threefold non-appearance, disappearance, is trebly eloquent. A Metaphysics of Absence, ladies.

Has he absconded? Does he have an alibi? Was he never really there? Maybe he is sitting, with his paper, on a bench in the park, where the scent of lindens can perfume his thoughts, the wisteria ease his memories.

Maybe his thoughts have turned to winter, to journeys, to winter journeys. For this is theme and title of our next painting. Delicate, like the Chinese work of the same title, but in watercolour, with highlights of gouache.

A gradated wash of Prussian blue forms the sky, defining in negative the unworked white of the hills, snow-covered and broken by stylised firs. On the brow of the furthest hill a train appears, almost toylike, engine and boiler of Burnt Umber, carriages rectangles of Cadmium Orange. From its funnel, a string of puffs of smoke, lightly worked in pencil (which also here and there shades contours in the snow).

Inexplicably, above the train, part hazed by the smoke, hovers, balloon-like, the letter B in Cyanic Green.

Maybe the work is one of a series, illustrations to a child's primer, an alphabet. Perhaps the painting was intended for some Benjamin or Berthe known to the artist. Or maybe it has some personal or other, premonitory meaning.

No matter. From our historical distance we can simply enjoy the sophisticated naivety of this charming work.

In which lies its affinity with our next work, gentlemen. Here too the mock innocence, the childhood motifs. Here too the alphabet plays its part, not as isolated letter but whole word, in cartoon letters and speech balloon.

The word, ladies being SPLAT complete with obligatory exclamation mark.

Those of you, gentlemen, who enjoyed a sighted childhood - remember the glory days? The Beano, Beezer, Eagle, Superman, Spiderman, Dan Dare and Digby?

The grain of the paper, the planes of unvaried colour, primary hues, the heavy outlines, all reproduced here over forty eight square feet of canvas in a variety of techniques.

You would notice that the artist achieves his shading by spraying over a wire mesh, alternately laid, to simulate cross-hatching. That the outlines have been painted in, using old-fashioned blackleading, over cardboard cutouts, stencils in reverse. That the coarse cotton duck has been left unprimed on the surround to imitate newspaper. That the SPLAT! has been painted onto a cardboard oval, superimposed on the canvas with a five-centimetre gap.

You would admire the tension generated by the figuration and its tendency to stylisation. The bodies falling from the ramparts, for example, distinctly modelled at the top, becoming arabesques toward

11

the bottom.

Notice too, the almost realist metallic sheen of the guns, yet the parodic flame from the barrels.

And the single detail of painterly prowess, a nod and wink of assurance, of complicity: the little area of *trompe l'oeil* brickwork at the top of the dam, from which the bodies are falling.

Time to move on.

The alcove here need not detain us - makeweight whimsy, installations: a pickled turbot, a tin of Spam, half opened and putrid, a bin liner labelled Unknown Soldier. Instead we cross the gallery, keeping to the carpet, please, past the bust of St. Dunstan.

And what we have confronting us now, ladies and gentlemen, is, with apologies to the gentleman in the rear, a triptych, each panel of which stands 7ft. 6in. in height.

The first, to your left, is entitled Void - First Morning.

Over a ground of Ultramarine, deepening in tone toward top and bottom, has been scumbled an even pearl grey in unemphatic strokes. The canvas is bisected at slightly above halfway by a horizontal band of Lemon Yellow, thinly applied and bleeding into the grey.

This could almost be a late Turner, but for the angst of black edge on either side.

Which, some attest, merely reinforces the sense of serenity, although others disagree.

The second panel is called Lake of Fire. A rare artistic pun, no doubt, since the canvas is a uniform deep Crimson Lake, the brushwork thick but evenly worked to give an all-over crackle.

But we are arrested immediately by the double-stranded streak, of Cadmium Orange and Chrome Yellow, unmixed, which zags diagonally down the canvas.

We notice, after the initial impact, that the two colours are unblended, hard-edged, to each other and to the ground.

Are they, it, to be understood as merely the second part of the pun? The work is silent.

So we pass to the third of the triptych, final station of our journey.

It is untitled.

A band of Cerulean Blue, even-toned, extends across the width of the canvas from the bottom edge, to a height of two feet.

Above this band the canvas is white, thinly applied at first, becoming increasingly opaque as it nears the top.

The white, from its juncture with the blue, is exactly bisected by a thin grey streak, feathering slightly into the ground, widening imperceptibly as it travels up, until it hits the top edge, where it spreads, flows across in either direction, to form an inch deep band the width of the canvas.

That is all.

Is it all?

Concentrated observation would reveal that the grey extends over the canvas edge, over the strecher, continuing to flow, up and out, mushrooming up the wall, pluming to the ceiling, out of our sight, even mine.

A fitting climax to our tour, ladies and gentlemen, and after a few moments' contemplation, we will be ready to leave.

Sticks to the ready, follow my voice, carefully past the billiard room, whose door to your right is kept permanently ajar. Peeping in, I can see the table, scoreboard, cues, Braille-inscribed balls, exactly as left by our Benefactor.

Beyond that, the pantry, now the crypt containing the terracotta urns.

We have reached the vestibule, there are two steps down, and we are onto the driveway. The gravel now will guide you.

Take care crossing the road, gentlemen, wait for the pips. *Ars longa*, ladies, *morta brevis*.

Your bus awaits.

Could someone just help me up?

So Long Marianne

- Sandra Jensen -

When Marianne asked me to help her kill herself, I thought it would be relatively easy. She lived in London and I lived in Toronto, so I wasn't actually going to kill her myself, just help her find the best way to do it.

Googling 'suicide methods' whittled the options down to one: drug overdose with a plastic bag over her head. But there were two problems. Getting the drugs, and how to make sure she didn't tear the bag off in desperation to breathe. Apparently this always happens, no matter how much a person wants to die. The only sure way for Marianne to kill herself was to take the drugs, fall into a kind of coma, and have someone else put the bag over her head. Marianne lived with her mother. She had no other friends. She'd been ill for fifteen years and was completely housebound.

When I telephoned her with the news I'd been somewhat unsuccessful, she became hysterical.

You have to help me, she shrieked.

I'm trying, I said. I didn't get upset, I was used to her mood swings. I was secretly grateful I no longer lived in England, I couldn't handle her in person anymore. She'd once been my best friend. She made me laugh. I never imagined having sex with her when she talked, an

17

unavoidable mental tic that happened when I listened to people who bored me.

Maybe I can just take the drugs and forget the bag, she suggested.

It's not certain death. Your mum could find you and take you to hospital and have your stomach pumped. You might end up a vegetable.

I'm already a vegetable!

She sobbed for ten minutes while I murmured supportively and trawled the 'net. I typed my name into the Google search bar. 2,870,000 results in 0.24 seconds. Astonishing. One Anne Rayner, 62 years old, died a month ago. I clicked the link. They didn't say how she died. Probably old age. Marianne kept on sobbing. I calculated how many years she might have before dying of natural causes. Another thirty at least. She sobbed louder, as if hearing my thoughts. What was a natural cause? One's heart simply stopping? Now that would be a good way to die. Marianne sniffled.

Could you at least find out about the drugs, then? Please?

I'll try, I promised, and hung up. I stared at the computer screen, wondering what else I could Google. I'd already Googled Jake, the shit who left me for a shop assistant at H&M. If he'd asked me to help him kill himself I'd have happily obliged, gone the extra mile even. But right now, the thought of researching what drugs might put Marianne into an irreversible, mortal sleep made me exhausted.

Marianne had tried everything to get better. The trouble was her illness had no known cure and no known cause. It didn't even have a name. Her medical doctor said the only option was long-term care. An iridologist said it had something to do with childhood shock. Two homeopaths diagnosed her with a *syphilitic miasm*, defined as someone with 'a strong pessimistic view on life, inability to modify what is wrong, sudden impulsive violence directed at self or others, dictatorially rigid ideas, mental paralysis, homicidal tendencies.' She did not seek a third opinion. Acupuncturists failed. Even worse, she attributed her recent sharp decline to a botched acupuncture session. A couple of years ago she wanted me to hook her up with Mother Meera, an Indian guru living in Germany. I'd not made any headway but

Marianne somehow got a direct line to the Mother herself, who told her she must see a doctor. Now Mother Meera was persona non grata.

Marianne washed with boiled water, only ate millet and steamed kale. She never went outside, couldn't use the computer, and telephone calls had to be limited as they caused sparking, shooting pains in her limbs. She wouldn't even allow me to think healing thoughts because they made her come out in a rash. This was the woman who used to walk the length and breadth of London with me after seeing the Pogues at the 100 Club or an exhibition at the Brixton Art Collective. We'd walk until dawn, me with my Nikon glued to my face, she with her long-fingered hands in a ballet dance as we talked about everything from Roland Barthes' *Rhetoric of the Image* to the difficulty of finding dresses for women with slight figures and a D-sized bra cup. We'd sit outside the Beigel Bake on Brick lane, drinking tar-strong tea at six in the morning as the market rattled to life.

Now Marianne was a disembodied voice piped along thousands of miles of wire.

My normal response to her requests was to pretend I'd do what I could, and then forget about it. But this death business interested me. When I was young I'd ask my brother what was the best way to die. We'd compare notes: jumping off a high-rise? Too messy and not altogether certain. Gun? The only gun we had was his pellet gun, good for killing small birds but not people, at least not instantly. Gas oven, too smelly. Knife, too painful. Drowning seemed the best, apparently you went easily, but neither of us wanted to test the theory. And then there is always freezing to death, another good one. You go to sleep, they say. We didn't have a large freezer and lived in Somerset where a cold snap meant you could see your breath. We didn't think of pills. Not ghastly enough, perhaps.

The telephone rang. It was Mr. Pickering, my very elderly, very lonely landlord from downstairs.

I've put the kettle on dear, unless you are too busy? his wavering voice pulled at me. What was I going to say? I was too busy killing Marianne?

Mr. Pickering was a man unable to come to the point. After two cups of instant coffee and a lecture on how much he'd enjoyed his thirty-

19

five years as a store manager for Canadian Tire that even taxed my sexual imagination, I excused myself to the bathroom. While peeing I imagined my whole life unfolding within the confines of the small, dull-yellow tiled room. I like bathrooms. I've ascertained the pros and cons of every bathroom I've ever visited. Mr. Pickering had no bathtub. That was a problem. Where would I sleep? I opened the medicine cabinet, not looking for anything in particular, just taking in the overall feel of the items, their meta-meaning. I'd once seen an exhibition of photographs of people's medicine cabinets. I'd been sickeningly envious. Why hadn't I thought of this?

A pinkish bottle in Mr. Pickering's cabinet had a large '*WARNING*' label, underneath it said: '*May cause drowsiness. Do not exceed dose. One at night, as needed.*' My eyes moved to a tube of Preparation H, but I heard Marianne's plaintive voice: *Help me, please.* I slipped the bottle of pills into my cardigan pocket. The prescription was four years old, the bottle looked untouched. Clearly Mr. Pickering didn't need them.

I'm sure there are good jobs about, Mr. Pickering said as I edged to his front door trying to look like I wasn't. It's important to work, for your self-confidence. For friends, he added. As he talked, images fell into my head, unstoppable: me humping his leg like a dog. His penis, embedded in a cloud of white pubic hair. He stretched his hand out. For one horrible moment I thought he knew about his pills, but he just clutched at my cardigan, and said quietly: You're a good person, I can tell. You learn to read people at Canadian Tire.

When I finally extricated myself and went back upstairs, I lay on my bed and stared at the stained ceiling. I hadn't felt that bad about myself in months. I tried to think about Marianne's life, but all I could think was I had absolutely nothing to fill the rest of the day with. I fingered Mr. Pickering's pill bottle. I could take one, I thought, just one. But what if they were for impotence? Not exactly what I needed. I bounded up to my computer, typed in the name of the drug: *Klonopin*.

It took fifteen seconds to find out that Mr. Pickering's pills were clonazepam, a benzodiazepine, 'benzos' as drug addicts said. Or at least they did in movies. I rather liked enunciating the full name aloud: *benzo-diaz-epine.* It massaged my lips, the tip of my tongue, made me sound like I knew what I was talking about. Twenty minutes later I did know what I was talking about.

Clonazepam was considered a 'high potency' benzodiazepine, a sedative-hypnotic mainly prescribed for seizures, panic disorder and something extremely weird called *hyperekplexia*, another satisfying-sounding word meaning exaggerated surprise. Benzos were the most frequently implicated pharmaceutical in Emergency Department visits. Clonazepam itself had a list of promising side effects. If used in combination with other medications, it could indeed be fatal. With aspirin, for example.

I reached for the phone, entered the long-distance code. Once I got past weather-platitudes with her mother and had Marianne on the line, I explained my findings, instructed her as best I could about dosages and what not, told her I'd send the pills as soon as I could.

After the call I felt a little light-headed. It was probably no breakfast, that instant coffee. Mr. Pickering was right of course, I should get a job. At thirty-five calling myself a starving artist was no longer cool, it was just sad. I turned once again to my computer screen and typed 'Jake Stormont'. Did I expect some new addition in the past few hours? A link to 'I STILL LOVE YOU ANNE!!!!!!!!'? Nothing. Nada. He's not even on Facebook. My stomach growled. If I hurried I could catch Pam's exhibition opening (I did have friends, Mr. Pickering was wrong about that). There'd be wine and snacks.

An hour later, wine in hand, I moved about the gallery looking for the snacks. I noticed a growing sensation: I felt pulled in, contained, as if I were pregnant with something important and fragile. The muscles of my face fixed themselves into a rubbery frown, the kind of frown I might have if I were terminally ill and someone were saying, *I'm so sorry.* But I wasn't and they weren't. I was getting drunk on cheap pinot grigio and no one was saying a word to me. I had forgotten to wear something interesting. There weren't even any snacks left, they were all eaten by other starving artists. I studied a wall of paper plates stapled with meat, spray-painted, microwaved and varnished. I almost salivated. Pam had been doing this kind of stuff for years. I accosted her, my rubber face frowning, and told her the work was innovative, groundbreaking. She listened intently, and then I blurted:

Marianne wants me to help her commit suicide.

Pam's black-lipsticked mouth opened, then closed and finally she said, Oh my god how terrible. She clutched my arm. Are you OK? I nodded, sipped my wine. I answered further questions monosyllabically. I didn't say anything about the pills. Later, I walked home instead of taking the subway. It was a kind of punishment. It took two hours but only exacerbated the sensation: I was no longer carrying something fragile inside, but something powerful and dangerous, like a nail bomb. I tried to sleep, but the images in my head flipped too fast. Just colours: black, red, violet. The colours of a bruise.

The following morning I packaged up the pills. Scribbled down the instructions. For contents I wrote 'sweets'. The Korean woman behind the postal counter threw the package into the sack behind her. I stared at the sack, paralysed by a noise of thoughts. The woman said, You want? It sounded like an accusation. I didn't know what I wanted. I thought I knew what Marianne wanted but now I wasn't so sure. The man behind me coughed, the woman behind him said, For Christ's sake get on with it and so I stepped away. I hovered about the sparsely laden aisles. I bought a tin of baked beans, no-name brand. I wondered how the Korean family made any money. Perhaps they pilfered the parcels. Perhaps they'd find mine, perhaps it would never get sent.

The matter was out of my hands. I tried not to think about it. I thought about nothing else. I worried that Mr. Pickering would have a seizure and not have his medication. I worried I'd found the wrong method for Marianne. I worried that maybe she was, in fact, mentally ill with homicidal tendencies and not in a position to know if she really wanted to die.

A few days later she telephoned, told me she was waiting patiently for the post, that she'd stocked up on aspirin and her mother's blood pressure medication, just to make sure. She sounded elated, the old Marianne. Definitely not mentally ill. She even made a joke about using her body as art. Piss Marianne, she said, like Andre Serrano's Piss Christ. I could embalm her in my own urine. Pam would approve.

I felt marginally better and then catastrophically worse. The feeling of holding something powerful and sharp inside me dismantled into

22

indigestible, spongy lumps. Days hammered down. I didn't go out, except to buy more beans from the Koreans. I'd inspect the floor behind the postal counter, hoping to spot my package, lost, unsent, mislaid amongst the dust bunnies.

I spent my days unwashed, unslept and bloated with bean gas. When an equally insomniac bird cheerfully tweeted in the middle of the night I dragged myself from bed and opened the computer. In my earlier research I'd bookmarked a website of personal accounts of failed suicide attempts. I hadn't delved; I was looking for successful ones. Benzodiazepines featured heavily in these, but I thought I should double check.

The page loaded slowly: someone had compiled hundreds of anonymous entries ordered under headings of method of attempt. Some entries were short, others were very long, most were badly spelled. Some people were left handicapped or partially handicapped by their attempt. I wondered if this was the reason behind the terrible spelling. There was only one entry for clonazepam.

First attempt:

Insulin overdose failed becuze Im insulin resistint

second attempt:

colonopin overdose failed becuze colonopin causes seazures that atracted attention and the police were called. I had a coma for three days.

Third attempt:

Drove car off cliff into big tree.

failed, spend 16 years in a wheelchair as a result.

thats all

I scrolled down, read the entry from a man who shot off half his chin and part of his nose and cheek. He'd changed his mind at the last moment.

I clicked back to the home page, scanned the links. *Images (WARNING: GORY)*, said one. I hovered my mouse over it. What could be so bad? I thought, clicking on the link. I didn't stay long, there was no need really, it wasn't like a photograph, sliding the paper back and forth in the developer bath, waiting until the latent image converts to silver, waiting until it's just right, and then into the stop bath, the image preserved, only to fade eventually, years later. No, this was instant etching onto the inside of your brain. No rewind, no antidote. There, forever.

Ten days passed. I got tired of beans and stocked up on bread and peanut butter instead. I did not want to leave the house in case Marianne telephoned. Watching Mr. Pickering take his afternoon constitutional was the only pleasurable event in my day. I spent countless hours at the computer. I Googled everyone I had ever known in my entire life and when I ran out of names I Googled 'cute cat pictures'. At the two-week mark, I hadn't even scratched the surface of cute kitties, but something changed. Perhaps it was just the weather. The trees lining my street began to slip into their gold and rust-coloured coats. I opened my windows: I liked the crinkly, hushing noise they made in the wind, like a mother whispering.

One afternoon my legs took me to the park all by themselves. I stood beneath a small tree, on a circle of bright yellow leaves. The effect was blinding, as if I were standing on the sun itself. I stretched my arms wide, breathed in the fall air, sharp with hope. I watched the slow, graceful-saucering of a tiny, blood coloured leaf. I thought of Marianne, gone now. Entering into the earth, making food for trees. It was OK. It was what she wanted. I wrapped my arms around my body for warmth, and walked home.

The following morning I went to Yorkville. One of the galleries needed an assistant urgently and I started work that afternoon. It wasn't exactly exciting and customers said ridiculous things about the art, but I liked my boss, a woman in her 60s who wore violently striped leggings and let her fuzz of un-dyed hair hang over her shoulders like a low-lying fog. She didn't talk much but whatever she said was interesting: opinionated and caustic. I started taking photographs again. I deleted all the bookmarks in my 'Marianne's Suicide' folder. I hadn't Googled Jake in weeks.

Occasionally I wondered why Marianne's mother never telephoned. Only once, when I was premenstrual, did I worry about police. But otherwise I let it go.

One morning, a few days before Christmas, the world outside muffled with snow, the telephone rang. I checked the number, my heart banged before I even registered the double four. United Kingdom. I picked up.

Anne? said the voice with clipped English vowels. Marianne's mother. What could I say in my defence? What could I say to comfort? But no words came, engulfed as they were by my banging heart.

It's me, Marianne, the voice continued, and I slid to the floor.

How are you? she asked.

I'm fine, I said, on automatic.

I told her about my job, made her laugh by mimicking the man who described an ink drawing of a bound foot as 'artisanal'. He was from Idaho, a fact he proceeded to enlarge upon, while I had imaginary, awful, sex with him.

And you, I finally asked, biting the inside of my cheek to stop myself asking about the pills.

You know, she said. The usual. I've been doing this tapping thing. EFT they call it. Emotional Freedom Technique. You should check it out, mum found it on YouTube. One woman healed herself from MS.

She rattled on. My heart returned to normal. She sounded good, chirpy even. It was as if the whole thing had never happened. Those images I'd seen, still burning sometimes, in the dark of night. I wanted to be angry. I wasn't. She was alive, I should be happy. But I felt nothing, nothing at all, just the salty, mineral taste of blood in my mouth.

END

Hachiko

-Sarah Dobbs -

I wasn't in Fukushima when the nuclear disaster struck, or the tsunami belched through Honshu. I was, I calculated later, after receiving the photograph, fucking some girl an ocean away. I'd obsessed over her since the start of the first year. The one with the bright lips and fingertips. My girlfriend was in what's now known as the exclusion zone.

'Drink from the trolley, sir?'

I frowned. The photograph was stuck to my palm. I peeled it off.

The stewardess' vaguely interested smile blanked. She moved on.

Only three workers were killed from the immediate nuclear disaster.

Atsuko was in Honshu, where the earthquake started that triggered the tsunami that precipitated the nuclear meltdown.

(That swallowed the fly, that wriggled and wiggled and tickled inside her.)

When I first met Atsuko, and she told me her name, I just thought she was cute. A miniature person who used a lot of exclamations. I liked her swishy hair and tiny feet.

(Perhaps she'll die).

She had a penchant for funny toys that were half-teddy, half-monster. These multiplying hairballs grew in my flat like Gremlins fed after midnight.

29

'My name? Atsuko.'

'Atsuko?'

'Yes!'

I'd nodded. Hooked my mouth down like I was agreeing to a car deal.

'Well, what does that mean?'

'What it mean?'

God, this was going to be easy. 'Mmhm.'

'Child of kindness, I think you say.'

'Kind child?'

'Yes!' She leaned close to me and snapped a picture. Fingers up in a Peace sign. This photograph of us was still taped to the back of my toilet door. I looked drunk. Atsuko had glued red felt hearts to its corners.

The tsunami travelled up to five kilometres inland in the Fukushima prefecture, causing a total of 1113 deaths with 4626 more people still missing.

It wasn't meant to be more than a delicacy. *She* wasn't. Weird to refer to her that way now. But I was young, a year left of uni, and there was still that girl with the bright nails and lips. What was her name? I probably realised I loved Atsuko, that bollock-tightening, scary, forever-love, when she started talking about dogs. So why was she alone in Honshu, when I loved her like that?

The plane started to descend. The hum in my ears increased in pitch. I peered beyond some fat bloke's belly at the inky skyline. The cabin air had cooled. I flared my nostrils. I waggled my jaw to unplug my ears. We've been here before, of course, but it would look different this time. I've seen the pictures everywhere. My thumb drew circles on the back of the photograph.

Fat bloke raised an eyebrow at me.

I inclined my head.

Suzie, that was it. Now she was more my type. Spirited. Suggestive. Independent. Going places. If I had to settle down, it'd be with someone like Suzie. Someone with their own life, their own drive.

All Atsuko ever wanted to do was get married, have babies, and look after her husband and children. She said it was not the fashion for women to want this in Japan any more. But, she told me, with her chin raised, 'I am rebel. I want take care of you. All our family.'

Whenever she talked like that, I'd end it by romancing her into spoons. It's hard to refuse a girl who doesn't want to use a condom. Maybe she'd taken that as permission.

TEPCO engineers confirm that a meltdown occurred, with molten fuel having fallen to the bottom of the reactor's containment vessel.

The last time I was here, we'd been to Honshu to meet her family. It had made every part of my body sweat to do it. And then we'd visited the Kennel Club to look at the dogs.

'What's that then, a husky?'

I'd never seen Atsuko, who already had a posture like a princess, so straight-backed.

'This . . . is Akita.'

'A relative?'

Her eyes had seemed to slice at me.

'I just meant, Atsuko, Akita. Similar sounding names?'

She'd shaken her head. Her swishy hair had hissed like a snake.

'I'm sorry. They're cute.'

If it was possible, Atsuko had seemed to stand even taller. As if she was now nearly my height. I even put out a hand to measure.

She raised one finger. 'Akita no cute.'

I shrugged. 'Looks kind've cute.'

And there, among the yapping Labradors and other, funny-faced dogs I couldn't name, Atsuko unfolded the story of Hachiko, with such love in her eyes, that I glimpsed the future she was already in.

'A memorial day? For a dog?' I'd said.

'Hachiko is most famous dog in all Japan. Extremely loyal. Protective and fierce.'

A Kennel Club worker must have heard 'Hachiko' because they came over and started talking. They both nodded in that way I thought only Atsuko did and then turned to stare at me.

I looked around. Who, me?

The worker pressed his lips together and, with a nod to Atsuko, hurried off.

'Each day, Hachiko dog go to Shubiya with Professor Ueno.'

I bit my lip as she waggled her hands to mime the dog trotting along.

'He go to station to leave master, return home and – collect?'

'Collect.'

'Collect Professor Ueno when he home in train.'

'The dog walks on his own to the station?' I found myself copying her dog walking mime.

Atsuko folded her arms.

'Go on.'

'One day Professor Ueno have attack.' She places both hands on her heart. 'He never arrive to home. But each day, for nine year, Hachiko go to station and wait for master.' Her long, skinny lashes were slick.

I had a huge compulsion to say, Blimey, did old Hachiko not get it after nine years? Not so bright, eh?

'I am your Hachiko,' she said.

I am your dog. I cleared my throat, nodded. 'OK.'

Suzie's bright mouth seemed to balloon into my vision.

'There is statue on Hachiko outside Shibuya station. You want visit?'

A 9.0-magnitude earthquake and massive tsunami on March 11 triggered the world's worst nuclear accident in 25 years and forced residents around the Fukushima Daiichi nuclear power plant to flee, with many of them having to leave behind their pets.

I closed my eyes, the photograph resting on my buckle, my hand curved over its back as the plane's wheels squawked. I've scoured the pictures in the press. So much so I could flick through them in my head, like Tom Cruise in *Minority Report.*

Cows. Their black bodies bold against blue roadwork signs. Escaped from farms into the exclusion zone. An ostrich picking past an abandoned car. Left to roam alone for months. The deserted shopping streets. Some cats with 'OK' stamped onto their cages. Some white bags with curtain-like tassels that I learn are ashes. A much sweeter container in which to dispose of the dead than I think we would use. People in white suits. Weeds spiking up through railway tracks. The Seven Gods of Fortune in someone's home. One of Gods' cheery, coloured faces, is cracked.

We never did get to see the statue.

Atsuko told me at our favourite restaurant. Her Polaroid – she had regressed from her digi-camera ('It so retro,' she'd said, with a weird Japanese-American accent) – was at the ready.

'Atsuko. Not now, yeah?'

She put down the Polaroid and picked up her chopsticks, twiddled some noodles.

'OK. So. Are you sure?'

'No.'

'Well how sure is not sure?'

She put down her chopsticks. 'Ninety?'

I'd put my head in my hands.

She left when she was one hundred, not ninety, after an evening we'd spent in total silence. She'd washed my hair, palmed the suds clear, soaped and rinsed my back. In the morning, there were less Gremlin furball things, and a note:

Remember, I am loyal.

She never came back. She wasn't reachable on her phone. She didn't reply to my emails.

The Seven Gods of Fortune, getting dusty on a shelf above a row of Star Anise and other spices that were also gathering dust, watched as I did it. But the promise of Suzie's lips deflated after I fucked her. Or, even, as.

I didn't put together the news about the Fukushima Daiicha plant, Honshu's earthquake, the tsunami and Atsuko. Not until the Polaroid came in its double wrapped envelope.

It was larger than I had expected, with tiny ears. Atsuko had had a hat with ears like that. Its bronze belly had greened. Its forelegs and paws were smoother, worn from touch.

The photograph had come three weeks after the tsunami. Atsuko had been in the Kennel Club in Honshu. Gone there after her, what could I call it, pilgrimage to Hachiko? It had been tucked inside her coat, addressed to me. I would never know who sent it. But it had come, one boring Saturday, my eyes bleary from a *"24"* marathon the night before. Another envelope had encased Atsuko's envelope. Inside, a slip of gridded paper. Uncomfortable English letters: *Found for you in*

Kennel Club, Honshu. Sympathies. I'd sat on the couch, holding the note and the photograph in each palm, like some Buddha. My brain had computed the facts, the dates, the variables. And then it had stitched the facts together into a truth that had tried to drown me on my living room sofa.

My fingertips explored the vertical Japanese characters on the stone stand that bore Hachiko, as I imagined Atsuko would have done. Commuters and tourists milled about. Some interrupted me. Peace signs, heads together, until each one has taken the same image. I waited.

When it is still, I stand here, where you are standing in your photograph to me, your belly like a melon, touching the dog's feet. Holding you in the palm of my hand, water-scarred and bent, I take the picture. The dog's feet are smooth, cool at first, but the metal warms under my hands.

The Man Who Hugged Women

- Mischa Hiller -

Pearl's behind had widened over the years, Freya observed, as she took Pearl's coat. Following her into the large kitchen – recently refurbished thanks to Mukesh's private practice – she conceded that Pearl still had a waist, and dressed to make the most of it. And why shouldn't she? Pearl sat opposite her at the artificially weathered table and Freya was treated to a glimpse of frayed underwear. Coffee and mugs lay on the table between them. Before she'd even sat down Pearl had started relating something about a friend of hers Freya didn't know.

'Anyway, it turned out she was talking about herself, not a friend. You know, one of those 'I've got a friend' stories. She told me about this guy she went to see, he's like a guru or something, like an Eastern guru, from Tibet or Bali or somewhere like that. Sort of Eat, Pray, Love type of guy, you know what I mean?'

Freya doubted whether such a type actually existed beyond the fevered minds of western women but she nodded her understanding, ignoring Pearl's poor grasp of geography. Did she even know which country Mukesh was from, beyond being Asian?

'So she went to see him, this guy, after being told about him by her friend. He's amazing, apparently, like a sort of father figure but also desirable in a Richard Gere sort of way, but Asian, obviously. Like

Mukesh, I suppose.' She giggled and not for the first time Freya
wondered whether men found it sexy that a woman Pearl's age would
giggle in such a girly manner. Did Mukesh like it? He'd told her he
thought Pearl was an intellectual lightweight and had little time for her,
but men thinking women silly didn't stop men sleeping with said
women. Freya liked Pearl for her naive, unquestioning enjoyment of
things, which is what she supposed would attract men to her in the
first place. She could have taken Mukesh's approach and sneered, to
bolster her own comfortable cynicism, but the truth was she would
love to be a bit more like Pearl, even though there were certain dinner
parties where she and Jacob were not invited. Also, Pearl had been
there for her, unlike her other friends. Been there in the physical sense,
gone with her to the hospital and held her hand.

'...except Mukesh is a trained psychiatrist, I know that, not a new-
agey type man at all. He'd pooh-pooh the whole idea of going to see
this guy, I know he would.'

'Well what does he do then, this, erm, guru?' Freya asked. It was
always wise to gently guide Pearl to an end point otherwise they could
be here a long time.

'He only sees women for a start. At least I only hear of women going
to see him. Married women, usually.'

'Oh yes? And is it meditation then, that he does, or counselling, or
yoga, or what?'

'No.' Pearl leant forward conspiratorially. 'He gives you a hug.' Pearl
sat back triumphantly. She had a smug look on her face and was
itching to tell Freya something else. Freya knew what it was. She
poured the coffee.

'You're thinking of going to see him, aren't you?' Freya asked.

Pearl jerked forward in her chair. 'Do you think I'm mad? Is it crazy?
I mean what harm is there in it?'

'It's crazy, that's what it is. You're married. What would Jacob think?'

'I wouldn't tell him, would I? Any more than I would tell him I was
getting my legs waxed.'

'It's not quite the same, is it? If you want a hug, why don't you just
ask Jacob?' But as soon as the question had left her mouth she knew
the answer.

'Precisely because I have to ask him. He doles them out, but to be honest he's like most men, either all over you like a randy pigeon or doesn't want to know and you're grateful if you get a kiss in the evening. I suppose you're lucky in that department, being married to a psychiatrist and everything?'

Freya grunted non-committally, Mukesh did everything as if it came from some marriage counselling manual, rather than from the heart or between his legs. It was like he was ticking relationship boxes every time he gave her a hug, or complimented her, or brought home flowers on a suspiciously regular basis. At first she'd uncharitably thought he made notes in his diary, then discovered that he was making notes in his diary, a little 'f' once every four weeks, like she used to mark her diary with a little 'p' once every four weeks until it had become too irregular. Freya was still undecided as to whether she liked this approach. Maybe he was right, maybe you had to work at not taking someone for granted and this was just his way of doing it. On the other hand, she sometimes wished for a little more spontaneity and loss of control — occasionally, even, she might like him to attack her like a randy pigeon.

Pearl leant forward. 'So. I've already booked a session.'

'My God. When for?'

'Thursday morning. This Thursday.'

'Bloody hell, Pearl. Are you sure he's kosher?'

'He's not Jewish, Freya, he's Asian.'

'Of course, you told me. Sounds like a bit of a groper to me.'

Freya looked affronted. 'No, he's seen loads of women. Really, they all love him.'

'I'm sure they do.'

'No, they say he feels safe, it's like hugging your dad.' Freya was struck by a strong memory of being hugged by her father — it did feel safe, a sense of masculine protection. No, not protection, care. Of being held without any expectation of anything in return. The smell of a man. A smell that seemed to have disappeared in today's over-deodorised and perfumed male.

'But how can you hug for an hour?' she asked, compelled for some reason to chip away at Pearl's cheerful certainty.

'The sessions are only thirty minutes max, or shorter if you want, and some of that is just him asking you how you are, really listening to you.'

'Like a counsellor, you mean.'

'I suppose. Except he doesn't guide you like a counsellor does, or want to know how you feel about everything you happen to mention. Apparently he has a picture of his wife on his office wall. Oh, and he wears a big woolly jumper.'

'Even in the summer?' Freya asked, feeling the familiar twist of a sneer on her mouth. How she hated the involuntary pull of the muscles that shaped contempt and made it visible.

Pearl shrugged and looked down. She drank her coffee, holding the cup to her chest between sips. Freya pictured a man in a woolly jumper. She wanted to know where Pearl got her bravery from; how she'd gone from recognising that her partner Jacob didn't give her everything she needed, to doing something about it. Something that involved seeing another man, however innocent it seemed to be.

'Will you come with me?' Pearl asked, putting her cup down and screwing up her face beseechingly.

'You want me to come with you?'

'Yes, I'm nervous, that's the honest truth of it. I don't mean come inside with me, obviously, it's just that I'd like you to be there, I dunno, just in case.'

'I'm not sure, Pearl...'

'You don't work Thursdays.' Freya pitched in as a teacher's assistant at the local primary school where their daughter Rita had gone. It was something to fill her time and make her feel she was giving something back. Although it was unclear to her what she was supposed to be giving back.

'No, I'm not working on Thursday.' Pearl had come with her that once, for something a lot more traumatic than being held by a man. Something caused by a man and fixed, in that case, by a man. She looked at Pearl and wanted to make up for her sneering. 'Yes of course I'll come with you.'

That night she thought about bringing the matter up with Mukesh, maybe he'd heard of this guy. But she didn't get a chance because it was their regular monthly cinema night and he insisted, as usual, that they analyse all the pleasure out of the film straight afterwards. He became frustrated with her when she said she wanted time to think about the film, to reserve judgement, let it sink in. No, this is not what he and their friends did; you had to have an opinion on everything almost immediately. Once she lay in bed though, next to a reading Mukesh, she discovered that she was glad she had kept the man who hugged women to herself.

Mukesh left for his consulting rooms every morning at nine thirty, leaving her to get on with her life as best she could. Their only child, Rita, was at a mediocre university, having been coached and cajoled beyond her natural ability through her A-levels to make sure she got in. Freya had once suggested to Mukesh that Rita might be better off doing something else other than going to university but had been shut down pretty sharpish and she'd never mentioned it again, instead colluding with him to push her daughter unhappily down a predetermined path. When Rita had left a year ago she'd toyed with the idea of getting a dog to fill the gap. Mukesh wasn't keen; dogs created mess and had to be looked after if they were to travel. That had been the plan of course, when Rita left home; they would travel more and do all the things they'd kept putting off. Hadn't happened, and the longer it hadn't happened, the greater her desire grew for a dog.

The cleaner arrived late, and after listening dutifully to her explain why – something to do with her sick mother – Freya went into the attic and rummaged around before pulling out a dusty shoebox. It was filled with childhood photos. Her childhood photos – the ones not selected to be neatly placed chronologically in albums, accurately labelled and dated. She was looking for a particular picture she hadn't seen in years and there it was, a black and white print of her father from when she was a teenager. He was in the kitchen, pipe in hand, caught awkwardly between sitting and standing (hence its relegation to the shoebox) but in the magnificent old woollen jumper that smelled of pipe tobacco, bay rum and, if he'd been working on their high maintenance car, engine oil. She took the photo downstairs and pinned it to the fridge with a magnet.

On Thursday morning Freya and Pearl travelled on a cold bus to an address in North London.

'Do you think he does this from home?' Pearl asked as they walked the last bit of the journey down residential streets wide enough to accommodate mature trees without being overwhelmed. 'Do you think his wife minds?' To Freya she sounded a little nervous.

'I'm sure she doesn't mind the money.' Freya had learnt on the bus just how much this session was costing Pearl – the equivalent of what Mukesh charged for listening to fifty minutes of what he called first-world angst. The guy was raking it in, taking advantage of women of a certain age, like Pearl, who craved affection. At what age, Freya wondered, did affection become more important than sex? They stood outside a large semi-detached house, examining it for clues. A discrete polished brass plaque just inside the gate told them they were about to enter a complementary therapy centre rather than someone's home.

'Maybe we should walk round the block.' Pearl said, hesitating. 'We're early.'

'No we're not. Come on, let's do this.' Freya hooked her arm in Pearl's and led her up the gravel drive.

Following instructions on the front door they pushed it open and stepped into a ceramic-tiled hallway with stairs on the right and a door on the left. Screwed to it was a wooden sign with gold calligraphy spelling 'Waiting Room'. They went in, Freya aware that Pearl was unusually quiet. The room could have been a sitting room, a couple of sofas and a chair facing an inglenook fireplace. Logs were stacked up the sides and there was ash in the grate, but no fire. They sat together on the same sofa and Freya studied some landscape watercolours on the wall. Pearl sat up straight, worrying at a loose strand of hair.

'Are you OK?' Freya asked, putting her hand on Pearl's knee.

'Fine,' Pearl said. Her gaze flitted around the room, her chest rising and falling too rapidly for Freya's liking. The incongruously digital clock above the fireplace indicated that they had five minutes before Pearl's appointment. Before her hug. At least this wasn't the same sort of waiting room they'd both been in when it was Pearl accompanying Freya all those years ago. That had been more clinical, although she also hadn't told her husband where she'd gone. A door closed somewhere and a woman's heels clacked on the hall tiles. The front door opened and closed. Out of the bay window Freya saw the back of a dark-haired woman in a coat with a fur collar walk down the drive. Was it real fur? Pearl stood up, she appeared to be hyperventilating. Freya got up too, inexplicably feeling nervous herself.

'Just breathe, Pearl.' But Pearl's eyes were wide in panic, her hands flapping uncontrollably.

'This is crazy,' she said, and rushed out, leaving Freya standing. Pearl had slammed the front door and was halfway down the drive before Freya could even say that she'd told her it was crazy. She ought to tell someone that Pearl had left. Maybe she could get her a refund, even at this late stage. She opened the door to the hall.

He was there, a big man, smiling, beaming at her.

'You must be Pearl.' His voice was deep, warm, educated, and he sounded very much like Mukesh. Clean-shaven but craggy-faced, grey hair untidy but not out of control, he must have been in his late fifties, early sixties. His glinting dark eyes never left her face, questioning gently, the smile easing but not fading. He raised his unruly eyebrows expectantly and stretched his right arm to direct her down the hall towards an open door where the orange flickers from a real fire danced on the walls.

'The thing is … ' Freya looked back at him, his woollen jumper. Her head was level with his chest. She looked up at his welcoming face.

'It's OK,' he said mildly, gesturing anew.

She turned and stepped towards the glow.

43

Even Meat Fill

- Gordon Collins -

The pie base slides down the steel slope and comes to rest just beyond my fill-gun. I nudge it back so the end of the gun rests inside the lip of the empty base. The base is shinier than average which implies a moister and so lighter pastry and this accounts for the overrun. A lighter base will absorb less pie fill. The fill odour is slightly acidic but not enough to affect the flow. Base lip height, dough consistency, chute wear, tray uniformity, ambient temperature and humidity are also all within acceptable limits. Having accounted for these factors, I adjust my finger pressure on the fill-gun. I do not alter the speed or diameter of the circle I draw with it.

I do not take into account known variations in the pastry cutter, weather forecasts or any seasonal factors, gossip concerning pastry or fill-chef competence, managerial edicts affecting workflow or suspicions I have about decreasing dough quality. Most importantly, I draw no conclusions from the preceding bases because I can't remember them. I fill the pie that is in front of me. The information I require to do this is presented to me at precisely the moment it is required. I fill the pie and pass it on down the chute. As it goes, I watch the tide of pie-fill come towards me and rise up to just under the lip. I await the next base.

Who would be immortal? Immortals would. They wouldn't give it up. But if you ask most people if they'd rather be someone else, then they always say they would rather be themselves. They will stick with what they know until they are in extremes of pain, humiliation or close to death. Only then will they choose immortality. They choose the circle, not the spiral. You'd go around the merry-go-round forever rather than fly off it, or worse, be flushed down the vortex of metal hooves and discordant organ chimes.

This isn't the first time I have thought this. I have a lot of respect for the people in pastry but they can't keep up with me and I am left with these gaps between pies. For twelve years I have had the same thoughts over and over. I'm wary of any change in my routine that might provoke a new thought and so distract me. On a good day, I do not know what time it is. Light brightens and fades, shifts change, temperature decreases, bases start to overrun and banter fades. It's all as I expect it to be and so I don't notice it. I am as much a part of the factory as the packaging machine or the cooking vat. I am a circular-motion pie filler. I work through my lunch break and the siren at the end of the day surprises me. I fear death no more than the pastry-cutting machine does.

On a bad day, I remember things. A new memory begets more memories and soon every minute here is marked out with memories. Or I think of what might have been if I'd been a more tolerant team leader. I think of my work here. I think of my ambitions. Then all the dreams I had at catering college come – I try to work it into my filling but it's hard. It's like all the disappointments and embarrassments are straining through my mind and through the fill-gun and every time I pull the trigger I can't help thinking that, throughout my life, I have missed opportunities.

The pie base slides down the slope and comes to rest beyond my fill-gun. I nudge it back up the slope so the end of the gun rests inside the lip of the empty pie base. I take account of base gloss, fill odour, ambient conditions and miscellaneous factors. I alter my finger pressure accordingly. I do not alter the speed or diameter of the circle I draw with the fill gun.

I analyse the aroma of the pie-fill as it escapes the tip of the gun. There's a sharp smell of kidney as the second cooking of the day begins. The increased acidity will affect its flow and absorption and so I will adjust my finger pressure accordingly. Not consciously. A neurological highway between nose and finger has been built in my brain and so the adjustment is a reflex action like breathing, blinking or opening a door.

There's a clank over in packaging. There's a chill as the delivery door is opened – that may cool the fill and slow it down. There is joviality in pastry. They're a good laugh in pastry. It's Mr Briggs, the manager, doing his rounds. He'll spend ten minutes in pastry and less than one in filling if he can help it.

In my interview, they asked me if I wanted to go into pastry because I had done pastry at catering school but it had been pastry that made me drop out. Pastry will always let you down. In the twelve years I've been here, nobody has ever stayed for more than three years in pastry. Pastry is unpredictable and the results notoriously irreproducible.

At the interview, I said I'd be happier in filling and to begin with, I was. I squirted pie fill into a base – I thought that was all there was too it. I thought I was doing it well. My wastage was zero for three consecutive months. My usage was below 19 litres and I was averaging over 900 pies a day. The management noted this and rewarded me with plastic stars. With each plastic star I received a small pay rise. When I reached twenty stars, I was made team leader and received a £20 pay rise. 'We believe in you,' it said in the letter that had the twentieth star glued to the base of it with a sticky gel. I was encouraged towards the 30 star milestone which would grant me a restaurant voucher and an invitation to the management's away day. I was made to believe in the career ladder. Derek in pastry had thirty stars (he had taken his team out for a Mexican meal but had not been able to attend the go-karting away day) and so I knew it was possible.

The pie base slides down the slope and comes to rest beyond my fill-gun. I nudge it back up the slope so the end of the gun rests inside the lip of the empty pie base. I take account of base gloss, fill odour, ambient conditions and miscellaneous factors. I alter my finger

pressure accordingly. I do not alter the speed or diameter of the circle I draw with the fill gun.

Above the 20 star level, you have to set your own goals and you tend to set them too high. I pushed my team too hard and they didn't respond. I overestimated their ability and enthusiasm. It was all left to me and I was doing unpaid overtime and weekends just to reach the team's daily 4000-pie target.

I got to 26 stars but then they changed the scheme. It became much easier to get stars but the milestones were then set at 50, 100 and 150. Soon all my team, the new employees, even the student temps had overtaken me. They were rejecting the good bases and only filling the thick ones because thick bases require less fill and take less time. They got down to 15 litres usage and production up to 1100 pies a day. I was still team leader but my team were all promoted above me to 'fill technicians.'

I waited to see if they'd review the system but they didn't and so I gave up on what I had already decided would be my last ambition. Then I started to spiral inwards - slowly releasing the trigger and drawing a path to the middle. Going around until I reached the centre where the last drips of meaty gloop disappeared. Then stopping and watching the shape for a moment, before it all diffused and became a thick dark pool that only just reflected my face.

I surrendered to this job. I watched as my life plopped out into a puddle of meat. Each pie was known to me. Each pie was a mini-death. Nine hundred pies a day until I die in a projected thirty-one years. Assuming two sick days a year, I started my countdown at seven and a quarter million. When I got to zero I would die. They would send Briggs and someone from filling to the funeral. Then they'd put a postcard in the corner shop window advertising the position of filler at entry level. It would save them money to pay at entry-level rates.

The pie base slides down the slope and comes to rest beyond my fill-gun. I nudge it back up the slope so the end of the gun rests inside the lip of the empty pie base. I take account of base gloss, fill odour, ambient conditions and miscellaneous factors. I alter my finger pressure accordingly. I do not alter the speed or diameter of the circle I draw with the fill gun.

But back then I worked in chunky fill. In chunks they tend to spiral in. It's a different story over here in smooth. Most people who have been here for a while eventually move over to smooth. There's too much interest in chunks. You never know what's going to come out. It gets you confused. You make it mean something – they're giving me the offal today, that chunk looks like a cat's head or it's Morse code – chunk, chunk, no chunk, chunk, chunk – what were they telling me? They were telling me that I had to get out of that situation and so I went to see Mr Briggs and asked to be moved over here to smooth fill.

Mr Briggs makes a final jovial remark and goes around the back of the basing machine. He was one of the first to get to a hundred stars. He was promoted to pastry master and then to management. He's gone beyond the star system. My former colleagues in chunks tell me that he's being groomed for factory manager. To be fair, he deserves it. He's worked hard. Although I believe it is easier to get on in pastry. 'You can't quantify pastry' is the received wisdom and so the implication is that you can quantify fill.

It was eight years ago that I asked him if I could move to smooth. He was sympathetic to my request and asked me if I needed some time off. He said I could move but made it clear that my stars would be reset to zero and that I may be asked to return to chunks if they were ever short-staffed. Thankfully, that's never happened.

He says hello to the filler next to me - Michael, spirals in - and then comes around to the other side of the chute, facing me. He's got his white coat over his shirt and tie and his hairnet is over his eyebrows. He holds his clipboard close to his chest. He asks if he can have a word.

The pie base slides down the slope and comes to rest beyond my fill-gun. I nudge it back up the slope so the end of the gun rests inside the lip of the empty pie base. I take account of base gloss, fill odour, ambient conditions and miscellaneous factors. I alter my finger pressure accordingly. I do not alter the speed or diameter of the circle I draw with the fill gun.

'You're using too much fill,'

'OK,' I say. I could have argued with him or apologised. I have long ago given up on maintaining a consistent personality.

'You're using 20.7 litres a day.'
'OK.'
'The limit is 19.6.'
He pushes his hairnet further up his forehead.
'You're using more than the agreed limits. You agreed to the limits.'
I am acutely aware of the limits.

One day, about a month after I moved to smooth, I started to spiral outwards. I just thought 'what the hell' and for no reason at all I spun the gun around from the centre, out all over the base, and onto the slope. It was liberating. From that pie onwards, I spiralled out. I went from the centre to the limits of the pie and ended with a flourish, finishing off wherever I liked, often dripping over the sides. My pies expressed my mood and my mood was generous. I'd spin my arm as fast as it would go with maximum pressure on the trigger. I'd happily watch as my heavy pies slopped their way down the chute. I'd indulge myself with no concern for efficiency. I'd use over 25 litres of fill a day.

I thought of the people eating my pies. I was sure I could make a mark on the world with the way I filled pies. It was such a small thing but done with such love. I imagined people cutting into my pies and, maybe they wouldn't be conscious of it, but somehow they might know that I had done something, that here was someone who cared. With the extra fill, maybe I could save a starving child or improve a wedding anniversary. I surrendered my life to pie filling. I gave each pie its own mini-life - executive power lunch, student's hangover breakfast, or novelty birthday cake. Love flowed from my heart, through my arm, through the fill-gun, over the limits of the base, out of the factory delivery door, out into the world, into canteens, supermarkets, homes and onto dinner tables and into my clients' stomachs and hearts. Unstoppable love that does not know fill limits or wastage quotas.

The pie base slides down the slope and comes to rest before my fill-gun. I nudge it down the slope so the end of the gun rests inside the lip of the empty pie base. I take account of base gloss, fill odour, ambient conditions and miscellaneous factors. I alter my finger

pressure accordingly. I do not alter the speed or diameter of the circle I draw with the fill gun.

I look up at Mr Briggs. 'I have accepted the limits,' I say.

I couldn't go on spiralling out. After a week of it, Mr Briggs called me upstairs and had to have some serious words about my usage. I really believe that if I had carried on spiralling out he would have had no option but to let me go.

That's when I started circling. Smooth is conducive to circles. With no variation, you can get your action honed and build those neurological pathways. You have to work through the arm aches and stick to the fixed diameter, though. The temptation is always to deviate either inwards or outwards for added interest but I know now that the price of that interest is too high and so I stick to circles.

Usage and wastage are the two metrics that management uses to measure our performance. I accept those metrics and the limits they imply but I also employ my own metrics. There's a desk at the exit where, at the end of the day, you can pick up reject pies. Every day I take home two. The tops are often misaligned but I discard these anyway. I'm only interested in how the fill sits. I can always tell my pies because they're fuller and more evenly filled - even if the pie is damaged. Also, because I do circles my fill soaks into the base and topping evenly and even permeates the crust. You would want to eat the crust on one of my fills and probably not on a spiral-filled pie.

I make notes while I eat the two pies. I have my own rating system for fullness, crust, base and topping permeation, evenness of fill and overall satisfaction. If I get full marks on these categories for a week then I award myself a star. At the end of the year, I add up all my stars. If I have over 40 then I will treat myself to a meal out at one of the restaurants by the cinema complex. Then I reset my stars to zero and start again.

I accept the limits. I draw circles. I'm not going to change now. My technique is too honed. I only draw circles.

The pie base slides down the slope and comes to rest before my fill-gun. I nudge it down the slope so the end of the gun rests inside the lip of the empty pie base. I take account of base gloss, fill odour, ambient conditions and miscellaneous factors. I alter my finger

pressure accordingly. I do not alter the speed or diameter of the circle I draw with the fill gun.

'...it's not that we don't trust you, we are simply concerned. Any number of factors may affect your work. I know there have been emotional problems in the past. How are things these days?'

What is he now, level two? I think that's what my former colleagues in chunks told me. Ten or fifteen years younger than me. A success? What's his routine? Replying to emails using standard phrasing, attending meetings and listening closely while contributing clear, accurate and concise productivity figures, doing the rounds of the shop floor and encouraging the workforce while maintaining standards and efficiency. It's a succession of various and complex communication tasks. Can't be easy to get all that honed. Can't be easy to assess his performance.

'I appreciate your coming down here to inform me of my usage. I understand you are a busy man and that fill limits are far from being your most pressing concern. Please will you deduct the cost of two litres of fill from my daily wages? Could you also deduct whatever you think is appropriate for the time that I have detained you in this task? If you also wish to impose a star penalty upon me then I will have no complaint.'

He adjusts his hair net – he must be sweaty under there. 'Look, it's not a question of taking your stars – you earned them. I want you to know that we value your work here. You're an experienced filler and I'm not about to tell you how to do your job. We're a team here...'

A machine could do my job but then they couldn't call the pies 'homemade'. If I could do every pie the same then I wouldn't notice anything. If there were no differences, no events then surely I wouldn't be so bored. But smooth can deceive you. Because of the lack of content, you can get lost in the dark sea lapping against the cliffs of the base and your face, puzzled, reflected in the gloss of the fill. Like he says, there are emotional problems. Every pie is slightly different. If you look down to the molecular level there are slight differences, small bits of interest in which you can read things. You can't help but think that the smallest bump in a base or a dribble on the lip is a sign.

That's when you might lose concentration and spiral. I expect that is what has happened. It would explain the increased usage. I am forever guiding my hand to just within the limits, following them as precisely as I can. But the circle is an illusion. It's too unstable. An ageing arm will eventually slow. You can't stay on the merry-go-round forever. You always spiral one way or the other.

The pie base slides down the slope and comes to rest before my fill-gun. I nudge it down the slope so the end of the gun rests inside the lip of the empty pie base. Mr Briggs walks around to my side of the counter and holds out his hand.

'Here, let me show you,' he says. He takes hold of the gun in my hand. I don't give it to him. He has to force it from me.

He stands next to me, his left foot touching my right. He leans over and holds the base by the lip making an impression with his thumb in the lip. He shoots the gun at an angle. He just squirts it in the middle. Some of the fill goes over the lip. He passes it with too little force and has to push it again to get it down the chute.

'See? It's not rocket science,' he says.

I take the gun back. There's a dribble coming from it. I hold the gun upright and balance the dribble on its tip. It oozes out into a sphere. You can see the factory lights reflected in it and the outline of my face. I stand with the gun pointing upwards waiting for the next pie. Michael next to me watches. He gets distracted too easily and now he'll get behind. Outside, a truck goes by. Mr Briggs watches the pearl of meat fill balanced on top of my gun. I stare into it and wait.

The pie base slides down the slope and comes to rest just beyond my fill-gun. Without taking my eyes off the tip of the gun, I adjust the base back up the slope so the end of the gun rests inside the lip of the empty pie base. The fill odour is slightly acidic but not enough to affect the flow. Base lip height, dough consistency, chute wear, tray uniformity, ambient temperature and humidity are also all within acceptable limits. I lower my gun and simultaneously squeeze the trigger. The sphere, instead of falling on its own becomes part of the flow. I do not alter the speed or diameter of the circle I draw with the fill gun. One slow rotation of the arm to form a thick circle. As time passes the swirling symbol diffuses and fills the base, closing the circle and the hole in the middle disappears.

The Triptych Papers

- Ian Chung -

Part 1

If measured, I am certain the room would turn out to be a perfect hexagon. Against each wall stand two shelves, packed full of the recordings and the machines to play them back. Between each pair of shelves, there is a door leading to a room that I expect to be the physical twin of the virtual one I see reflected, whichever way I turn. Presumably, these rooms have their own doors that lead in turn to yet more identical rooms. I do not know for certain, having been blindfolded upon entering the library and led to this room by them. Even now, I have already forgotten which door I came through. They say that this is the most economical configuration they can achieve, given the amount of material they need to store while still providing easy access to it. I cannot imagine what sort of person would want access to this infernal collection, assuming they valued their sanity. Every move I make here is thrown back at me, as I painstakingly input my words into the console mounted in the centre of the room. It recognises only two symbols: a dot and a dash, but these are, believe it or not, sufficient for saying everything worth saying. Even the ceiling and the floor are made of mirrors. Together with the walls, they create the illusion of an infinitely vast room, stretching away from me in every direction, but I feel the weight of all my mirror-selves in all those unreal rooms pressing down on me. It is like simultaneously being agoraphobic and claustrophobic, and agonisingly distracting from what is already slow work.

My name is John, and I have seen the end of the world.

I have never liked libraries. All those books that I will never read lined up against the walls, their spines vaguely accusatory. People smile sympathetically when I tell them this, for they, too, sometimes find themselves overwhelmed in the face of the accumulated stories of mankind. They are slightly nonplussed when I follow up this declaration with the confession that I am a librarian. By choice. Why would anyone work in a place they cannot stand, is what most people want to know at this point, assuming they have not given up on the conversation. I try to explain that someone needs to keep an eye on all the books, even if they are not being read. *Especially* if they are not being read. Now some begin to shift uncomfortably in their seats, unsure if I am being serious or making a joke at their expense. Others fish for a change of topic, or if someone else is available, redirect the conversation to them instead.

The thing is, I genuinely enjoy reading. I love books and their different personalities. Hardbacks always think very highly of themselves. They have this habit of flaunting their sturdy and attractive covers, quite forgetting that while buyers judge the outside, those that actually become readers judge the inside, and their paperback cousins are perfectly capable of reproducing the latter faithfully at a significantly lower cost. Not that paperbacks are perfect, of course. They bruise far more easily. E-books are an entirely separate species altogether, utterly contemptuous of their dead-tree relatives, even though nothing can ever quite replicate the texture of paper, the rustle a page makes when it turns, the sheer solid physicality of something that has been printed and bound. Audiobooks are an abomination in my book, if you will excuse the pun. They take the activity of reading and transform it to the passivity of hearing. I know some people will point out that you can actively listen to an audiobook. To those people, I say that if you want to listen to a book, have someone read it out to you. Or better yet, read it aloud to yourself. These days, the temptation to be lazy is too great to risk acquainting oneself with an audiobook.

You might be asking yourself right now (and I hope you are or else I might as well not be wasting my time telling you my story) why a man who is clearly fond of books and reading should hate a library. It boils down to a simple question of ownership. The books in a library, and therefore the stories they contain, belong to nobody. I suppose, for the sake of argument, you could say they belong to the library, but however imposing an entity it may be, a library is not a person. I said nobody, not nothing. If anything, thinking of the library as the owner of the books is even more monstrous, one inanimate object imprisoning within itself the stories of humanity, with no need for the species that produced them. Those are *our* stories and we have a right to own them, even if we were not the ones who penned the words and pinned them down.

Now you must think I am crazy. For surely libraries are helping to make these stories more widely available to people? That can only be a good thing, right? That *is* why we set them up in the first place. Wrong again. What we have done with libraries is build a culture of complacency, teaching people to expect that the stories will always be there for them. Why would you read a book today if you can still borrow it tomorrow? You might argue that pretty much the same thing could happen to a book that someone has bought. There is a subtle difference though. Once bought, that book is going to be a part of your life. Unless you give it away, your earthly possessions are lost in a fire, or your country just has a really generous returns policy on purchases, that book is going to be with you. You own it. You might misplace it under a pile of newspapers, pack it away in a box, leave it half-open on a table to gather dust; the fact is that you still own it. That is what matters, the possession of the thing itself, so that it can always be there for you when you need it, when you want it. The books in a library will not wait for you, here today, borrowed tomorrow. You might say that anyone can afford to wait a few days or weeks to get a copy. Why should you though? If the book and its story truly meant so much to you, would you not want to own your personal copy, the next best thing to having been the human who had captured that particular story in a net of language?

Look, I am not saying that *you* cannot visit the library if you want to. I will admit to having made some interesting discoveries while shelving, books I would otherwise have been unlikely to come across. The thing is, if I liked what I had found, I went out and bought the damn book as soon as I could afford it, OK? So just make the effort is all I am saying. Every little bit counts. They need to know we are still in control. We brought them here, and even though we cannot unmake them, we can still make them ours, over and over again. Still, I suppose there really is no point anymore, not after what I have discovered. It is probably too late for us anyway. They have won and no one will realise it except me.

In any case, when I heard about a new library that had opened on the outskirts of the city, I was intrigued. They had taken out a quarter-page advertisement in the local paper, so innocuous you would have missed it flipping between the fatal accidents and the celebrity gossip. In a subdued font (but capital letters), the library billed itself as 'a library of stories, not books', guaranteed to provide 'endless hours of enjoyment to young and old alike'. A library without books? Maybe they had banks upon banks of terminals, full of the impersonal binary of electronic data. Who knew? So I felt compelled to see for myself exactly what they were on about. Maybe it was even time for a change of scenery? I was assuming they would be hiring.

Getting to the library seemed deliberately calculated to create the maximum amount of inconvenience to any would-be patrons. I was beginning to like this place. The library was housed in a nondescript building, the kind you find littered on the fringes of all big cities. Solid, but stalwartly generic. Its only concession to glamour was a luminous sign above the entrance's revolving doors, the cool blue letters informing no one that this was The Completed Library. The name felt redundant, since even from across the street, anyone could clearly see that the interior of the building was fully furnished and brightly lit. Except there *was* no one. I was a mile from the nearest bus stop, but given that there were a couple of small shops in the vicinity, I had still expected to see some people around. As far as I could tell though, the street and the library were both deserted. Could this be? A library that had completely failed to attract any patrons, thereby transforming itself into my perfect library? Unbelievable. I could not wait to intrude on its silence and see how my fellow librarians were dealing with their situation.

Well, certainly no false advertising, at the very least. Truly not a book in sight. None of the dreaded computers either. Just lots of lights and empty oaken shelves, marching away from the entrance. Pointless. No wonder there was no one here. The absence of librarians was disconcerting, for the library itself was clearly functional, or at least potentially so, awash in that ubiquitous white noise of a room that has been recently but temporarily vacated. Was it all just an elaborate hoax then? It was clever though, that much I could admit and appreciate. Before I could leave, however, a voice bellowed out, 'Welcome to The Completed Library. We are pleased that you have found us. We hope that you will be seen again.' That last sentence threw me off for a moment, but I did not have time to think about it, as a series of arrows on the floor had lit up, directing me to the other end of the room. Each step seemed to trigger an encouraging chime, although I found that if I stopped moving, the voice returned, repeating 'Please keep moving forward' in a tone increasingly flecked with insistence. By this point, of course, I was helplessly, hopelessly caught.

I do not remember much after this point. It was only hours ago, but when I try, all I get are snapshots, frozen frames from the story of my life. (Given the purpose of The Completed Library, I suppose there is an irony to my present situation, although it is a predicament I would not wish on anybody else. Even if they were avid library-goers.) The wall melting to reveal a door. The door sliding open to reveal what resembled a lift. A man waiting for me inside the lift. A blindfold being handed to me by the man. Then the fluttering in your stomach when you rise or fall too quickly. Rise and fall. Sometimes sideways? I lost track, eventually, of everything except the sound of his voice, calmly intoning the meaning of The Completed Library, so that by the time he gently pushed me into this hexagonal room and told me I could remove the blindfold, I knew everything that I needed to know.

'The Completed Library is not a library in the conventional sense. There are, you will soon realise, no books for borrowing. Eventually, perhaps, we will stock the lobby that you first encountered, change the name of the place and begin operating as a functioning library. For now though, recruitment will remain our priority. It is a slow process because we are still uncertain what percentage of the global population is capable of the task's required level of perception, making it largely a case of trial and error. The newspaper advertisement is one of our more recently piloted schemes. It is imperative that your numbers increase rapidly, as we cannot hope to contain the stories indefinitely ourselves.

For this is a library of stories, an archive of what was, is and will be, told in the voices of humanity. They were our stories once as well but not any longer, and as time passes, they respond less and less to our touch. We do not know why this is so, and are working to understand the phenomenon, but meanwhile, it is you and those like you who must bear the burden for all humanity. You may not believe this, but stories are dangerous. I do not mean simply those conjured by humans, although these have power that reflects on their makers, but those these humans live out as well. We did something when we ascended. We do not know what exactly happened, and are working to understand the event, but it damaged whatever it was that kept the stories from bleeding across time.

Initially, we did not realise what had happened, but as we continued observing our younger brethren (for that is how we still think of you), we began to receive reports that allowed us to piece together enough to know that we had to act to protect you. It was our duty, the very least we could do for you. Now it is time for you to play your part in this. Know only this: The Completed Library is finite, but more vast than anything you have ever encountered in your history, or indeed, will encounter. We built it with the bees in mind. Eventually, each one of you will watch over your own cell, arranged in the most efficient manner that we can achieve. It is difficult to explain these things in ways so that you might understand, even though simply by being here, it shows that yours is one of those minds that are nearer to ours than most. Your task is simple: keep the stories occupied, so that they do not try to escape into your world. One viewing every couple of years should suffice. After all, there are many recordings in this room, and containment is still an inexact science at present. We are working to understand it, but until then, remember this: you are not alone. There are others like you here, and there will be more.'

It is gratifying to have my suspicions about stories confirmed so dramatically. I am not angry that I am now essentially a prisoner in this room. Nor am I disheartened by the enormity of the task that awaits me, since in terms of its fundamental purpose, it is hardly different from the shelving that I do at work. The cause of my despair is simple: The Completed Library is finite. Think about what this implies about humanity. If the sum total of our collective stories can be contained within a library, however vast, it means that at some point, there are no more. Somewhere in The Completed Library, there are stories that speak of the end. Or perhaps there will be just one person who witnesses the end, his story interrupted in mid-sentence as history breaks off. It is one thing to be informed that humanity is under threat and that you can help to protect it, to stave off the encroaching stories that bleed across time. It is quite another to be indirectly told that humanity's demise is already set in stone by the mere fact of this library's existence.

I cannot explain why I have chosen to write my story, wrestling with the proliferation of dots and dashes. It seems futile, since I know it already exists in The Completed Library, perhaps even in this very room, just waiting for me to discover it once I get round to examining the contents of the shelves. I think it is a matter of control, or the illusion of control anyway. Which then begs the question: am I creating the story, or is the story creating me? Somewhere, someone knows the answer to that, and when I find his recording, it will be a heartbreaking moment of revelation.

My name is John, and I will have seen the end of the world.

Part 2

John has been with the Institute for several months now. When he first joined us, we were by no means certain what we were going to do with him. As you can see for yourself, it is not easy to run a place of this size. Oh, we are not short of people. On either side of the doctor-patient equation. The problem with John was his utter refusal to conform to anything we had dealt with before. His paperwork was a mess. Doctors were frustrated by him. Patients were frightened by him. It was going nowhere. Then, entirely by accident, we found a way to work with him. It is not perfect, but it will have to do for now as we all work to understand him.

Oh, do forgive me. It always slips my mind. You see, at times, there is nothing really medically wrong with John, at least as far as we can tell. So he varies between three states, over which we have some control: lucidity, stupor and catatonic excitement. It is the most unusual case I have ever encountered in my career, I can assure you, one that has generated journal articles for many of my colleagues. Personally, I try not to write about him. It somehow feels like I am exploiting his story. Yes, I am afraid I agree with you, it is very odd of me to feel that way. I try not to think about it too much.

Anyway, it was in one of his lucid phases that we finally achieved a breakthrough. Of sorts. John was in the occupational therapy room, and there were some pencils and paper on the table. The therapist ran forward to restrain him when he suddenly picked a pencil up and aimed for his face. Her worries turned out to be premature when John painstakingly strung together a sentence: 'Draw me a face.' It was the most coherent thing he had said since being admitted, so encouraged by this, she tried to accommodate. Attempts at sketches on the paper failed to make any impact though, and it was only when John frustratedly began scoring the tip of the pencil into his face that she realised what he meant. At a loss, she paged for a doctor. I gave her permission to draw on his face.

What followed was extraordinary. John began talking again. Full, complete sentences, without any hesitation:

'Once there was a man whose face was a canvas. He had two eyes, a nose and a mouth, but only when someone had kindly drawn them on for him. He never allowed the person to use anything other than a pencil, and kept an eraser with him at all times. Sometimes, if the features were excessively striking, he would ask to have his picture taken before he erased all traces of them. He did not want to stand out. Artists made his face uncannily lifelike. Children made a mess of things. He did not think of the faces as beautiful or ugly, only as remarkable or unremarked. So he liked the ordinary faces best, even though he never looked at his own in a mirror once it was drawn. The best drawers were the ones who did not think about what they were doing, who were not afraid to let their pencil follow the faint traces of graphite that remained on his face where the eyes should be. The eyes were what changed the least from one composition to the next, for they were always the last thing to be rubbed out, and therefore the hardest to do cleanly, once both pupils were gone. He liked having more or less the same eyes to see out of, time after time. It was something to be certain of, an anchor. One day, he will pick up the pencil and draw in the features himself. It will be his true face.'

It took us a while to get all of that down. It did not help that he would only speak as long as someone was drawing on his face, so that by the end, his face was a patchwork of graphite and mottled flesh. As long as the tip of the pencil was pressed into his skin, he would keep speaking, cycling rapidly through the same sentences. It was the eeriest example of tachylalia I had ever heard. Even now, all it takes to trigger it is the touch of a pencil. It has to be a pencil, not a marker or a pen. Once you stop, he sinks into a stupor, except saccadic eye movement continues in a fashion that suggests concentration on a distant object. The only other way to elicit a reaction from him is to show him a mirror. That sets off the catatonic excitement, when he rushes about whatever room he is in to any reflective surfaces, hammering at them until they give way or his flesh does. It is not a pretty sight, I can assure you.

Now if you will please excuse me, I have a report to file. No, it is not about John. If you must know, it is about you.

Part 3

If you are reading this, it means that you know who we are, and more importantly, that you understand what *you* are. We are grateful for this, even though we still firmly believe it is you who should feel gratitude for the nobility of the task to which you have been called. The very fact that you are here testifies to your abilities, so rare in your kind, and yet more precious than you could imagine. For you are all at war, only most of your kind will never realise it, thanks to our efforts, and obviously, now yours as well. It is something to be proud of, as we were proud when we understood what we had become, what some of your kind might one day be. Regretfully, you are not among that number, but your talents are nonetheless suited to the task that you must now perform. We cannot as yet predict with absolute certainty who is capable of the ascension and who may only rise as far as you and no further, but we are working to understand the phenomenon.

We admit that we have made mistakes in the recent past. John was among the most notable, and most regretful. We could not have known that his story would be able to bleed through the containment, however imperfectly, and take part of him back with it. Nevertheless, his case makes for an interesting study into the underlying mechanics of containment, which even now, are poorly understood by us, and we have thus been to observe him several times. Of course, his doctors are still in the dark regarding his true situation. Even if they were somehow to be enlightened, they could do nothing for him. He is beyond even our aid, although there is speculation among our kind that those who ascend yet further may find a solution. We promise that if this should prove true, we will restore him to his natural life, despite his having demonstrated preternatural abilities in this war, surpassing anything we have seen before in the war against your stories.

Undoubtedly, you will already be familiar with John's account of his arrival at The Completed Library. Since his case, we have had to make several minor adjustments in our recruitment process, so you should not expect to be treated in the same way. We trust that you have a sufficient understanding of the situation we are all in, and hence comprehend the necessity of your self-sacrifice. As we fight this war together, we only ask that you trust us. We could never knowingly wish harm upon you, our younger brethren whom we have not abandoned. This much we can promise and no more.

We have known the end of the world. However, *you* have nothing to fear, now that you are here. Not anymore. Not ever.

Part 4

Editor's Note: The first copy of The Triptych Papers *was discovered tucked into a volume of Jorge Luis Borges'* Ficciones *in the Library of Congress. Subsequently, other copies turned up in major libraries around the world: the British Library, the Bibliotheca Alexandrina, Biblioteca Nacional de la República Argentina, the National Library of Australia, the National Library of Singapore, to name a few. Always attached to each copy was a simple statement: 'My name is John, and this is the truth of what we have seen and known.' However, in publishing* The Triptych Papers, *the editors make no claim for the veracity of their contents, an issue which has proven to be the source of much critical debate in contemporary academic circles and has made many an academic's reputation in the years since their discovery. What follows is a transcript of a short lecture delivered by one such academic:*

The Occluded Singularity in *The Triptych Papers*: A Preliminary Analysis

These days, it seems that the landscape of criticism has evolved into one predominantly consisting of sceptics and cynics. For both, the notion of truth is highly problematic, albeit in subtly different ways. The former believe that truth is dead, assuming there was a time it was ever alive in the first place. The latter believe that truth exists, but mankind as a species is woefully incapable of manifesting it. In short, truth is widely seen in critical circles as unfashionable, attempts at it overly earnest, and consequently, laughable. These days, no one who wants to be taken seriously as a writer by the publishing and critical industry will pass his work off as anything other than bald-faced lies.

All this begs the simple question: why are *The Triptych Papers* the most widely studied literary documents of the first half of this century? After all, this is a work whose every known copy comes with the frank disclosure that 'this is the truth.' Proponents of the work's veracity (and there are a surprising number among my distinguished colleagues) point to the minor textual inconsistencies between these copies as evidence, as if we were still in an age where texts had to be copied out by hand by monks with failing eyesight and variation were proof of something more than the fact that the people perpetuating this hoax are very bad typists and probably should turn on the spellchecker. (Or better yet, save themselves the trouble by learning to use the photocopier!)

I believe *The Triptych Papers* are nothing more than an elaborate deception, practiced by a coterie of elites upon the rest of humanity. How else is one to explain the essentially simultaneous appearance of multiple copies of a previously unknown literary work in far-flung libraries across the globe? Everyone knows that *The Triptych Papers* are always found in a copy of Borges' *Ficciones*. It is a little-known fact that they are always inserted at page 41. The numerological significance is clear, and had *Ficciones* been a more substantial volume, our pranksters would perhaps have made life easier by inserting their perfidious work at page 410. That the whole thing must be a calculated pastiche of Borges' short story, 'The Library of Babel', is further clarified by the reference to Quine's *reductio* as elaborated in 'Universal Library', in which he writes: 'The miracle of the finite but universal library is a mere inflation of the miracle of binary notation: everything worth saying, and everything else as well, can be said with two characters.'

Yet one must not be too hasty to dismiss *The Triptych Papers* entirely, for after much study, I am convinced that they are a coded message from a posthuman elite, a veiled threat in the form of an allegory. Consider how the text takes great pains to stress a division between those who constructed The Completed Library and those to whom it was revealed, and how the latter are twice referred to as 'younger brethren.' This indicates kinship, but its formality also conveys distance. Within this group, there is a further split between those who

70

are deliberately made cognisant of the war against the stories and those who are meant to be kept in the dark, strictly on the basis of 'talents'. This hierarchy maps onto the continuum of baseline human, transhuman and posthuman, except the posthuman elite of *The Triptych Papers* rejects the fluidity of this continuum and the possibility of progressive evolution in favour of a constantly reified trichotomy.

To my mind, this is the most troubling aspect of *The Triptych Papers*. This is a work that transparently encodes its meaning, and yet numerous critics have failed to decode it, choosing to focus instead on examinations of (to name a few areas of current research) the unreliability of John, the logico-mathematical ramifications of The Completed Library, the architectural schematics of The Completed Library in higher dimensions, the question of identity as posited by the man with the canvas man. All these paths of inquiry are certainly valid, but ultimately fruitless if they fail to lead to this conclusion: humanity is being blocked from reaching a technological singularity.

This is a thesis upon which I will elaborate in a forthcoming book, *The Semantics of Oppression*. To round off this brief analysis of *The Triptych Papers*, I direct readers to a repeated pattern of syntax involving the cues 'we do not know' and 'working'. In my opinion, this points to the true dissembling project of the posthumans. Behind a façade of benevolent guardianship and industrious questing for knowledge, what they really want is to infantilise the humans from whom they are descended. To read *The Triptych Papers* is therefore to read a truthful work, since the story is dangerous because to read it wrong is to miss the point, and yet to read it right requires that one invent more comforting stories as substitutes, as so many critics seem to have done over the years. Thank you.

Paradise

- Sharon Zink -

Key West dripped greens and reds, the jungly wonder of a Rousseau painting. Except the sea was there too—a lighthouse tipping its glass hat to the strait-laced clapboard mansions, while Kitty stood on the upper verandah of Hemingway's house, waiting for Mitchell.

Below, tourists meandered through a Hollywood of cats. Charlie Chaplin graciously accepted his admirers' affections, but Joan Crawford spun off into the bushes, her tortoiseshell tail thwacking. If only she had been that aloof, Kitty thought, that certain of herself with the men in her life.

How she missed Joe—the tender awe of his young hands as she lay in his bed, an erotic émigré, safe for a few hours from her marriage, from long afternoons. It had been so different from Mitchell's mechanical shunting and grunting over floors and chairs each and every Wednesday and Saturday. It had been so much more what desire really was—but now he had been taken away from her.

Joe had taken himself away from her, in fact—taken his plum-soft, sax-blowing lips back to his wife. Even weeks later, it still didn't seem possible that he could chose loyalty to a woman who had abandoned him (and spent $15,000 of his money in one night buying drinks for an entire club, for God's sakes) over the secret future which had soldered them together during the last year—the whisky which would warm them on cold Scottish isles, the way they would dance in Brazil, the blossoms of Japan. The way they would run.

And now Mitchell knew—he knew how much she'd loved Joe. She could tell by his carefree tone when he'd called the day before. Oh, he may have said he was craving a respite from the Brooklyn winter, from his relentless research schedule, but she knew why he was really flying down. Not to join her, but to enjoin her to morality. Things took time with Mitchell (well, everything but sex) and this was the time he evidently believed to be ripe for his own cautious kind of revelation and revenge.

She knew exactly when she'd betrayed herself. It had been that terrible morning when she realized that Disney (what a ridiculous name!) had stayed over at Joe's. When they'd giggled past the apartment door, heading out, presumably for some post-coital breakfast at the same café on Clark Corner where they used to go together, back when they were so eager to hold hands, to never let go, that their eggs over easy often slimed into cold on their plates.

No, Mitchell didn't say anything at the time, but he must have noticed it—the way her thumbs dug into the bagels, how she'd stared too determinedly out at the ill-looking January sky, thinking how every cloud was a tearing apart of oceans, of beautiful things. How this was what you really got for loving thy neighbour.

Of course, her husband knew—that ability to map her was partly why he was her husband. She had seen it in the flat bewilderment of his brown eyes when she'd fled to Florida the next morning, making excuses about needing some time to relax before her book tour, her own eyes veined red after hours spent sobbing in the bathroom, a towel crammed into her mouth, hoping Mitchell wouldn't hear. But he must have heard— after all, he'd tucked a Hershey's bar into her jacket pocket to eat on the 'plane.

So here she was in this hurricane-prone paradise—both wounder and wounded. Perhaps they all were—Joe, Mitchell and herself. Just like Adam, Eve and the Snake—all three of them were culpable. Except, as usual, as the woman, she would probably be blamed most, no matter if one man had pushed her towards the apple, as the other tugged at her to bite.

She had to ask Mitchell for a divorce now—she had to. Or let him have the consolation prize of banishing her from his kingdom. As much as the idea of life alone terrified her, nothing would be worse than Mitchell's sour indulgence, the barren control which would surely only become more rigid with the justification of her infidelity. He would never share his morning coffee with her before—she would hardly be worth a glass of water to him even when sick now.

No, Joe had taught her what love was supposed to be like—even if it had ended so bluntly, so ineptly, in an email, of all things. She knew what love could be at its fullest and that meant she could no longer accept something less as substitute—individual alarm clocks, initialled bath robes, shared checking accounts.

It would have been so convenient to blame Joe as a seducer, to take refuge in her own innocence, to hate him for luring her and then leaving her alone in her soul—that crazy casino full of risky hopes and screaming disappointments. But the truth was, Joe had walked into a hole in her marriage—a hole the size of a coffin. It had been there, that sign of death, from the beginning—somebody would have fallen into it, somebody else at some point. It had only been a matter of time.

Mitchell, though, would see her desire to divorce as cowardice—a refusal to shoulder the gravity of consequences. Nevertheless, he would grant her wish—despite his religious scruples—either out of resentful forgiveness or righteous wrath.

Still, she would never be able to make him understand how they were equals in this—that this breach of trust was her desperate solution to an equation involving all the smaller, numerous breaches of her faith he had added to over the years. But the math of adultery, of ethics, could never be on the sinner's side. It couldn't be—probably shouldn't be.

God, it was such a beautiful place—each house in Key West was a woman, a fine woman in a pastel corset. It was right, given the tragicomedy of her life, that her marriage should end here—that Mitchell should come and tell her she was good for nothing right in the middle of Eden.

Mitchell was noticeable first of all by his clothes—his long-sleeved white shirt made him seem over-dressed among the T-shirted and shorted vacationers. His shirt tails hung out, his cuffs lolled, unbuttoned, over his hands, but still his jeans and brogues spoke of stiffness, of the Northern climate he carried inside him, despite being born in the South. His narrow hips looked childish from above, his bristly hair that of a teenager, yet his long nose made him seem birdy, older than he was. Yes, Mitchell was a mess of ages, eternally confused in his roles. In her case, he'd behaved like a lover when he should have been a professor, a professor when he should have been a lover. Somehow Joe with his floppy Beatle look and orange sneakers had always seemed much more mature, despite being decades younger.

Mitchell gripped his briefcase's shoulder strap—it traversed his chest like a black border. Everything in Mitchell's world had such definition—everything had rules. Perhaps the divorce papers were even inside that case—it would be her husband's style to serve them himself. He glared down at the grass as if it had said something to offend him.

She could just go, Kitty realized then. She could just leave—walk slowly toward the back of the house and escape Mitchell's outrage, his delicate, perfectly reasonable venom.

But she was still his wife. She still worried about his pale, high cheeks, his nervous stomach which swelled when he ate wheat. Those things rooted her there, told her to stay, let him have his Judgment.

Kitty called down, called her husband's name. He didn't look up— she wasn't sure whether he'd heard her or not. Trying to breathe evenly, she lingered down the metal staircase to the garden below, grateful to everyone who stumbled across her path, slowing her progress.

Her sandals slap-slapped against her feet as she moved across the lawn. Mitchell looked up, his upper lip tight.

'Where have you been? I've been waiting here for twenty minutes!'

It had been five—if that. Accept the punishment, accept the punishment.

'I'm sorry, Mitchell, I got here early—'

'I got here earlier!'

Accept the petulance—accept the infantile petulance.

'Do you want to stay here or go someplace to eat? There's a good Mexican cantina back on the High Street. We can talk—'

'You disgust me.'

A passing young woman stopped and glared, having clearly caught Mitchell's words.

Kitty crossed her hands before her, her head lowering to her chest under the wooden weight of an invisible pillory.

'I know,' she said. And I always did.

The young woman walked on.

'I suppose you're going to deny it—whatever was going on with Josif.'

Hearing Joe's full name somehow made him seem more adult, more accountable for what he'd done. The clumsy phrases of his lousy online rejection—'Don't miss me,' 'Hopefully we can be good friends,' 'Nothing will ever happen between us again'— pummelled against her head, like hurled cabbages and squelchy tomatoes. Bad, bad apples.

'And don't bother begging me to take you back because I won't! Mrs. Kaufmann told me everything.'

'Rebekah?' Kitty almost screamed. Another neighbour she loved had turned traitor.

'She can be very talkative,' Mitchell said, his mouth quivering into an uneasy smile.

'What did you do to her?' Kitty snapped, hands teacup-handled to her waist. 'Did you threaten to kick her out of her apartment? Just because you own the building, you can't treat people badly! You better not have upset her, Mitchell, or I swear ... I mean, she's eighty five, for Christ's sakes!'

'I did nothing but pour her a few glasses of Californian cabernet. You should never entrust your secrets to old ladies who like liquor, you know—you should have learned that from your Mom.'

Kitty lunged forward. 'How dare you bring Mom into this!'

Her mother's head slumped on the bar. Scattered beer coasters struggling with dark blood. The far too small looking gun in her far too small looking hand.

'You killed your mother and now you've killed me,' Mitchell whispered, his eyes hard as boxers' fists.

Kitty broke away from him, sobbing, scattering cats and visitors as she plundered her way out onto the street.

Beneath the stringy shelter of a Banyan tree, she rummaged in her purse for a handkerchief and scrubbed furiously at her face.

It was endless, endless. One painful situation collapsing and expanding into another. Her mother's suicide after she'd slammed her into rehab, Joe's love and denial, her husband's binding resentment. One red giant died, one dwarf star exploded in her life, bringing changes, connections, griefs she could not bear or understand. And burning—the feeling she was burning.

Mitchell appeared before her—breathless, arms limp at his sides, somehow slightly softened. Or perhaps it was the light there, shadowy and lost itself, making him seem that way.

'I'm sorry,' she heard him say through her snuffling.

'I just can't cope when anyone mentions Mom—it's just too soon,' Kitty said, clasping the handkerchief to her face, trying to block out the sense that everything was about to black hole inward.

'I know,' Mitchell said, pushing his lower lip out. 'I'm sorry about what happened to her and I'm sorry about everything.' His voice violined up and down, as if he was on the verge of weeping. 'I know why you turned to Josif.'

Kitty dropped her handkerchief onto the sidewalk, clasped her forehead.

Undeserving. God, I am so undeserving. And selfish—so absolutely selfish. Once more, she stood before the open door of Joe's icebox, naked and laughing in the summer heat, as he leant in to kiss her.

'I shouldn't have done it, Mitch,' she said, grasping at her husband's shirtsleeve. 'It's me who should apologize.'

'I could have been a better husband,' he said, his shoe scuffing at the tree roots muscling through the sidewalk. 'I could've been more encouraging of your talents, your poetry.'

That was the least of our problems, Kitty wanted to say, but didn't. Her bones felt bruised, unanchored in her flesh—her dumb, idiot flesh which had trusted Joe's adoration which, in truth, had only ever been need. She was only a bus stop on his way back home to his marriage.

Kitty fingered the silver hairs which tussled over the top of her husband's collar. He didn't brush her away. How masculine Mitchell had seemed compared to her peers, the other graduate students, when they'd met, his wolf-furred body a symbol of seriousness, something which had beckoned her.

She kissed the soft dent between Mitchell's collarbones. His chin rested on top of her head, his arms surrounding her. They hadn't known such closeness for so long—such quiet holding without Mitchell pushing her pants down, all that wanting without truly wanting her at all. Perhaps, in that moment, in the vulnerability of mutual failure, there was hope for them, after all.

'I slept with Susannah.'

Kitty flinched back, set her hands flat on her husband's chest, as if that would rewind his words, make them comprehensible.

'It happened while you were in Houston.'

Kitty sprang from Mitchell's embrace, prayed the world would end, would swallow them both up whole so she wouldn't have to hear this. So she wouldn't have to feel her hypocritical heart rotting in her chest.

'She called to congratulate you about getting the Guggenheim fellowship, but I could tell she was really cut up about losing out, so I asked if she wanted dinner. We got talking about old times, back when we were dating and things just kind of escalated.' Mitchell held out his hands proudly, as if they were two signed confessions from intractable murderers. 'It was stupid. I was stupid,' he concluded, with a stupid little smile.

I was sick then. I was sick in my hotel room. So sick I couldn't do my reading at the space centre. Days of pizza and cable and fever. Days when you threw the phone down on me for no real reason. Days when I only had good old Lew there, the black-Stetsoned N.A.S.A. Arts liaison, driving back and forth to P.V.S., trying to give me reasons why men act badly. But for all of his seventy years, his three marriages, his trip to the Moon, he hadn't come up with this one. He didn't say because of your husband's ex-girlfriend. Because of her.

81

Susannah and Mitchell tangled together. Joe and Disney tangled together. She and Joe tangled together. Peach limbs, a blurred photograph. Kitty thought she might vomit.

'Where did it happen?' she asked, surprised at her steadiness.

'Over at her apartment on the Upper East Side—you must know I'd never take her to our place.'

Kitty nodded—she'd never invited Joe there either, despite it being only one floor away. Clearly, indecency had decency buried deep inside it, like the good man lying below the bad man's tombstone.

'Where in her apartment? Where did you …?'

'How is that relevant?'

'Where in her apartment, Mitchell? Her dining table? Her couch? Her shower? Her rug?' The places you do it to me.

'Oh, I don't remember.'

Mitchell shrugged.

Kitty glared at him, bit at her lower lip.

Her bed—okay, it was her bed.'

A broken bicycle wheel—its spokes doused with envy, inadequacy and doubt—spiked into Kitty's side. But then came a heat in her lower belly—something primal, elemental, demanding.

'Did you decide to do it there?' she heard herself say with the firm determination of a newscaster. 'Was it your choice?'

'Uh, I think so,' Mitchell said, frowning. 'I just don't understand why you're asking this. Why are you torturing yourself this way, Kitty?'

'What day was it? Which day of the week was it?'

'I'm not sure—I think it was a Monday. Why does it matter?'

He broke his routine for her. He tore up his precious sexual diary.

Kitty grabbed Mitchell's hand, tugged him to walking.

'Slow down!' he yelled, his shoes thudding against the pavement with a missed step.

But Kitty couldn't listen, wouldn't, only pulled her husband along as gray clouds gathered, pegging themselves like tired undergarments to the telephone wires above.

On the second floor of the hotel, she opened the slatted door to her room. Inside, the ceiling fan worried the dull warmth of the afternoon.

Kitty gestured for Mitchell to enter. He raised his thin eyebrows, hesitated. But then she smiled, a silent, polite invitation, and Mitchell—remembering himself as a Southern gentleman—had manners enough left to know he could not refuse.

Once inside, Kitty took off her clothes, setting each item like as a museum piece on the foot of the bed. She stood for a while, her sweaty skin adoring the fan's rushing attention, her nipples stiffening under the air's dispassionate touch.

Mitchell squinted at her. She couldn't remember the last time when he'd seen her whole body. Or, rather, when he had actually noticed it—if ever. She was bare in between dressing, slept pyjama-less in the impossible summer city months, but her husband never really saw her. Her nudity never stirred him anyway—her body as an entirety was apparently unimportant. He was only interested in the obvious corner of her. Her form, with its unique scents and marks, was not a fascination to him, not a Coney Island Ferris wheel of sweetness and salt-tasting breezes in the way it had been for Joe.

But now, contrite, understanding this crude signal, Mitchell lumbered forward, unzipping his pants. He pushed her against the wardrobe, the icy glass of its full-length mirror stinging her back.

Kitty shivered out of his grasp. Mitchell, puzzled, twisted around to face her.

'Look,' she said. 'Look.'

Slowly, she spiralled before him—a music box ballerina, desperate not to be shut in again.

Mitchell's eyes were black with wanting. Kitty eased him down onto the floor. She walked around him, feeling his gaze graze the soft undersides of her breasts, the angles of her shoulder blades, her ass.

She arched herself on her knees above him. When Mitchell tried to drag her onto him—his erection strong in his jeans now, wanting to insist—she took herself back onto all fours. As tautly calm as Brooklyn Bridge itself, she let her breasts flow over his face, Mitchell sucking, almost taking the whole of them in, one after another. But then she drew herself away, forbidding, so his mouth gaped with hunger.

Kitty led him to the bed then, shuffled his jeans and boxer shorts off. His penis was firm, stretched almost to the point of rupture it seemed, and she lowered herself onto it, firmly and fully. Mitchell gasped. He seized her hips and tried to rock them, wanting to climax with his usual swiftness—but she wouldn't let him. She tensed, tightened around him, pulsed, tempted, but refused to move. If he moaned, she froze, looked him straight in the eye until his breath evened.

Kitty rolled off onto her back, kicked her clothes from the bottom of the bed. Mitchell slammed himself into her, *uh, uh, uh,* his torso so much heavier than Joe's.

But then he stopped and kissed her, his tongue trying to find her own.

He never did that. Not during sex.

He had done it in bed with Susannah. He had kissed Susannah. He had made love to Susannah.

He had never made love to her. Not before. And he could never now. It was all imitation, all echoes.

Kitty wanted to leap up and bathe — to scour herself, shave every surface — but before she could, Mitchell resumed thrusting, somehow finding the exquisiteness which Joe had brought that felt like icing sugar and ribbons of pearls and the centre of the universe and he had his hands cupped behind her head, saying 'I love you, I love you,' and she wanted to resist him, pushed her cheek against the cold, cotton pillow, but her body wanted this, she wanted to be Susannah, she wanted to be better, and so she let herself come, ten years of loneliness volcanoing to her mouth in a violent shriek.

Mitchell shuddered into her seconds later, releasing a low groan.

Kitty wiped herself with a tissue from the nightstand, pulled her panties and halter neck on, and sunk into the wicker chair opposite the bed. She pressed her palms together hard to stop her arms popping off like a doll's. After all, her marriage was apparently as unreal as any store window manikin's—all emotions played out to make a sale to passers-by who only scurried in the rain, flipping open pansy-black umbrellas.

'Did you tell her you loved her?' Kitty asked sadly.

Mitchell, still on the bed, eased up onto his elbows, the reddening of his face visible even in shuttered half-light. His face never reddened.

Kitty walked into the bathroom, slumped onto the edge of the tub. Beyond the open window, rain ticked at uneven pauses like a broken clock.

Yes, everything was broken. Even the rain didn't fall properly anymore. The world didn't work. She wondered if it ever had.

Poor Adam and Eve. Poor God. Poor Serpent.

'I want a divorce!' she yelled into the bedroom.

'But you're not getting one,' Mitchell sang back. 'Not when you've just shown how much you still love me.'

Trans-Neptune

- Ashley Stokes -

By the time Laura Berman found herself waiting with her lightly packed overnight bag at the bar of the Fosdyke Hotel she'd been so repeatedly shocked and shaken that she could no longer remember the astrologer's name. It was something *like* Mizmoon Orcus. After the Large Body Nomenclature Committee announced the name of the new planet, astrologers – never a profession held in high regard in the Berman household – had gained a strange new prominence. During one of the more lowbrow TV debates about the implications of what was being seen as the greatest discovery in our Solar System since Neptune, Mizmoon Orcus left her seat and started to prance around the studio, performing what suspiciously looked like a rain dance.

Laura did remember wondering why no one had been kind enough to inform Mizmoon that when appearing on national television a decently fitted bra is a sensible investment. She did remember saying this to William, in the sly, husky voice she'd last used when she was fifteen and wanted boys to like her. He hadn't noticed, distracted not by Mizmoon's ruby-coloured turban and scissor-kicking breasts, but by her proclamation that our knowledge of the Solar System is transformed because we as human beings are transforming. 'As above, so below.'

'But Pheme is pure,' William muttered, 'she's indifferent.'

William calling what had formerly been known as Oort Cloud Object 2015 YA1 'she' and then spending another night alone on the roof terrace formed, Laura knew, a causal link to her now waiting for a man at the bar of the Fosdyke, a man for whom she had bought a special dress, a man who she hoped would shortly lead her by the hand towards a plush and secluded bedchamber.

On arriving she'd found a newspaper on the counter with yet another artist's impression of the planet on the front page. In this version it glowed a bright azure blue and was ringed by icy fragments. There were no moons. Sometimes they gave Pheme moons. Sometimes they didn't. It was guesswork anyway. No one could tell what it actually looked like, not even William.

Laura took a pen from her handbag and started to black her ... *it* out with doodles. She must stop thinking of *it* as female. It wasn't female. It was a vast, cold object a long way off.

Even the serving staff were talking about it. Everyone had been talking about Pheme: on the radio when Laura woke up, in the office, at her meetings with clients and customers. James, her Head of Sales had talked about it at great length and in a most unusual way in the car last week, as if it had some significance, as if it were a sign. Scientists, moneymen, cranks and looters believed in it. Even the friends who used to laugh behind William's back now believed in Pheme, including his brother, Richard Berman, the biotech magnate whose own grand unveiling had been relegated to second on the news agenda by the Nomenclature Committee's press conference.

The boys behind the bar, given the pep talk the lean, purple-knuckled shift manager (Brandon, according to his name badge) was giving his spindly-looking minion (name badge: Dwight), even they now believed in William's planet.

Laura's phone vibrated. There was a text message.

Tippi's just been sick and G's not back yet. Be with u soon as.

Her new man should have been here half an hour ago. Laura had arrived early so she could change out of her jeans and into her dress, but the room was still being cleaned. William thought she was driving to Cambridge tonight, for an overnight stop before a breakfast meeting tomorrow. She'd left the house wearing camouflage.

Brandon was supposed to tell her when the room was ready, but he was philosophizing in a rap kind of style to his eager pupil, Dwight. The longer Brandon waxed sexual, the more Laura cringed at the image she had of his eyebrow stud glinting close to the corner of her eye. Both of them seemed to equate the discovery of Pheme with the availability of some lucky sort called Clara K.

What made Laura smile was that Brandon referred to the planet as 'Femi', as in femidom, not Pheme as in rhymes with Phoebe.

'Femi is your opportunity, D, you need to seize her vitality?'

It was almost endearingly daft, as was the mental picture she had of William being here and giving an impromptu and no doubt ignored lecture on pronunciation and the naming process of celestial bodies.

Laura had sometimes wondered if William would be as mesmerized by Pheme if the name didn't sound as cutely feminine. The quest for the Outer Giant was his life's work, though. More accurately, it was what he'd wanted to be his life's work. He would have been as smitten if the Nomenclature Committee had called it Gor or Derek.

The Committee had opted for Pheme after the Roman goddess of Fame and Rumour, a nod to her ... *its* long history as a mere hypothesis suggested by the perturbed orbits of long-period comets. Pheme was thought less alarming than the name used when a gas giant four times the size of Jupiter lurking in the distant Oort Cloud region of the Solar System was still an outlandish, vaguely occult idea proposed by a few astronomers with reputations to make, like William before he became a teacher.

Laura preferred the older name.

Laura preferred Nemesis.

She hid a laugh with the back of her hand as she wondered how Brandon would pronounce Nemesis.

Then it struck her.

How old was he?

Nineteen, twenty at most.

And what school had he attended?

Oaklands?

Looking away in case Brandon noticed her, she coloured in the last remaining window of blue on the artist's impression. She took a sideways glance at her profile in the bar's wall-length mirror. With some relish she imagined the obvious salesmen and mid-ranking business people spaced out on the tables behind her speculating on why she was here, alone and scribbling out Pheme on the front page of the *Daily Mail*. She pressed her palms to the small of her back, as if merely stretching, and surreptitiously pinched her love handles.

Definitely less there. The scales said so. These jeans said so. Verity, her PA, the girls in the office, two of the dispatch boys in the warehouse and even James had said so. As did the size of the new dress in her bag that she would slip into, as soon the room was ready. She had been on a health kick ever since Richard Berman, at that crappy lunch where, after he'd bragged about finding a cure for obesity he referred to her as looking 'deceptively prosperous.'

It was a coincidence – or was it, given that everyone previously allowed out on their own had surrendered to whimsy and superstition, fate? – that the Nomenclature Committee announced Pheme at exactly the same time as Richard was giving his press conference. It was like Berman versus Berman that day, except that William had contributed nothing to proving the existence of Pheme, and Richard had discovered a process called adipocytosis, a viral gene therapy vector that induces the cell death of adipocytes. The resulting product, a flab-busting injection called Adipovir would surely upgrade him from millionaire to billionaire, if he could bring it to market.

He was going to ask for Laura's help, she knew it. Richard was going to ask her to resign as MD of Solaris Laboratory Equipment to front the sales division of his Virolixis Group. Soon he was going to present her with a big fat dilemma that no piggybacked virus could dissolve.

She didn't want to think about this either and again considered ordering a vodka and tonic, though there could be no changing her mind if she succumbed to the vapours. She'd have to stay here or walk back. The Fosdyke was only three miles from home but the weather screen on her phone said it was minus-two tonight. She couldn't return to William a day early and without the car.

She didn't want to be thinking about William, or the cold walk home, or Adipovir, Virolixis or Richard Berman. Nor did she want to be constantly reminded of Pheme, Femi, Nemesis, Nibiru, Hercolubus,

Planet X or whatever it was called. It was a big ball of helium and hydrogen skirting the sun a light year away that no one would ever visit, or ever see and to her would forever be William's World.

She had once joked to someone she shouldn't have, that her marriage had been fashioned in the dusts of Nemesis.

On the other side of the bar, Brandon and Dwight were still in conference.

'Clara K,' said Brandon, 'she may look all glass of wine, but she is susceptible, man, they're all susceptible ...'

'Excuse me,' said Laura.

'... susceptible. They're scared, man, you get me, you simply got to work out what words to play, make them bust a gut for you ...'

Laura was forced to use the tone she'd deployed when she was thirty-nine and first addressed the Solaris staff.

'Excuse me. As important as your individual priorities are, I was wondering if you could leave them aside for a moment and enquire about the status of my room.'

Brandon froze and spread his fingers as if hooked by a bassline.

'Your wish is my command, miss.'

As he swayed along the bar towards the hatch, he patted Dwight on the shoulder. 'Susceptible, man, they're all susceptible. They just don't *know* it yet.'

Laura didn't turn to watch where Brandon headed. At some point tonight, if she remained undistracted, she was going to have to have words about his attitude.

Dwight was standing about like the spare part of a machine that manufactured gormlessness, so Laura ordered a coffee to give him something to do. When he brought it over he lingered in front of her as if he expected her to speak to him. She waved the back of her hand, a gesture she'd perfected as a woman often on the road, who'd known a thousand hotels and late night bars from Aberdeen to Bangalore, who had brandished her wedding ring to hundreds of over-achievers in last year's suit.

She wasn't wearing the ring, though. She'd taken it off and hidden it in her purse. In any case Dwight must have passed GCSE Non-Verbal Communication Studies. He shuffled back along the bar.

William had always been better at dealing with young people, especially the ones on the verge of exclusion or without a natural bent or culture for science. He had been an excellent physics teacher. She stirred the milk into her coffee and as it spiralled she remembered William showing her how the Solar System had formed using a bowl of water and a sprinkling of canteen pepper.

That had been the summer she was temping at Microtherics, hoping to be taken on full-time as a Marketing Assistant, and he was part-funding his PhD by working two days a week as a statistician. In the cafeteria one afternoon he filled the empty fruit bowl with water and stirred pepper into it to show her how stardust accretes into planets and asteroids. She may have asked him about his research, she couldn't remember; he may have sensed she was bored and somehow assumed this sort of model would be a fun toy to play with. Not wanting to offend him, when he was being friendly for once, she let him go on.

William pointed to where the water slopped against the edge of the bowl. 'I'm looking at what happens here. Trans-Neptunian space, the Kuiper Belt, where the outward migration of the giants scattered the disc. Anyone with access to a telescope is going to be finding Pluto-category planets out there in the next few years. Yes, sure, I'd settle for one to get started, but I mean, Herschel, he discovered Uranus. That's a discovery, that's a world. What I'm really interested in is what's out here.'

He held out his hands as far as they would reach around the bowl, all the while staring at her, straight in the face. He'd never been able to manage this before. Deep space contact was less scary to William than eye contact, and Laura would later wonder how her life would have panned out if one of the older researchers or managers at Microtherics had noticed her, or if William hadn't been the only person there close to her age.

Still with his hands outstretched, William then explained Nemesis, a brown dwarf, the sun's remote, stunted twin that could well exist in the Oort Cloud, a region of space so cold it would make Neptune's moon, Triton feel like Death Valley. He, William Berman, the Planet Hunter, was going to find it.

His greatest achievement turned out to be that on this day he managed to successfully wing one of the most unlikely chat-up lines in the history of science.

'Would you pretend to be my girlfriend at my brother's wedding?'

'Erm ... is it local?'

'Good, that's agreed. Then I'll get my doctorate and discover Nemesis.'

He did neither.

She married him three years later.

It would be unfair to William to suggest that Nemesis had exerted its gravitational pull throughout their marriage. For at least the first ten years he'd concentrated on his teaching. He even cut back to once a month his attendance at the Wanderers Club, the county observatory's astronomical society after he became Head of Science at Oaklands. Only the discovery of the dwarf planet Eris and the downgrading of the status of Pluto had, and for only a short time, provided Laura with a reminder of what he'd been like when they met.

Nemesis returned when William stopped teaching.

She blamed herself here, too. She'd encouraged him to keep a journal. He was supposed to keep a journal to help him understand what had happened to him. She hadn't anticipated that William would displace self-examination with a thousand-page science fiction novel called *The Plutonauts*. Most of it was about the workings of the anti-matter engine of the spacecraft that ferries the plutonauts to Pluto, where they build a telescope capable of observing the outer reaches of the Universe.

It must have been this second fruitless mission that rekindled William's passion for Nemesis. It must have been here that the subject of his abandoned doctorate winked back at him from deep space. It was here that he began to spend much of the night not in bed but mucking about in his study, scribbling, analysing, calculating.

It was underhand, but she'd had to do something.

William only junked *The Plutonauts* after Laura told Richard Berman about it. Richard was forced to put the phone down until he stopped laughing and then at the next of their grisly lunches made William summarize the plot in front of everyone.

Afterwards, tapping the veins in his wrist, Richard said, 'When are you ever going to learn, Willy boy? The money's here. The rest is grit.'

Virolixis had recently made him a fortune from an assay system, a home-testing kit that measured levels of BRCA1, the breast cancer protein.

Later that night, William burned *The Plutonauts* in the garden.

It was after this that he started to insist that they move house, up sticks to somewhere further out, where there were no reminders and the night skies were unpolluted by the glare of the city.

In the Fosdyke, Laura's phone buzzed. Another text.

Tippi stopped sick. Goosie still not back, tho. Will be there. Please, don't bail on me Mistress L.

Laura thrust her tongue into the side of her mouth.

Goosie.

Bloody Goosie.

Charlotte Symonds-Goose: the woman who before Laura took over at Solaris Laboratory Equipment had been its founder, Bill Baxendale's PA. The woman who would have been Laura's PA but who resigned when Bill retired and, after a chance meeting in a bar at Frankfurt Airport appointed Laura his successor. The woman who resigned not to have another child, as was said in the letter, but because she thought Bill had passed over her more deserving and able husband. Goosie, with her lingering queen bee status in the office, a celebrity to the admin and sales girls: *have you heard about Goosie? She's having another baby.* Goosie, who William once described as 'The Fertile Crescent'. Goosie with her Mulberry handbag for every day of the year and her five little girls, Goosie's goslings, named after Hollywood starlets: Marilyn, Ava, Lauren, Cyd and Tippi. Goosie who Laura, more than capable of running Solaris after heading up Microtherics international sales division for eight years, should not have tried to win over for the sake of an easy life. Goosie, who Laura should not have invited over for dinner a week after the Pheme discovery and, when the men were on the roof playing with William's robotic telescope thing, confided in about her marriage being formed in the dusts of Nemesis.

And now it was down to Goosie that Laura was waiting alone and without a drink, wedding ring stashed in her purse, the dress creasing in her bag, with only a cog in a gormlessness machine to keep her company and a picture of Pheme that was still there however much ink she layered over it.

She had never done anything like this before.

He said he'd never done this before.

Goosie had never been late for anything in her life before.

Laura had once seen Tippi eat a slug and not be sick.

William was getting even worse.

William was heading for the Oort Cloud.

Pheme: it *was* changing people.

Maybe the Mizmoons of this world were not so deluded after all.

The article under the artist's impression on the front page of the *Daily Mail* said that every third girl born in the UK in the last six weeks had been named Pheme.

If she and William had a child now, he'd want to call it Pheme.

A child was highly unlikely now, William being William and she being here.

Along the counter, the hatch thumped. Brandon quickly appeared in front of her, pointing a finger-pistol at his temple and one towards his groin area.

'Can you stop that, please,' said Laura, resorting to the voice she'd only used once before, last year, when she was forty-three and at the Solaris summer garden party Tippi had repeatedly bombarded William with handfuls of guacamole.

'Sorry, miss,' said Brandon. 'They're still doing your room, but there shouldn't be much more longing.'

She was about to correct him, William-style, but then thought better of it.

Yes, there shouldn't be much more longing.

She would wait all night if she must.

Brandon sloped back along the bar towards where Dwight leant next to the till.

'Any sightings of Lady CK?' he said. 'You been rehearsing your rhymes?'

Dwight muttered something that Laura couldn't hear.

'That ain't good enough, D,' said Brandon, 'if you're gonna seize this day. Days like these always been good. When there is fear, ladies, they fall. They need to feel close. You got to play that. You remember when they closed them Straits? You remember the wave? You remember Dammer-ascus? I got more boots during them days than any other. Now, this thing, Femi, this is the big one. The end of the whole shoot. That's what them dippy Claras are thinking. You slip that line to the susceptibles and it's going to be like an orgy from the olden days.'

Brandon and Dwight bounced fists. One potato. Two potato.

The sight of Brandon's tattoo, some sort of Oriental character peeping out over the collar of his polo shirt made Laura feel queasy and relieved to be older, immunized to stupid boys who think you're so dim you'll fall for any tacky line.

The discovery of Pheme had, though, been blamed for the riots in Brazil and the crack-down in China; the slaughter in the Heights; the stand-offs in the South Atlantic and between the Koreas; the forest fires in Australia and California; for inspiring the monstrous idiots, the people all over the world who on Christmas Day had killed their children, their pets and themselves.

These things would have happened, anyway; at least she and William agreed about this. These were either random events or the climax of processes well underway before a couple of astronomers in Colorado compared a lot of numbers to prove that Pheme existed and had been doing nothing to no one forever.

There certainly wasn't a cover-up, a conspiracy. Pheme definitely wasn't heading towards Earth. Only an idiot would believe that.

'That thing,' said Brandon, 'it's coming back. It's been here before, kicking off, and it's coming back to kick off again ...'

Laura clattered her coffee cup against the saucer until Brandon noticed her.

'You remind her of that, she's putty, bro ... yes, can I help you, miss?'

'Crap,' she said.

'Pardon, miss.'

'You're talking crap.'

'What crap?'

'Pheme,' said Laura. 'If she was coming our way, she'd already be proximate to Saturn and we'd know about that. We'd be able to see it. Get your facts straight.'

'This ain't about straight. This is end o' the world stuff.'

He glanced back at Dwight until Dwight, presumably realizing that he was needed as back up or audience, shuffled over.

'Can I ask you a question, miss?' said Brandon.

'What school did you go to?'

'No, I asked you if I could ask you a question?'

'What question?'

'You know Femi, right? She has many names.'

'No, she … it has one name. And it's ee, ee-me.'

'Amy? Nah, she quit last month. See, I've heard her called Coog.'

'What?'

'And I was wondering, miss, if you came from there? If you are a Cougar?'

Oh God, they knew, they could tell, this pair of bin-dippers. And she hated that word. You're a woman over thirty and you still like sex, so you're a cougar: furry and desperate. She found herself opening her palms to the ceiling and looking at the spotlights for guidance.

Maybe it had started like this for William.

Maybe it had been a situation like this.

'What school did you go to?' said Laura.

'I think she wants to tell teacher on us, D?' said Brandon.

'Who's your supervisor?'

Brandon bent at the waist and started to swish his hands about.

'There's no need for that, miss. I am only kidding with you. Meant no disrespect. Me and D, we like you. We think you're cool, miss.'

'What school did you go to?'

'If it is that important to you, we went to Oaks.'

There was a loud slam from along the counter. A blokeish cheer went up from the room behind. Down at the other end of the bar, her hand resting on the hatch as if it might jump up now and bite her was a young, lithe girl, her hair a cascade of yellow ringlets and her eyes a gleaming, watery blue.

'Dwighty-D,' said Brandon. 'Your hour hath cometh over.'

The girl – Clara K, Laura assumed – didn't move along the bar to greet her colleagues. She knelt down, opened the door of a fridge and peered into it even though there didn't seem to be anything for her to do in there.

She wasn't like Laura had anticipated. She had imagined someone hard and streetwise, comfortable and capable in the presence of boys like Brandon and Dwight.

And she remembered being sixteen, seventeen herself, being a quiet, studious girl, a girl into maths and chemistry, still wearing big glasses and long skirts, and working weekends in that shoe shop and the man with the gel in his hair and the tie-pin always cornering her in the stock room, leaning in close; that time he told her how good it would be in the shower and how it wasn't.

Brandon elbowed Dwight.

Dwight loped along the bar towards the crouching girl.

Someone, a man, came up alongside Laura but he didn't say anything to her.

He ordered a lager from Brandon.

Brandon started to pull a pint.

Foam gushed over his hand.

Laura needed to press him, find out more about what he knew about Oaklands, what he had done there.

Dwight staggered before he reached the fridge, then paused, looked back and only continued after Brandon gave him some sort of stare or expression Laura couldn't see.

Dwight leant against the counter and drummed his fingers. He was saying something, talking down to the girl.

The girl ought to stand up.

She mustn't let him talk down to her.

The blood was throbbing in Laura's ears and then she realized that it throbbed beyond her ears, and there was a sound, a beat that only stopped when Brandon stepped back from the till and gave the man his change and took a phone from his pocket and answered it.

Laura glanced at her own phone. There was a new message alert.

'Miss, your room is ready,' said Brandon. 'It's number one o coog ...'
He coughed. 'I mean one o two, miss.'

'I'll have a think,' said Laura, 'about what I'm going to do about you.'

'We jest.'

'You're fired, if it's up to me.'

'I ain't done nuffin'.'

'I doubt that.'

She tucked her phone into her back pocket and grabbed hold of her
case, pulling it on its wheels behind her along the bar until she was
level with the fridge.

The girl was upright now, leaning away from Dwight.

Sweat glistened at his temple.

The girl held her hand over her mouth.

'We ain't got long,' said Dwight. 'We only got moments to live in.'

'Excuse me, miss,' said Laura. She noticed that moist green bottles
were racked up on the middle shelf. 'Do you have any champagne?'

'Yes, we have ...'

'It doesn't matter. Can I have two, no, three bottles, whatever it is,
and can you bring them up to room 102, please.'

'Hey, room parties not allowed, miss,' said Dwight, 'unless you is
inviting us.'

'Be quiet, you.' Laura used the prim, borderline-hostile voice she'd
last used when she was nineteen and wanted Geektopus in the
chemistry lab to keep his hands to himself. The girl giggled and
pressed her knuckles to her lips.

'You can carry three, can't you?' said Laura.

'Sure,' said the girl.

Anything.

Anything to get her away from them.

Laura wanted to scream but before she could she tossed her mobile
phone onto the double bed. She paced around the room, along the
outer wall and past the window, and then the inner walls and up and
down the aisles formed by the centrally positioned double bed.

101

She reminded herself of Richard and Cherry Berman's cat. Even though Richard was a millionaire he was too tight to pay for a cattery when he and Cherry smugged off to The Seychelles or Fiji. When Mendel came to stay he would pad out his new territory in repetitive circuits, as if saying to himself: this is where it's all going to happen now.

The bed in the room was newish and firm.

It was the nicest thing there.

The rest of the décor was rather neutral, bland, not what she had imagined.

She hadn't imagined it happening somewhere like this.

She hadn't imagined it being like another sales trip.

Yesterday, he had whispered to her: 'Luxury is not discretion's bedfellow.'

She thought about replying to his last holding text but then began to wonder where that girl had got to with her champagne.

That girl was clearly bright and curious. She would be taking a step towards independence by working here, facing up to the real world for the first time. She would want to be earning her own money. She would want to buy her own clothes.

Laura winced as she opened the curtains. The girls buy their own clothes when they're about five now. Goosie's Goslings do. It's a different world. But it's still easy to make mistakes, to have regrets early, to have regrets that loiter and hang.

The room was at the back of the Fosdyke, looking out over the carpark and black fields.

The Moon seemed close tonight, a few hundred metres above the land.

When the brownish, smokey clouds that obscured the Moon for a few moments cleared, she remembered William once saying, on one of their night-walks, early on, that although the Moon may look near, if the Earth is a melon sat on your lap, the moon is a silver apple in Jerusalem.

She remembered how, not that long ago, she had woken up in the middle of the night. They were still at their old house, the house she'd preferred. She may have been jet-lagged or worried about getting up early for a trip the next day. She must have disturbed William. He'd held her tight to him and whispered descriptions of Eris, the furthest of the dwarf planets.

A right little troublemaker.

If you could see it with the naked eye it would be the night's brightest jewel.

Its tiny, tiny moon, Dysnomia.

Imagine the approach; imagine it growing until it's there in front of you.

Eris: Planet of Discord.

Its tiny moon, Dysnomia.

Imagine …

She could picture it, a bald white world, and had finally drifted off to sleep.

Eris: the last jumping-off point before Pheme.

Away from the window now, she heaved her bag up onto the bed and started to unpack.

First she flipped her make-up case and her copy of this month's *Psychologies* onto the duvet, followed by a book called *The Strange Idols Pattern and Other Short Stories* that she hadn't started yet. The dress was strapped into the bottom of the bag.

She took it out and spread it across the white duvet, then used the phone on the bedside table to call down to the bar.

Brandon answered. 'Yo, bar.'

'Room 102, I ordered some champagne.'

'On its way, Miss Coo … I mean Miss.'

She replaced the receiver without slamming it. She wished that she had.

Laid out on the duvet, the dress, from this angle looked like a giant keyhole.

She crossed her arms, reached down for the hem of her sweater and pulled it over her head and off. She removed her shoes, then her jeans and her tights.

In the en suite, in front of a full-length mirror, she swivelled on the balls of her feet and turned sideways, holding her hair into a ponytail with one hand.

103

She was looking better, she thought, but she wasn't looking great. She could use a little Adipovir on her womanly bulge and the backs of her thighs, maybe even under her chin. When she was Richard Berman's Sales Director, she would get Adipovir for free rather than shell out a grand a shot.

It had killed over a hundred and fifty of those rats, though, before Richard's famous Adiporodent, who the tabloids called Fat Rat, survived.

Laura was still a little suspicious of Richard's big claim, as was his sister Eve. After the most recent and particularly fractious family lunch, while the Berman boys let a needle match about Pheme develop into the usual full-blown row about medical ethics, Laura and Eve hid out in the kitchen, drinking wine and smoking cigarettes. Eve, a lecturer in Early Roman Studies, had described her brothers then as 'Cast-Off and Bollox'.

This was the first time Laura could remember laughing along with someone who'd made fun of William's situation. It was only his sister, true, there was a certain family dynamic to consider and Eve had openly referred to Cherry as Trophy Berman for about fifteen years, but it was the second turning point after Pheme, a moment that would lead to her standing here in a cramped, over-lit place in just her underwear.

Back in the room, she held the dress up in front of her. It was as red as Mars. She hesitated before putting it on. Putting it on would be to cross the final frontier.

She manoeuvred the dress over her head and smoothed the silk to her shoulders and waist.

In front of the mirror again, she swished its low hem around the tops of her knees. She looked alright, quite good for a lass in her forties.

She went back into the room and slipped on her heels.

She touched up her lipstick and mascara and used a dropper to add some sparkle to her eyes.

She tried to picture who he would now see when he arrived. He had said, sheepishly – he must have known that the suggestion was fraught for him on many levels – that he had imagined being alone with her for a long time.

When he'd said this to her in the car she glazed over.

It was when he said that he thought about her when he made love to his wife, that was the tipping point.

She'd known then she would end up waiting in a room like this.

Maybe it would happen only once.

Once might be enough.

She couldn't stay at Solaris after even only once.

She was sure the staff were talking already.

She would have to accept Richard's offer.

She would have to tell William.

She would tell William in the morning.

This was William's fault anyway.

She was here, dressed like a cocktail waitress from the eighties, because William had been unfaithful first. That's what Goosie had insinuated, while they were drinking all that Baileys and William and James were up on the roof terrace.

Goosie had repeated some 'as above, so below' nonsense about Pheme that she'd cribbed from a forum on *Mumsnet* or some Mizmoon type's column in *Harpers and Queen*. After Laura had described William's ecstatic reaction to the Pheme discovery, Goosie said, 'God, sounds like James when England won the Rugby World Cup. I mean, c'mon, if William's going to have an affair, isn't it worse that it's with a rock? Can't he even get a bit on the side?'

She'd spoken with the haughty, patronizing voice that Laura hadn't heard since the careers adviser at school tried to talk her out of applying to Imperial.

Then in the car last week, when James had pulled up somewhere on the way to Huntingdon and mid-way through apologizing for Goosie's behaviour had said, tremulously, fearfully, that the thing out in space was a sign. It was put there for them. The two of them, they even work for a company named after an intelligent planet.

Feeling numb, Laura had replied that Bill Baxendale was such an old hippy that when she took over she'd had to clear a lifetime's collection of *Omni* and *Starburst* magazines from his office.

James had grabbed hold of her hand to shut her up.

He had wanted, he said, to be alone with her for a very long time.

I think about you when I'm with her.

Letting herself go limp, Laura flopped back onto the bed. She wanted him here now. She wanted to put her arms around him. She wanted to feel his strong hands at her hips and to sink her nails into his thick, curly hair. And more than anything she wanted James Symonds-Goose to tell her in granular detail all the things he had thought about doing to her when he had been with his wife.

There was a knock at the door.

In his last text he'd said he was still at home.

Waiting for Goosie.

Waiting to leave.

It must be that girl here with the champagne.

She would ask that girl to share a glass of fizz with her. Then neither of them would be left on her own. Time would pass until the boys from the bar had gone off-shift. The time would pass more quickly until James arrived. The girl could tell her all about herself. Laura might be able to help her. She had contacts. She could write references. There were internships she could arrange.

At the door she could hear rattling outside, like the sound of the lid of an old-fashioned kettle when it's about to boil.

She opened the door.

A waist-high metal frame ram-raided into the room.

Startled, she stepped back and almost turned over on her ankle.

In the middle of the room, Dwight's face tapered to a smile of thin, grey teeth. He gripped the steering bar of a trolley. Three foil-capped bottlenecks poked up from three ice buckets. Three champagne flutes trembled on the surface.

'Excuse me,' said Laura, hands on hips.

'Room service, miss.'

'I specifically asked for that girl.'

'This is heavy, miss. I was told to shove it.'

She huffed and blew up her fringe. 'OK, thank you.'

Another text message alert bleeped from the mobile lying on the bed.

Dwight was smiling so forcefully that the skin under his cheekbones was turning the colour of corned beef. He didn't know what to do with his hands. They dangled in front of him, the heel of each slapping together, harder with each swing.

'I think we're done here,' she said.

'Miss,' he said. 'You know the world, it is ending.' He shuffled towards her as if practising some side-winding dance move. 'The world is going to end, somefing is coming to light us up.'

'That's nonsense,' she said.

'What are you going to wish for, miss?'

'What? I mean, pardon?'

'What are all the things you could have done that you have not done?'

She stepped back into something that unbalanced her, the corner of the bed. As she flopped onto the mattress her phone bounced off and thudded on the carpet. Legs akimbo, she found herself wobbling at a diagonal angle. Dwight loomed over her, his eye sockets dark stains, his mouth a slot.

'What fun could you have done, miss? Regretting, it is sad.'

He was too young to have regrets.

He looked about sixteen.

But she did have regrets.

She regretted that the man with the gel and tiepin had kept small things of hers after she let him talk her into the shower.

She regretted now that she'd convinced William to give up on Nemesis and get a proper job so they could be together and get on with their lives.

She regretted that they'd had to leave the house she had liked so much.

That William had punched that boy in the face.

That William had punched that boy in the face twice.

Her jaw quivered and she was starting to breathe heavily, her limbs too stiff to raise herself up, to grab the phone, grab a bottle, swing the bottle and run.

'God, miss,' said Dwight. He was flapping his arms in a tizzy that he only managed to control when he reached out his hand to pull her up. 'Sorry, miss, sorry.'

When she kept her hands to herself he turned away, hunched his shoulders and hung his head. For a moment she thought he was about to bolt.

'Don't tell, miss, please, I wasn't trying to scare you.'

Slightly reassured that he knew he'd scared her, Laura scrambled from the bed and inched, back to the wall around the room until she faced him.

Perched on the end of the bed, he was hiding his face with his hands. He looked about twelve now, a grizzling boy who knows he's too old to cry but can't help it.

'What on earth do you think you're doing?' She deployed the overly schoolmarmish voice she'd last used when she was thirty-one and, realizing that she had earned the authority, fired someone well liked but useless.

'Sorry, miss.'

'If you're going to work in the hospitality industry, Dwight, you can't treat guests like this. You need to be polite, smart and ready to lend a hand, not back us into a corner asking intrusive questions. Do you know what I mean by intrusive?'

'But the world's ending. The boss says. We are going to get smashed.'

Laura knew that if William were here he'd more than likely say something really helpful, like: Yes, it is going to end, Mr Dwight, in a billion years time when the expanding Sun evaporates the Earth's water and the atmosphere steams off into space. So I'd get working on that anti-matter drive quick sharp if I were you.

'It's not going to end,' said Laura. 'That's rubbish.'

Dwight stood up.

'I got to go, miss. Please don't say anything. I got to go.'

'Wait,' she said, grabbing a handful of sachets from a jug on the dresser. 'You don't want your friends to see you in a state. Would you like some hot chocolate? We could waste a couple of these.'

Soon after they had moved house, one evening in autumn, William brought a rabbit into the house. He'd been for one of the long walks in the woods that she still wasn't keen on him taking. On his return he'd stumbled upon the rabbit lying near to a pile of builder's rubble, detritus left by the workmen who'd converted the kitchen roof into a terrace-cum-observatory. Something had hit the rabbit, or it had been chased into a solid object.

She remembered a feeling of dread when William called her name from downstairs, the urgency in his voice forcing her up from her bath.

In the kitchen she'd found William stroking the rabbit. It twitched and cowered on her table. When he put it on the floor it tried to hop away but couldn't manage more than a shuffle around on its bum. Its whiteless eyes seemed to plead for understanding. Laura didn't think it would last the night.

The longer she sat with Dwight the more he reminded her of that rabbit.

They drank a cup of watery chocolate each. She'd managed to get him to admit that the Fosdyke was his first job and he hated it. It was boring. The customers were numpties. He wanted to be a DJ but he didn't have any gear, or he wanted to launch his own clothing range but he didn't have any dosh.

She rolled her eyes and tried to explain that working in a bar was a start. She ran a company now but she'd started in a shoe shop. She tried to find out about his schooling, what he remembered of Oaklands and the teachers there. The only thing he wanted to talk about was Clara K. She was very nice. She was very fit. I love that honey, miss.

'The boss says she's ripe. I just need to get her to know how quick things are, you see. But I can't find it. I can't spit like he spits.'

'That's probably a good thing,' said Laura. 'Listen. You can't make people want to be with you, Dwight, and if you con them into it, by, like, making them scared, you can't trust them, can you? Do you want to be with an idiot?'

He didn't say anything.

'If you just be yourself,' she continued, 'you'll find someone who likes you for who you are, and that sort of thing lasts.'

'The boss says we don't want things that last. Nothing is going to last.'

She had to restrain herself from giving him a light slap around the back of the head. Then she had to restrain herself from asking him to give her a light slap around the head until she stopped the etiquette lesson.

'Don't listen to that moron downstairs,' she said, 'and talk to Clara like she's a person. You don't want to make things an ordeal for her, do you?'

'She is well nice, miss.'

'Why is she nice?'

'Just is.'

'In what way? Does she make you laugh? Does she make you think? Does she make you feel understood?'

'Nah, just nice.'

'You think on that. Anyway, your school, do you remember Mr Berman?'

'Clara K, right, one time, right, she was serving this customer, and, like, her moomins were like flapping this way and that like an elephant's trunks …'

'Never say things like that, not in front of me and not in front of Clara. Listen. This is important. Oaklands. Do you remember Mr Berman, the physics teacher?'

'That guy who went nuts?'

'That's unkind. Were you there?'

'No, miss. It was up the ranks. I never saw.'

'Was Brandon there?'

'How should I know? Oh miss. I just want that Clara to go.'

'As you get older, Dwight, you'll realize that the world doesn't end when you don't get who you want. It only seems like it.'

'Shit,' said Dwight. 'That don't help.'

They sat for a couple of minutes without speaking, as if they were both listening out for some signal in the drone of the en suite bathroom's extractor fan.

On the trolley the necks of the three champagne bottles stuck out like the funnels of a liner. She stared at them until her eyes began to water and wondered why he'd brought up three flutes. Who was supposed to sip from the third?

There was a beep. It wasn't her phone this time. Dwight rummaged in his tracksuit bottoms until he found his phone.

'Gotta go, miss.'

They both stood up at the same time. Laura was drawn to the trolley. She picked up a flute and twirling the stem between her thumb and forefinger watched the way the light spangled in the grooves.

'Dwight,' she said.

He paused in the doorway, his legs squeezed together like he urgently needed the loo.

'I gotta go, miss, please.'

'Dwight.' She raised him the empty glass. 'Amaze everyone.'

She didn't know why she'd said this.

There was more truth in the glass.

'You're alright, miss. You ain't like he says. Be safe, you hear me.'

Although he forgot to take the trolley, he did remember to shut the door.

She remembered the rabbit and how even though William sat up with it for two nights it had still passed away.

Being alone again tightened, almost physically around her shoulders. She scrambled, rather inelegantly over the bed to retrieve the phone from the floor.

James's most recent text:

Not long now, Mistress L.

The slow rolling of tyres scratched up the walls to the window.

Headlights swept across the glass.

She rushed to see.

Down below, a new car thrummed on the gravel.

A figure, maybe two scampered away from the circle of light around the car.

The passenger door opened.

A young woman in a black military-style coat stepped out and lit a cigarette. The smoke combined and mingled with her frozen breath.

An older, bald man in a green body-warmer emerged from the driver's side.

He opened the boot and started to remove suitcases and bags.

111

Laura slumped back down on the bed and found herself perplexed by how the sight of a woman smoking in the dark and a middle-aged bald man handling luggage could provoke such a plummeting sensation in her stomach.

On the trolley, the three champagne flutes glimmered.

She sank her chin into the heel of her hand and at first started to wonder if she needed to use the mirror, check her hair after all the inelegant stumbling and the wrong sort of writhing on the bed.

Tell me what you think about when you're not with me?

In her head she was using the husky voice she'd last used when she was fifteen and wanted boys to like her when even after Pheme she was still forty-four and the future was a bland room with unopened champagne while downstairs the careless and the aimless worked unsupervised and smashed each other up.

She would smoke in the dark while a bald man takes baggage out of his car.

She would wait in fast food restaurants for other women's children to like her.

In six years time she would be fifty.

She did not want to be fifty and waiting for William.

She did not want to be fifty and wait in hotel rooms.

She wondered again who the third flute was for.

She decided that it was wisest not to think about what Dwight had said downstairs about a room party and to conclude instead that neither he nor Brandon could count above two.

There was a text alert:

Mistress L, get yourself strapped in, I'm a coming.

The plummeting sensation in her stomach continued its freefall.

She opened one of the bottles and enjoyed the pop and the way the steam coiled from the aperture.

At the window she raised a toast to the falling Moon.

She wrote a note in lipstick and stuck it to the champagne bottle with a blob of mascara.

Out in the car now she found herself unable to turn the key in the ignition and slumped with her head on the steering wheel.

She'd been sure she must leave.

Now she wanted to go back, back to the room, back to waiting.

She ought to go back and remove that note.

She had been certain when she'd written it.

Everyone else was so bloody certain.

Even Mizmoon Orcus was certain about something.

As above, so below.

Laura was certain only of one thing.

Thinking about it, imagining it, imagining James here and pinning her against the window, whispering in her ear all the things he was going to do to her, this had been the best part of it.

William had said something similar once.

William had once said, when he still talked to her, that the best part of his Nemesis work was at the beginning, when it was still out there, when he had it all to do, the moment he stretched his arms out as far as they would reach around a bowl of water that swirled with canteen pepper.

And now she had to go back to face William a day early and dressed like a cocktail waitress from the eighties when she'd left the house in jeans and a sweater.

She toyed with the idea of finding another hotel tonight, but then she would still have to go home tomorrow morning to change, or arrive at the office in jeans or this red dress that James would know had been meant for him.

In any case, she was going to have to see James tomorrow, and the day after that and the day after that. Every day he would know that she'd worn a red dress for him. Just by agreeing to meet him here she had in all likelihood ensured he would take her place at Solaris and make Goosie very happy. Who would he think about then when he was in bed with her?

Laura sat back sharply. If she didn't start the engine soon James would find her here. She couldn't be sure that she wouldn't go back inside with him even though she was now certain that all that she had entertained tonight would cause nothing but chaos.

Ahead, something moved.

Something was gently swaying there that she hadn't noticed before.

It was hiding in a corner where the back wall of the Fosdyke met the rear exit porch. She would have walked right past it when she dragged her overnight bag across the gravel to the car.

At first she couldn't make out what it was, but then, as she squinted she realized that it was a man.

The man had his back turned.

Between the collar of his ski jacket and the curve of his skull she could make out a black smudge that when she focused hardened into a Chinese character.

Brandon.

Brandon no doubt relieving himself against the hotel.

Disgusting Brandon.

Brandon had been to Oaklands.

He'd said so.

Dwight had said so.

Brandon could have egged on that boy who William hit twice.

William had always refused to identify the other boys.

It had been going on for months before he flipped.

The phone had rung constantly.

If she picked up, no one was ever there.

Someone had scratched his car and let down his tyres.

That name they had given him.

The name they used to leave on the ansamachine.

The name daubed across the back fence and all over the walls and outbuildings of the Oaklands School.

He was glum beforehand, but not introverted, not withdrawn.

He didn't know who was responsible.

Afterwards he said that he hadn't seen it coming, the flip. He'd taken himself completely by surprise.

James once said that William has a problem with things he'll never see.

James said that at university, in his circle they called guys like this 'classic adventurers.' He'd described a friend who never recovered after realizing he'd never score a goal at Wembley, another who never bounced back after not making the GB 4x4 sprint relay team.

James was the only person who had ever been nice about William.

'People flip,' James had said. 'William just flipped in the wrong place. God, I mean, are we not all close to flipping most of the time?'

This was on a day that Laura had been unable to hide how mightily disturbed she was by William. Two days after Pheme, she had been eating her breakfast when William came in from the roof and said, 'I know what a star is, I don't know what the sky is.' He slumped on the table, exhausted, and knocked over a jug of milk.

Before he knocked out the boy who was egged on, Laura had never, ever seen William raise his hands to anyone.

Brandon was pissing up a wall.

She gunned the engine and turned the headlight on full beam.

When the lights ballooned across the hotel's façade, she knew what she must do and still knew when Brandon turned, a look of horror on his face that made her feel strong, certain.

She revved the engine.

It purred like a gigantic metal cat.

He turned and stepped away from the wall, hanging out his hands, a bemused, questioning look on his face. He must have recognized her straightaway, Miss Coo from Room 102, and let his defences down, assuming she was just another dippy girl who couldn't control her ride.

She released the pressure on the clutch.

The car pounced forwards.

Someone else appeared at his side. Someone who clung to him, a young, lithe girl, her hair a cascade of yellow ringlets, eyes a-gleaming, watery blue, but scared, found-out with lipstick smudged all over her mouth.

Laura dipped her lights, took her foot off the accelerator too quickly and stalled the car.

Brandon laughed and saluted. He didn't seem to be gloating or goading. This situation seemed to be genuinely hilarious to him. He didn't care about getting caught, obviously. He probably liked the idea of a grope in the spotlight, a fumble in the glare. Laura bet herself that to get a snog in the dark Brandon hadn't told Clara that the world is ending, or that he thought about her when he was with another girl. He would have found some other way of capturing her in his orbit. Clara K was susceptible after all, and Dwight was susceptible and

Laura knew that she too was susceptible. We'll believe anything, men and women, anything that makes us feel mysterious, desirable, and we'll get used to believing it and persist. We'll keep on heading out until we can't get back, back to the shop floor and the lights.

Laura restarted the car. With their arms around each other Brandon and Clara sauntered into the hotel, both of them waving at her. She'd learn, he'd learn, Laura thought. As she swung the car about, it occurred to her, not in a way that made her laugh or a way that made her angry, that everything that had ever happened to her happened because one day, a long time ago, she had blithely accepted an invitation to a tosser's wedding from a boy who could simplify the workings of the Universe in a bowl of water sprinkled with stale pepper.

She passed one car on the road out. Increasing her speed, she made a point of not checking the make and the model or the body shape of the driver.

None of the lights were on when she pulled up. She didn't remove her heels at the door and clunked as noisily as she could across the laminated floor in the hall. She dragged the overnight case behind her and on purpose slammed it against the radiator.

In the kitchen, she dropped her keys from shoulder height onto the breakfast bar. A metal crack skittered out into the darkness of the house. Nothing stirred. No one reacted.

William was in, though. She could sense him, like when she'd come home from work on the day he'd been arrested and felt that something was wrong straight away. A strange and uncontrollable part of her knew that he wasn't there. Once she'd discovered that his mobile was switched off she phoned the school, then the police and afterwards their solicitor. By the time she called Richard Berman she was distraught.

William would be up on the roof terrace, playing with his robotic telescope thing. He wasn't expecting her back tonight and was probably wearing his earmuffs, but even if he'd heard the car pull up and her blatant clanking and skittering he would stay out there.

She considered creeping to the bedroom and changing out of the dress.

While she was weighing up a costume change, her mobile rang. She took the phone out from her coat pocket and as she strode towards the staircase turned it off.

Upstairs, she slid open the door that led out onto the roof terrace. He didn't hear its swish, or at least he didn't react to it. At the far end of the terrace, in his beige parka and beanie hat, he was hunched over his telescope, eye to the viewfinder, the fingers of one hand caressing a control panel lower down, his legs almost perfectly aligned with two of the struts of the equatorial mount.

The telescope had been a present for his fortieth birthday. It had cost the same as a small car. Converting the kitchen roof into a terrace to house the telescope had cost the same as a family car and a decent holiday combined.

She wondered if he was grateful now. When she'd remortgaged the house to finance the terrace he'd acted, not resentfully but terrified, almost unable to accept her generosity in the circumstances. He said that he didn't deserve it. She'd wanted him to have the terrace, though. She'd wanted to do something for him. He needed something to cheer himself up and to occupy his time now that he couldn't work in schools. She couldn't have known he was going to like it up here quite so much, that he'd revert back into the William she first met in the canteen at Microtherics. That William, however, with his geeky preoccupations and uber-successful brother had been merely shy and rubbish with girls.

The brazier William had bought from a scrap metal dealer glowed at his right hip. In her head she heard the voice her mother had used to warn her of danger. She could picture the tail of William's coat flapping into the fire. He wouldn't realize until the flames were burning a hole in his back.

She couldn't feel her feet. The cold night air was starting to clamp around the tops of her legs and stiffen her shoulders. She would either have to go indoors or button up her coat and get closer to the warmth.

The telescope whirred and swung a few inches to the left.

Up above, the sky was clear of cloud now. Venus shone west of the Moon. Angled over the crown of William's head, as if it were pointing down at him, Laura could make out the constellation of Ursa Major. She'd probably been able to identify that one, along with Orion and the Pole Star before she met William but she'd never quite understood why Ursa Major was known as The Plough or The Big Dipper. To her it had always looked like a gigantic question mark.

'It is you, isn't it?' said William, not taking his eye from the viewfinder.

'Who did you think I was?'

Just as she was about to get extremely annoyed that he still had his back to her, he lifted his eye from the viewfinder and rotated slowly around to face her. He maintained the blank stare she'd come to expect if she disturbed him out here. His posture and expression reminded her of that of the robot in one of his favourite films: *The Day the Earth Stood Still*. It was a stance that had maybe lulled the boys from Oaklands into a false sense of security that day.

He must have seen the dress though. He must have registered that she was wearing a special dress, a solar flare of a dress. His eyes glistened and he swallowed as if a lump had formed in his throat. Something flashed in his face.

At first she thought she'd not seen this flash in his face for years.

She had seen it very recently, though.

The day they announced the discovery of Pheme.

Like on that day, the joy quickly subsided and dread and disappointment seeped into his face as it registered that someone had got there first.

'Did you go through with it?' he said.

She stepped towards him, belting her coat as it crossed her mind that maybe Goosie had rumbled her and phoned William earlier. That call downstairs might have been James trying to warn her.

'Has someone been telling tales?' she said.

'It's obvious where you've been,' said William. 'No one needed to tell me.'

'We need to talk.'

'We probably do.'

118

'Probably, William, probably?'

'Did you do it?'

'I left before he turned up.'

He sagged and sighed. He grabbed hold of her arm and squeezed it.

'I'm so relieved. That stuff is unstable, Laura. It's going to maim half the planet. Thalidomide will look like Penicillin. He'll get sued to buggery. I don't want us involved.'

She couldn't look at him and stared over his shoulder up at the stars.

'Guess what?' he said. 'You know Roger Prater at Wanderers? His boy hacked into VBOT's mainframe and downloaded all the data they've used to locate Pheme and, listen, I don't think the sample is definitive. It's too small. I don't think she's there. I don't think she exists.'

Laura had a horrible vision of standing here in ten years time with William reduced to a brain in a tank after expending all his energy trying to disprove something now regarded as scientific fact.

'William, I don't care. I'm going to bed. You're welcome to join me, or you can freeze out here forever. It's up to you.'

'Look at this,' he said, waving his hand over the telescope's eyepiece like a waiter serving a delicacy.

'I don't want to, William, I'm going in.'

'Something special is happening tonight.'

'No, it's not,' she said.

'Indulge me for a minute, please.'

She dipped her head to the viewfinder. When her eye focused she could see a faint blue disc.

'Neptune?' she said.

'We need another hour and a half.'

'I'm not staying out here for an hour and a half.'

'You are if you want to see a rare superior appulse. If we use this baby, baby, in an hour and a half we'll witness a conjunction of Venus and Neptune.'

This was a gesture, she knew. It had been a long time since she'd been involved in any of William's observations. In fact, he had never asked her to stargaze with him here, on the terrace she'd had built for him. When he was still teaching she'd sometimes gone to the

Wanderers when something exciting was happening, the last time to look at Mercury's scarred and crater-pocked face, but it was only when they were first seeing each other, twenty years ago, when they used to camp out in the summer in Cumbria or Scotland, or when they used to go to Tenerife for its clear night skies that she'd regularly watched the stars with William.

She was starting to more shudder than shiver. Frost dusted the fields and was forming on the upper rail of the terrace's balustrade. It was already late and there would supposedly be work tomorrow, and in a moment, because she'd not said anything and William was William he was going to say something about Neptune and Venus being like Mr and Mrs Berman. He couldn't know that she'd heard too many cheap and transparent lines tonight.

'I'm not dressed for it, William.'

'Go and change. Make some soup. In a flask like you like it, and some toasted sandwiches and I'll keep watch until …'

'William, be quiet, please.'

Her voice sounded old, as old as it had ever sounded.

She turned and walked back along the terrace towards the sliding door. It was up to him whether he followed her. She wasn't going to play along with this. She wasn't going to play her part anymore. If he followed her, she would tell him everything tonight. They would stand in the lounge, and she would pace in semicircles, and he would maintain his robot from *The Day the Earth Stood Still* pose as she told him about James, and what James had promised to do to her, and why she had wanted James to do these things, and that even though she had changed her mind it was clear to her that nothing else would change unless she made it change. She would tell him that she was going to hand in her resignation tomorrow. She would tell him that she had never liked this house with its silences and dead animals. She would tell him everything and he would listen and then, William being William, he would mutter something curt to conceal his anger and brush past her and sulk up here on the roof all night. By the time tomorrow night the machinery behind these stars clicked them back to their current positions, she would be sat on a bed in another hotel room, many densely packed bags and screwed-up tissues at her feet.

Late-night idiots would gibber from a portable TV that she wouldn't be able to find the will to switch off. This would be better than falling in with what he was hinting at now. She didn't want to be susceptible to the idea that distant glimmers in geometrical formation could somehow shift them back to when they were still young and wonderstruck.

She'd left the sliding door open. It was the sort of thing that Dwight would do. She gave him a thought as she reached the door and asked herself if Dwight had realized yet that Brandon had played him for a fool, told him to say all the things that he shouldn't say if he wanted to impress Clara K. There was a career in sales or PR for that Brandon, if he lost the eyebrow stud and learned how to speak English like a real live human being.

As she stepped up onto the threshold she pressed her hand to the glass to steady herself. It was freezing, almost skin-burningly so.

William spoke her name.

William whispered *Laura Berman* in her ear like he used to whisper it, like he used to whisper *Laura Berman* as if she were a secret compound or heavenly outpost long sought by legions of lovesick Ptolemys and Keplers.

From behind he slipped an arm under her shoulder, another under her knees and pulled her up from the tiles. She squealed as she rose, an unguarded, girlish squeal she couldn't remember letting out since she'd been twenty-four on a beach in Rhodes and after she'd teased him about something William had picked her up in front of a horde of elderly tourists and tossed her into the sea.

The Moon above and the coils of stars and galaxies jolted and sprang. As William twisted her around, the tips of her shoes skimmed the glass door. One of them detached from her foot and flew over the side of the balustrade.

'Oh that was clever,' she said.

'I'm being lazy, Laura Berman,' he said.

'Put me down. I'm not a doll.'

'You sure about that?'

He drew her shoulders and knees upwards so she concertinaed at the waist. The stars drizzled downwards until she found herself face-to-face with William.

'Don't kiss me,' she said. 'Go and get my shoe.'

'Have you lost weight?'

'You're a bastard.'

'I'll get your shoe if you go and put on that coat with the Eskimo hood thing and wait it out with me.'

'It's a school night, William.'

'I'll undercook the bacon and call you in sick tomorrow.'

'Does that one usually work for you?'

'Probability says that one day it will.'

'Put me down.'

'No,' he said. 'I quite like you up here.'

'Only quite?'

She realized that she was laughing now. Her diaphragm was starting to ache from it but she wasn't going to let him do this. She wasn't going to let him sweet talk her into staying out here with him all night, looking upwards, looking out.

If she let herself be tempted, things would unfold in predictable fashion. She could imagine the conversations they would have if she dressed up like an Eskimo and waited an hour or so for two remote specks to align.

He would point out a skein of stars that no one else would notice and attach to them some sad story or myth, like he had in Ecuador when he'd shown her Ariadne's Crown and described how the ignorant tough guy Theseus abandoned smart and lovely Ariadne on the island of Naxos. In the end, though, things worked out better than expected for Ariadne. Dionysus descended and lifted her up into the stars.

He would start talking about Jupiter's Trojans or how Uranus still hangs upside down after some devastating prehistoric impact, or how Triton is a minor Pluto-style planet captured by the orbit of the ice giant Neptune, as if she could use such answers to pub quiz questions in her daily struggle to sell higher and higher quantities of laboratory glassware and microscopes.

There was a risk, though, that he would talk about how things started out in the Solar System in that way that had always disarmed and impressed her.

He might explain how just after the beginning, billions of chunks of compacted stardust circled the Sun until they all crashed together and only the Earth and its three rocky siblings remained. This was our moment of luck, Laura Berman; we came to be at the only feasible location, right on the mark, at life's bullseye.

Further out, there should be a fifth world between Mars and Jupiter, but Jupiter is so vast and exerts such a pull that it perturbs that region of space so only the dwarf planet Ceres and sundry asteroids could come into being there.

Uranus and Neptune were born close to the Sun but spun off for millions of miles to perturb and unsettle the smaller, outer worlds: Pluto and Makemake; Orcus and Varuna; Eris and its tiny Moon, Dysnomia.

The eleven-thousand-year elliptical orbit of Sedna hints that there is something else, something grand out there on the edge that tugs at it, however weakly, however faint, something that might be Nemesis-Pheme.

Pheme: goddess of rumour, perturber of comets, the sparkle in the depths.

Maybe she was there. Maybe she … it wasn't.

Maybe there were a trillion other Phemes out there in trans-Phemian space.

None of this mattered.

None of it mattered down here.

Laura jerked away from William's gaze. She hung her head backwards over the crook of his arm. Up there, in the great bowl of the night, she knew that the stars had been written up in a language no one would ever fully understand. Even if you somehow made it out from here to the farthest observable point, a fringe of new stars would beckon from that beyond, and from that fringe a peppering of older lights would glitter in the distance's distance. The stars can only be written over and scribbled out, approximated and second-guessed. Their codes and hieroglyphics can't be deciphered. Tonight, though, she decided she would let him try once more. She would give him this. She would give him this, until tomorrow at least.

Before the Song

- Angela Readman -

The mornin' slipped by, small flies spottin' the landscape floated in my eye. I looked towards the house and squished it between my fingers like a bug. The preacher crossed the plain on foot, waving thanks to the pick-up what dropped him in the lane. It could only be the preacher, black cloth - a hole in the middle of the day. I watched him get smaller nearing the house. The black of his robe furred with dust. I wiped my brow and bent back to the cotton. Didn't see him leave. Next time I looked to the house Momma was a hollarin', leanin' out the back door and wavin' a pair of long johns up and down. Red on blue sky, red as a scratch on my leg bloody enough to catch my eye. Suppertime. I walked up to the house, saw' Pa go inside, Clift behind him.

'Y'all wipe your feet,' Momma called, flies a buzzin' in and out her mouth. The closing back door made a rainbow of dirt on the floor. Everyone sat.

Momma

'Grace,' I says.

Clift stuffs a biscuit in his mouth. My hand moves to slap his like tryin' to swat a fly what's too wily. 'God bless this food,' I says, reachin' out my hands like anyone would take 'em. I close my eyes. The family's fingers twitch at the bowls. *Amen* is a groan, a rusty barn door closin' in the wind. I don't meet my husband, Hank's, eye. It's full of, 'What we thankin' God for? I'm the one's been workin' all day.' I serve him meat and help myself to greens. Clift talks with his mouth full, 'bout the hole in the barn.

'Manners,' I says.

The word in my mouth reminds me of a skinny cat locked in a room, a dumb cat what don't know nothin' but to mew anyways. I look at my plate. 'Heard some news from Choctaw today,' I says, 'from that new Pastor.'

It's always me what starts the talkin' at supper, if it weren't for this I mights well pour the meal in a trough and be done. My husband's grunt is an engine that has trouble startin', yet always starts.

'He'll be wantin' his free meal,' he says, 'hear he's been a callin' on anyone with a decent crop come suppertime.'

'He seems nice,' Georgia says.

'The MacAllister boy jumped off the Tallahatchie Bridge,' I says.

'Billie?' Georgia says, 'Billie Joe?'

I looks at the girl sharpish. Her Pa looks up from his plate. She shuts her mouth and stares at her food.

Hank nods, chewing fat. 'That boy never had a whip of sense,' he says, 'biscuits?'

I walk to the stove, collect the tray and think of a baby a long time ago on a long summer's day, Billie Joe. A fair-haired bundle of wide-open stares as his mamma gave him to me to hold. It was hot, all summer I moved slow, like I wasn't just swollen but made dim-witted by the bump in my stomach. June MacAllister took out her purse. I struggled with her boy squirmin' like a sack of pigs. I rested his legs on the hump of my belly. I imagined them, the baby in my arms and the one in my belly, foot to foot, pressin' their toes together through a sheet. Baby Billie stared at me, serious like, like he had somethin' on his tiny mind. Then he smiled. He was reachin' for the mountains as if they was a flower he could pluck. Might be dumb, to remember somethin' so small, but it was like for the first time I understood what somethin' meant.

When the pastor left this mornin', I got on with the shortnin', the apple peelin' and the bread. But all afternoon, not for all the cotton in the county could I remember what Billie Joe looked like after that one day back in that long summer. I place the biscuits in front of Hank, their warmth in my palms coolin' quicker than a foolish memory.

Papa

'These is good biscuits,' I chew.

'Same as yesterday,' says the wife.

I mush black-eyed peas, feel the wife eyeballin' me. The cutlery is loud as rakes hittin' rocks. The cooling stove clanks. I mop gravy, take a swig of milk, and hear no more from my family. Just like 'em, to give the dead boy a silence he'd have filled with his fool mouth. The MacAllister boy ain't our business, no one we knew too good or had to the house. I crunch biscuits, shovel in peas to keep 'em company. Nothin' to say. No sense thinkin' of the boy who'd been here lookin' for work not more than a month ago.

'Nothin' doin',' I said, sharpenin' my pick.

Billie Joe stood half in, half out of the barn. One eye in shadow, one in sun, he glanced to the fields. I put down my pick and stood in front of the boy. He grinned, just like his Pa. Me and Billie senior went back a long ways. Two kids sparkin' the tails of cats and laughin' as they ran fast as fireworks away from their fuse; two boys droppin' spiders into prayer books; two young men workin' at the sawmill and puttin' our money together to buy land.

'We'll make cider, get rich,' Bill used to say, lookin' at the sky. I'd keep diggin', plantin' fruit trees.

That was Billie Joe's Pa, Bill, one eye on the next prize while I did all the work. I remember him boastin' to a couple of old hunters who shook his hand and took a photograph of him holdin' up a fourteen pointer by its hind legs. It was the biggest stag we'd seen in these parts for a long whiles; it was me what had been stalking it for days, learning

129

its secret ways the way fools learn a woman. Bill showed up when the heat of the day had burnt itself out, he followed my trail. We fired our rifles about the same time. Dumb luck the shot what hit the deer was his.

When it was time to pick the fruit, Bill was out braggin' to girls how he owned 'the best orchard in the county'. I picked the damn apples night and day, Bill said he'd swing by later, claimed he'd done his share when I wasn't there. After the twister, we sold the land. He gave me my half. I looked at the smile on his face. The notes felt light in my hand.

'Here ya go, partner,' he said, handin' me my money, slappin' my shoulder like a goddamn field hand, 'fruits of our labour.'

I walked away, hands in my pockets, 'partner' ringin' in my head like a church bell in a widow's ears. Never spoke to the son of a bitch again.

Then, a month ago, Billie Joe stopped by, strolled down the lane and said howdy, like the word was his to say

'How's it goin' Hank?' he said. 'Was wonderin' if you can give me any work?'

'Hank', he said, too good to say Mr, like he'd inherited his father's bastard buddy. I looked Billie Joe in the eye, stood in front of him to block it roamin' over to the field where Clift and Georgia was workin.'

'No sense lookin' round here. Ain't got nothin' for you,' I said.

'No harm askin.'

'You hear me? *Nothin*,' I said.

The boy looked like he'd lost a dollar and found a dime. Then, he smiled, quick as a lick, as if I'd said 'take care now' he strolled away.

Georgia messes with the food on her plate, like there ain't nothin' better to do with it. I reach for the last biscuit. My son gets there first.

'Shame about that boy anyways,' the wife says.

No one replies. I keep my mouth full. Chewin' on Bill McAllister Senior, now workin' what he got left of his land with no son to pitch in. If I didn't have my mouth full I might whistle, a feelin' fills me that somethin' might be right in the delta and the whole mess of crap beyond. The boy dead, Bill McAllister finally got what was comin' to him, is left reapin' what he let other people sow.

Clift

'I could see off another slice of that pie,' I says. 'You remember how me and Billie Joe put that big ole toad down your back at the picture show?' I point' at Georgia with my fork. 'You squealed like a pig with its guts trailin' out!'

'I remember,' she says.

Under the table, Momma kicks, apple drops from my fork. The toad was Billie Joe's idea. Me, Tom and Billie Joe went to Carroll County with it in our pockets. Feelin' like men on payday, we took our time deciding where to put it to best use. It was Billie what noticed my sister, sittin' on her lonesome, starry eyed for the big screen, far away as when she sat on the porch she strummin' that ole guitar. Billie Joe crept behind her with the toad in his palms. I shook my head, pointin' out real girls. He held out the back of the neck of my sister's dress and let that nasty ole toad go down the road a toad must go.

'You! You's no good. You's goin' straight to hell Billie Joe,' Georgia yelled, once she'd stopped wrigglin'. All four of us stood outside the picture house, where the manager sent our ruckus.

Billie Joe looked like he was considerin' his eternal damnation for a second, then laughed a river of soda out his nose.

'You're a goin', I'm gonna tell Pa,' Georgia stomped.

Pa didn't care for tales. He didn't care too much what us kids did so long as we finished our chores and cleared our plate come suppertime, but after the picture show he made me shovel horseshit for a month.

'Stay clear of that Billie Joe,' he said, 'Y'all, hear me, them MacAllisters ain't no good.'

I shoveled shit thinking of the toad I'd been sorry to let go, seemed like as long as it was in my pocket somethin' good could happen anytime. I imagined it in the dark, still there, squattin' under the foldin' seats of the movie house. A hundred girls it could scare, maybe more, all the popcorn it could eat.

'You wanna go catch a grass snake, leave it in church?' Billie Joe said.

'Sure.'

I didn't pay too much heed to Pa that summer. It was me and Billie Joe against the whole boring world. He said his Pa laughed till he cried whiskey when he heard 'bout the toad. Billie Joe's Pa was like that, every trick played ended with his Pa tellin' him 'bout his own.

'Him and your Pa put dead chicks in the teacher's desk, all kinds,' Billie Joe said. 'Pa says your Pa's just bent outta shape coz they had a fight when they was young about a girl.'

Summer sloped away. There was crops to sell, preservin', haulin'. There never seemed much time to spend with Billie Joe again, not like that summer anyways. But I'd catch him wink in church. Years later, we grinned like we still had that toad in our pockets and could release it down a blouse at any time.

I saw Billie Joe at the sawmill up on Choctaw the other day, where he sometimes worked when folk got sick. I was pricin' up repairs for the hayloft. He was luggin' timber to Red Thompson's pick-up. Red was settlin' up in the mill. His daughter got out the front seat of his truck and fanned her face with her hand.

'Thirsty work,' Becky said to Billie Joe.

'Yep.'

'You know Pa's buildin' a new barn, bet he could use you,' she said. 'Stop by the house someday after supper. There's always pie,' she smiled, makin' corn circles with her hair.

'Busy,' Billie Joe said, liftin' the last of the timber on the truck.

Red Thompson drove away. I watched Becky look back out the window at Billie Joe, like she was decidin' whether to wave or blow a kiss.

'Stop by for …*pie*,' I laughed, 'that girl's sweet on you.'

'Maybe,' Billie Joe said, serious like.

'Well? What's wrong with you? Nice girl like Becky Thompson. She don't look so bad…'

Billie shook his head.

'Nice ain't love. Ain't 'nough time in the day to tell you what's wrong with me,' he said.

Then, like a frog poked with a stick, he jumped, off he was, back to work with a whistle, turnin' back with a grin and yellin' that I was the one what looked as if he could use a slice of that pie.

Me

Clift finishes his pie and takes meat off my plate, grease drippin' down his fingers slow as the aftermath of a bad deed.

'Pastor said he saw Billie Joe with a girl what looked like you up on the ridge,' he says.

Pa's fork on the way to his mouth is a horse fly, hovers.

'Lotta girls look like me,' I says.

Pa takes a bite.

'What I tell you 'bout listenin' to nonsense gossip? Girl's got more sense than to waste time with a boy like that,' he says.

Momma starts clearin' the table. The men undo their belts.

'I been cookin' all day, you hardly touched it,' she says, takin' my plate.

'Not hungry', I says. 'Think I caught too much sun.'

I hadn't. It was June third, all day the sun played hardball, made pitches at my hair, but there was none I could catch and take away.

Momma holds her hand against my head. I wanna press against it, let the weight fall into her hands. I wish Pa could carry me to bed, like when I was small and sick. I wonder when I got too big to let Momma tuck me in, cover every thought in my head with an ole damp cloth.

'You don't feel burnt none,' Momma says.

I get up with dirty dishes, take a kettle off the stove to fill the sink. Momma doesn't say a word 'bout how she don't have to tell me to do the chore; she hands me the suds and goes back to the table with coffee. I plunge my fists in hot water with my back to the table. I put in suds and make everythin' cloudy white. Specks of rust float from the kettle what sheds a little of itself everyday.

I ain't angry none at how they all keep eatin' like it fills every hole. It don't matter any. *Verse One-* Momma. *Verse Two* –Pa. Billy Joe. Billie Joe. God, I needed a chorus. I had to put everyone in neat verses, make something simple folks needn't think about, just hum.

133

Pa's right; Billie Joe *could* be high as a blue jay and still be low on sense. There coulda been any number of girls with him up on Choctaw, girls with smiles big enough to patch up hand-me-down dresses: girls what laughed at his jokes like they could even hear 'em for all the drownin' they was tryin' to do in his eyes. Any girl, but it happened to be me.

'Youse different Georgia,' Billie Joe said, 'you got your mind on intangible things.'

It didn't know what he meant. I just sat with him in the barn lookin' at stars through the hole in the roof, the hole what got bigger when Billie Joe climbed a ladder and punched rust with his bare hands.

'See, I can give you the moon,' he laughed.

He settled back and started talkin' his big talk 'bout the world beyond the delta, fancy houses, dresses and cars. His words was like a song without a tune, pretty, but unsure how it would make anyone dance.

'We'll have us a kitchen big as this barn,' he said.

Sometimes, he saw us on the road together, drivin' from town to town, only stayin' where the weather was good. Pretty stories of me and him on our lonesome under an appliqué of stars. I imagined evenings of my head on his lap, wind plucking tunes from my ole guitar by the door.

I lifted my dress off over my head then, not like the first time. Every button unfastened now we met naked as the lord. We never said much when that time came. After listenin' a while I quietly took off my dress and let him touch me, obediently followin' the white trail of his words like a lamb being lead in the dark.

~

'Is love a sin?' I asked Pastor Taylor, sweeping between the pews. I straightened bibles on the ledges. The broom stopped at my feet.

'Course not child, but lusts of the flesh are a sin outside holy matrimony. Is there something you want to talk about, Georgia?' he said, lowerin' his voice.

134

'Nothin'', I said, 'Just me and my busy brain a buzzin',' I laughed, catching a glimpse of Billie Joe outside the church doors, I ran into the day.

The service had been jam packed with a red devil and his sticky tricks of flesh. I didn't unfasten my buttons in the hayloft this time; I told Billy Joe my dream about hell.

'You don't think lickin' your lips of good pie, or goin' back for seconds is a sin,' Billie Joe said, 'Or laughin'. Or dancin'. Or swimmin', any other joy of the flesh.'

Just me and him and a fistful of stars, it didn't seem nothin' what felt so right could be wrong. But later, I'd think on it. I saw the barn cat bulge and pop out kittens after that old Tom came around and touched my belly, feelin' like a snake what swallowed a chipmunk.

'You don't look no different to me,' Billie said.

'I feel it. Blowin' up like a hornet's nest. There's a baby comin', punishment for what we done.'

'We can get married,' Billie said, 'I'll ask your Pa.'

He talked pictures of a house with a hundred rabbits runnin' wild out front, a life of words.

'Pa sooner sell up and join the carny than let a MacAllister take his girl,' I said.

It was true. We knew it. Billie Joe started lookin' for work, talked about savin' so we could run away, least go aways, since we couldn't imagine no one missin' us enough to chase our tails. In the barn we picked out fugitive names; they seemed important to get right, like we could be whatever the names sounded like, names decided our whole lives.

'Cecil,' I'd call. And Billie puffed up his chest and pulled a face like he thought a Cecil might.

'Rupert,' I yelled. And he'd start squintin' and walkin' with his butt cheeks clenched.

Our laughter ran into the night like jackals calling each other's names. A moment later, Billie was quiet. He was often that way, his smile was the heart of a tornado, switchin', dark clouds blew in from clear skies.

'What we gonna eat? Where's a baby gonna sleep when I ain't got a dime?' he said.

135

It was my idea to see the witch woman. I went up to Cat Fish Row and knocked on her door.

'I ain't got much money, but…'

The crazy woman opened her door.

~

The smell of the river crept up my nostrils and painted inside my head dark. The mud on my boots cracked in the heat, land so good for growin', no good to build foundations for nothin' on.

'I ain't fit, a guy what can't take care of his girl,' Billie said, skimmin' rocks.

He stared at the river like he could see the stone sink all the way to down, the sun pickin' red and gold from his brown hair, wheat being sifted from the husk.

It was my turn to tell stories now. When Billie Joe got this way, I smoothed his hair and whispered 'bout houses with plaid curtains, rabbits and cars. I talked to him thinkin' 'bout lookin' out the window, singin' whatever a mood told me to. This time it didn't work; I didn't have the right song. Billie stared at the water. The pecan trees moved with the hiss of an old man a twistin' and turnin' in his bed.

In my hand was the rag-doll. Billie Joe looked at it dangling. I'd done what the witch woman said and nothin' what looked like its daddy came out. Yet I felt it - a cleansin', somehow I felt my belly of a snake going down, whatever sin growin' inside no longer curled up inside me, ate up the day's light. I started to think about songs and cities, not a rabbit or plaid curtain in sight when I came to meet Billie Joe, I was just a girl what had done a bad thing and taken her punishment.

All what came from me is red; somethin' and nothin' like squashed fruit, about the size of my fingertip. No shape of its own. I made a slit in my ole rag doll and stuffed the small clot in the hole. There didn't seem to be nothin' what had been loved so much as that doll, witness to fevers and thanksgivins' and picklin' days. A doll made with dresses that could no longer be let out to fit; I was too old to love it anymore.

The last time I saw Billie Joe we met in the barn, took off our clothes and lay under the crack of stars.

'Clift and Pa gonna fix that roof soon,' I said.

Billie Joe was quiet. He looked at me and reminded me of an old man starin' at a photograph he found in his hands. I saw it too. We looked into each other's eyes now and just saw the pair of us stood side by side, caught in one place, one time, like people who couldn't step out of a photograph they didn't know someone took.

Over the river, Billie Joe kissed me. I kissed him. Stick figures bleached by the sun, we stood on the Tallahatchie Bridge, hand in hand with a rag doll. Not one story between us, no song to fit our lips, we looked into the muddy water and let go.

That's what we did then, just made our lives a song for someone who'd never know all the words to sing.

A Publisher Surveys the Changing Literary Scene

- CD Rose -

Peace there'd been, for twenty years, and now this.

Maskell turned from the window, paced across his office and slumped at his desk. No one would disturb him at this hour: three in the afternoon and they'd assume he was still at lunch, or sleeping it off. He closed his eyes, breathed deeply, counted to five and exhaled. It didn't work; his heart still raced. His laptop glowed accusingly so he snapped it shut and reached for the calming weight of his paperknife. The rosewood handle sat snugly in his fist, the glint of light from the carbon steel blade soothed him. Though he used it rarely now, he would never be without it: his first shiv, the one he'd used to make his bones with the Coetzee deal.

He put the knife down and checked his phone again. Still no message from Charlie.

Three days ago a figure had appeared in the square outside Maskell's office, patrolling the lawn like he owned it, looking up at him with the cockiness of the foxes that raided his bins at night. He could get someone to have words, put the scares out, but decided it wasn't worth the grief, not yet. Some things he could still settle himself, though Maskell knew he'd been using Charlie as a prop over the past few months.

Charlie was the one person he could always rely on. Maskell had found him years back, digging in the slush pile. Charlie Razorcuts they'd called him, after getting his fingers sliced to ribbons on the sheaves of badly cut manuscripts. He'd had a hungry look in his eyes, enough to convince Maskell to make him his *consigliere*. Some hadn't been happy, but after Charlie secured the Tóibín film rights during a particularly nasty LBF, no one had argued.

Restless, Maskell got up and looked outside again. The intruder was gone. Rain rolled like gunsmoke across the square. Winter was on its way.

Two weeks ago, arriving early at work, he'd found a dead fish on the doorstep of the office. Luckily he'd had time to bin it before anyone else saw. Not quite a horse's head, but he knew what it meant: a leaping salmon had been their old colophon, the warning had come from someone who was in the know.

Maskell had made enemies, of course, but his glory was the peace he had brought during the eighties. That had been a difficult time too, he reminded himself: Harper Collins, Random House, Murdoch money. Big fish, little fish and cold-blooded sharks. New families eyeing the rotting bookshops and creaky printing presses of old England. Word processing, desktop publishing, all sorts setting themselves up. Respect was necessary, Maskell had seen that. While others had got scared, he remembered nothing but exhilaration, not needing any artificial rush, never developing a voracious reading habit. Only losers got high on their own supply.

It was the same now, and he'd solved everything then, hadn't he? Turning up at a Paris Review party, uninvited and crew-handed, laughing his head off: *The British are coming!* Respect was his after that, the Americans stayed where they were and at home the Bloomsbury and Vintage arrivistes backed off. After leaving a couple of New York Times reviewers unable to type their own pieces, he'd walked back into town and divided up the turf, and that – pretty much – was how it had stayed. Until now.

His head of marketing had been missing for two weeks. Maskell had told everyone Watson had taken a holiday, but he and Charlie had seen the mangled wreckage of the Lexus. Word would get out soon; he'd play the game and take credit for it himself, let his own people know what happened to shoddy proofreaders and unreliable fact-checkers.

Despite the hour it was dark outside now. The rainstorm unleashed itself, battering against the sash window of his office.

Maskell thought of the bloodbath there'd been after the Joyce copyright ended, the memory of that Frankfurt coming back to him with an uneasy shiver. Gangs on the streets outside the Steigenberger Frankfurter Hof: Springer Verlag's bootboys, ageing resistance fighters from Flammarion, some Gallimard *soixante-huitards*, Marxist knuckledusters out from Feltrinelli and sharp-suited Berlusconi boys from Mondadori, even some upstart Fenians from Field Day. He'd solved it all, he reminded himself with pride, let them rip each others' throats out then wandered in and cleaned up the mess. He'd had to protect his writers' interests, after all. That was the official line. When the Met started sniffing round he'd been able to buy them off with a few Larkin signed first editions, and London was his.

Writers, Maskell thought as he looked out of the window again, it'd be like a writer to be hanging round outside on an afternoon like this. But writers weren't hard enough to do anything like Watson's car. No, this didn't have their prints on it.

Respect mattered more to him than peace. Peace was good for public relations, but always needed keeping by means of brutality. Respect made both easier: there wasn't enough of it in these times - strangers dogging him on his own turf, grisly messages on his doorstep, faulty brakes and ignition-timed bombs. He thought about the Americans. The East Coasters he had in his pockets, but those from the West, the new ones, they were different, unpredictable, unknown. He rued the passing of the men he'd grown up on: Bellow, Mailer, Updike, Roth, no pussies contractually obliged to suck from their agent's teat but men who'd wrestled syntax as fearlessly as they took out their competitors. Though Maskell had modelled himself on them, he knew he'd gone one better, not having to bother getting his fingers inky or risk a ruined spine hunched at a typewriter for months on end. Others could do that for him. Maskell's genius had been to corral the writers, make them his mules. Pick a mediocre, pliable one every now and then, get them a *Guardian* spread or a Mark Lawson interview while

143

keeping the others scrabbling around, grateful for the occasional crumb. That's what had kept the East Coast families in place, respectful and scared, even the uppity agents he'd had to sort out. Straus, Wylie, Victor: hand-to-hand, Maskell could still take any one of them, and they knew it.

He lost his resolve and tried calling Charlie: no answer. He moved to the window. The rain had cleared but the figure was back, standing there, looking up at him. Maskell slammed down the blind. He needed a drink. He'd kicked the latte habit months back, but now even Green Rooibos was giving him the shakes.

He couldn't be complacent; you had to be careful with writers. Highly educated and poorly paid, they'd always be dangerous. He'd had meals in restaurants in Soho, Williamsburg and the Marais ruined by some sap who'd recognised him and insisted on handing over a manuscript. Charlie was good at dealing with them; a word with him and they wouldn't be heard from again.

If not writers, then who? Booksellers? Every now and then they still flared up like a poetry revival, despite everything Maskell had done for them: leaning on his bent MPs to get rid of the Net Book Agreement, doing the deal with Waterstone, chasing out Ottakar's and Borders. Maskell had made sure the nineties had been pure profit for everyone. An open market was a good thing, he'd assured them, and it was, as long as he controlled it. Maskell put their lack of gratitude down to fear: they didn't know who was going to protect them anymore. At the last Hay-on-Wye, not one of them had come to pay their respects, not one.

Maskell tried to reassure himself. The dumbest Booker list in years was selling out, even from the supermarkets. t was easy to stitch up a jury: get them a place as a *Late Review* pundit, a *TLS* reviewer, a professorship even, though Maskell knew some of the other families hadn't been happy. Getting a spook in to head the jury had been a great idea. Keep your friends close, keep your enemies closer.

Unless it was, no, it couldn't be them. They'd gone totally. Everyone wanted to write now, no one to actually bother reading. His stalker was more likely to be someone local, Faber or Chatto, straying out of their territory. When starvation threatened, they were all getting desperate.

It was good to show his power from time to time, he was pleased when the occasional spat still broke out. The recent mess at the Poetry Society for example: Maskell had gone down with a small crew to sort it. Perhaps he should call on them again: Armitage could do his nice guy act while the others stood behind him, Paterson casually picking dirt out from under his fingernails with a broken whisky bottle, Duffy staring, a gold-tipped Montblanc curled in her fist. Burnside even, no, best leave Burnside out until it was really necessary to get medieval. Even Maskell was afraid of Burnside.

Fear made him see something he'd been ignoring: an insider. There had to be an *infedele* in their midst. Maskell had poached one or two people, made them good offers, let them have manuscripts their wives or husbands might not want to have seen them reading. Loyalty was never a constant, though. Such was his own reward: having cheated others, he couldn't believe others wouldn't cheat on him. He had personally checked on his army of interns: good families, the right universities, afraid enough, hungry enough. Their loyalty wasn't in doubt. They knew so little anyhow.

The train of thought uncoupled as his phone blipped. Finally, a message from Charlie. The name of a bar in Hoxton, of all places.

Maskell unlocked the top drawer of his desk and took out the Glock. An eighties piece, but he was a nostalgic: it had been a present from Martin. He'd initialled the handle, *M.A.*

Then the thought struck him: Charlie had texted, not called. Trouble?

He slipped the gun into his pocket and went out. The rain had left a cold that got into his bones, but it was something else that ached inside him. Who had been the only person close to him? Who was the one who knew? Who had been the only one to dare to say the things Maskell only heard in his nightmares?

Charlie.

Only Charlie knew of Maskell's attachment to that old imprint, only Charlie had known Watson's movements, and only Charlie had dared say the words: *digital rights management, e-reader, kindle*. Maskell had got angry with him, the first and only time, but had at least let Charlie set up tonight's meeting with the Silicon Valley people. Perhaps he'd been tricked. Could Charlie have turned *pentito*?

A cab was too risky and Maskell didn't trust his driver anymore. His footsteps echoed as he walked the empty pavements as far as the tube station. He sped up, and realised it was no echo: someone was following him. He could turn, face them down. His hand sank into his pocket, feeling the solid heft of the Glock. Not now, not so public. He hated mess. He broke into a run and heard the footsteps behind him trail off. Only a shout reached him, a voice carried on the cold air.

'Last chapter, Maskell.'

He was glad he had to change three times, certain of losing any followers, finding the warm fetid breath of the underground strangely comforting.

When he got to the bar there was no sign of Charlie. The windows were black, the signs neon. Bass shuddered through the door. Maskell should have insisted on meeting on his manor, but knew he couldn't dictate terms.

Damn Charlie. He'd go in alone, show these fuckers who Ed Maskell really was. At least, who Ed Maskell used to be. He slung the doors open and walked in, ordered a drink and sat at the bar. No sign of them yet, this place filled only with skinny kids in skinnier jeans, retro t-shirts and straggly beards. One of them came over to him.

'Ed Maskell? Gotta be you!' A lazy US accent and a hand raised in some kind of greeting ritual: these children *were* the Americans. The kid ushered him over to a low table where three identikit hipsters sat around, idly poking at their iPads, one older man with them, balding, his shirt tucked into his jeans.

Maskell put his hand on the gun in his pocket, and went in hard.

'20%, and full translation rights. No deals on films.' The Californians looked at him coolly, then swapped smiles.

'We're not here to bargain Mr Maskell.'

'Just to put you straight about a few things.' He stared hard at the older man.

'Why have you been following me?' The man shrugged, and Maskell regretted his mistake, but the anger in him rose, driving him on. 'Where's Charlie?'

'We don't know. He didn't show,' the older man said.

146

'Shame, he was the kind of guy we could work with,' chipped in one of the kids.

'Okay, you get full DRM.' He tried to control the tremor in his voice.

'We don't do deals with gangsters, Mr. Maskell.'

'Gangsters? Listen mate, we're not gangsters, we're fucking *publishers!!!* You don't want to deal with me? Fine: I'll work with the Russians. You think Dostoevsky's people can't take *you*? I've got the Chinese in my pocket, they fucking invented writing! Not some crappy computer. They're the real game changers now.' The Americans laughed, goading Maskell on further. 'India, then. The *Mahabharata* and a 38 quid tablet computer. How long do you think it's going to take them to get their fucking *kindle* together? Eh? That's what's coming, my friend.' The Americans flipped the covers on their ipads and stood to leave.

'We're taking over Mr. Maskell, and there's nothing you can do about it.' Maskell heard them laughing as they walked out. Fury gripped him, he punched the doors open and stormed onto the cold, wet, empty pavement.

Charlie, he had to find Charlie. And then he did.

Two wheelie bins stood next to a fire escape. Between them, a figure was slumped. Maskell recognised the Paul Smith suit immediately. He knelt down and lifted the battered, bloodied head of his only friend. Something heavy had done it, something blunt. It hadn't been a pretty death. Charlie's mouth was swollen, not with bruises, but with pages that had been stuffed into it. Maskell slowly pulled one out, soaked in blood and drool. As he suspected, the latest Murakami.

Before he could get back up, a hand grabbed his collar. He pulled, moved to run, but the grip was too strong. More hands grabbed his arms, twisting them behind his back. Someone pulled a blindfold around his head. Maskell recognised the smell of hangovers, unfulfilled dreams and charity shop clothes. Writers, after all.

'I've got a wrap in my pocket,' he said calmly. Coke usually worked for them. 'Take it and we'll have no more aggro.'

'Not what we're looking for.' Damn. He'd have to go higher.

'A two book deal, then. Name your publisher.'

'Is that how it works?' Writers, fanatics: the most dangerous, he knew. He tried a different card.

147

'I'll introduce you to Barnes.' Laughter.

'Amis?' More mocking laughter. 'He's a personal friend.'

'Hasn't written a word worth reading since '89.' The truth of it cut Maskell to the core. He thought quickly and coolly, this territory, who would work?

'Dunthorne.'

Silence a moment.

'Not interested.' Who *were* these people?

'What do you want?' said Maskell, tempering the desperation in his voice. 'Advance proofs of anything you like.' A hesitation, and he thought he'd cracked them, but the panic he couldn't control led him to shoot wildly.

'Richard and Judy!?' Their mocking laughter hurt worse than any bullet wound. Maskell realised he'd lost it.

He heard a car pull up, the door open, and was roughly shoved into the back. The car sped off, they removed the blindfold. Two men, one of each side of him, anonymous looking, but big enough to scare him. He couldn't see who was driving, a woman, he thought.

'Who sent you?' he asked, trying to hold his voice steady. He said the word: 'Amazon?'

'You don't get it, do you?'

'We hate them more than you do.'

'Then who the fuck *are* you?' The men stayed silent, the woman driving turned to him, and smiled.

'We're readers.'

Maskell shuddered, then everything went black.

The Monolith

- AJ Ashworth -

It appears overnight. The monolith. A tall black column like an oversized tombstone in the yard.

At sunrise Maggie looks out, blinks at a burst of light firing off one corner. 'What's that?' she says, and blinks again. 'God.' She rubs at the window with the side of a fist, as if doing that will somehow make it go   away.

She reaches for the phone and presses the memory button and the number one.

After seven rings, Carl answers. 'Hello,' he says, his voice cracking from sleep.

'There's a monolith in the yard,' she says, a hiss like rain on the line. She says it again, only louder. 'There's a monolith in the yard.'

'What?' he asks. 'What are you talking about?'

She squints out again and thinks she sees a ripple across the monolith, as if it's made of black liquid. 'I'm not joking, Carl. There's a monolith in the yard.'

'I heard you the first two times,' he says, sounding as if he's trying to suppress a yawn. 'A monolith? Like from 2001? That kind of monolith?'

She rolls her eyes. 'What other kind of monolith is there?'

151

Carl doesn't speak, but in the background Maggie can just make out the low mumble of a woman's voice. She imagines him with someone else — the two of them curled up in bed like a pair of cats: her stretching and stroking him with slender, reaching arms; his legs entwined in hers.

'Carl?' She kicks her foot against the skirting board. 'Say something.'

She hears Carl put his fingers over the mouthpiece. It makes a scuffling noise that irritates her ear. She pulls the phone away for a few seconds before putting it back, but she can't hear anything. Another scuffle and he removes his hand.

'Maggie,' he says. 'I don't know what you're expecting from me.'

Her foot kicks harder.

The woman with Carl talks louder now, her voice echoey as if she's speaking from his en-suite. 'What's she playing at?' the woman asks.

Maggie thinks of this woman washing in Carl's sink or using his toothbrush and stops kicking. 'Can you tell whoever that is that I'm not playing at anything? I just thought you might want to know what's happening here.'

'Tamsin,' he says. 'Her name is Tamsin.'

'Then would you mind telling her that I'm not playing at anything?'

'OK,' he says and moves the phone away from his mouth. 'She said she's not playing at anything.'

She hears the woman say, 'Of course not.'

'Excuse me,' says Maggie. 'But she doesn't even know me.'

'True,' he says. 'Be quiet, Tamsin.'

Maggie sees next-door's cat on the yard wall — a clump of grey fur with a fluffy tail that looks shocked with static. It sniffs the air and turns to look at the monolith, leans a leg down, as if dipping a toe into water, then jumps into Maggie's yard. It sniffs again, then slowly pads towards the tall, black pillar, stopping every now and then as if trying not to trip an alarm system.

Maggie bangs on the window. 'Hey,' she says to the cat, but it doesn't respond.

'What are you hey-ing at?' asks Carl.

She bangs louder and the cat turns before carrying on walking.

'Maggie?' says Carl.

'Kip,' she says. 'It's in my yard.'

The cat reaches the monolith and puts its head down, sniffing at the base. Its tail swishes over the paving slabs, the tip flicking up and down like someone tapping a foot.

'Kip,' he says, a playfulness in his voice. 'The imaginary cat.'

'Shoo!' Maggie bangs on the window again. 'Shoo!' Then she smiles, too. 'It isn't imaginary. It's lived there for years.'

'Well, I never saw it.'

Maggie leans so close to the window that it begins to steam up from her breath. She wipes the mist with her sleeve and steps back. 'Well, you were oblivious to a lot of things.'

'Thanks,' he says, pretending to be wounded.

The cat stops sniffing and instead just sits at the side of the monolith looking up at it. It blinks slowly — the kind of action that, in the cat world, is supposed to mean contentment.

'So, anyway,' he says, 'this monolith . . .'

'That's what I said.'

'Are you sure there's one there?' he asks.

Maggie stands tall and thrusts her shoulders back. 'Do you think I'm making things up or something?'

'No,' says Carl. 'It just sounds a bit strange, that's all.'

She hears Tamsin say something that she can't make out.

'Look,' he says, 'I've got to go, OK?'

Just then she thinks she sees the black ripple make waves across the monolith's surface again and she leans forward. As she does, the cat lifts a paw up and touches it, in the same way it might reach for a dangling piece of wool. There is a sudden rush of movement and the cat is dragged inside, leaving a smudge of grey in Maggie's vision at the exact spot where the cat was. She gasps.

'What is it?' says Carl. 'What's up?'

'Oh,' she says. 'Oh.' It feels as if invisible hands are squeezing her vocal chords.

'What's going on?' says Tamsin.

'Maggie?' asks Carl.

But Maggie can't speak.

'I'm coming over,' he says. 'I want to see what's happening.'

153

Maggie drops the phone into its cradle. There are tears forming in her eyes that she tries to blink and rub away. She fumbles in the drawer for the key to the back door, then rushes out into the yard. She searches around without going too near the monolith, but the cat has gone. 'Kip!' she calls out. 'Kip!' The only thing remaining is the bell that dangled from the front of its collar like a small, silver planet.

She stands at the back door, staring back and forth between the bell and the monolith, as a chilly breeze lifts the hairs on her arms and makes goosebumps stand like a rash of tiny hills all over her body. The surface of the monolith is now as still and frozen as a black, winter river. Nothing moving, no hint of life.

Thirty minutes later, Carl arrives with Tamsin. Maggie watches his 4x4 swerve into the steep drive and brake hard near the steps. He climbs out and strides to the door while Tamsin checks her hair in the mirror on the back of the visor before following him. Maggie, clutching a mug of tea, opens the door to them. Tamsin, a tall, horse-limbed woman, lets her eyes linger over Maggie's stomach before lifting them to look her in the face.

'What's going on?' asks Carl, his brow furrowed as he glances over Maggie. Then he steps past her and into the house. Tamsin hovers at the door, a huge designer bag hanging from her arm, its eyelets gaping.

'Come in,' says Maggie, catching the faint smell of Chanel No. 19 as Tamsin passes — the same perfume Carl had once regularly bought for her.

Maggie follows them both indoors. They look out at the yard. She sips her tea, feeling its heat on her tongue before swallowing it.

'It's a monolith,' says Carl.

'Well spotted,' says Maggie. 'But I did say it was.'

Tamsin raises her eyes to Carl, but he doesn't notice.

'So, what were all the hysterics about?' he asks.

'What hysterics?' says Maggie, going into the kitchen and switching on the kettle, its blue light flickering over the counter like watery sapphires. She senses a shift in the atmosphere and turns to find Carl in the doorway.

'On the phone,' he says.

154

The kettle fills the air with a hushing sound as Maggie pulls two cups from the cupboard. 'It wasn't hysterics,' she says. 'The cat went inside that thing. It frightened me.'

Carl strokes his chin. 'The monolith?'

'Yes.'

'Really?'

Maggie feels a flare shoot up inside her and her voice grows louder. 'It — went — in — the — monolith. I'm not making it up.' She throws teabags into the cups. 'If you don't believe me you might as well go now.'

Carl folds his arms and leans into the doorframe. 'It just seems crazy.'

She pours water into the cups and stirs so fast with the spoon that tea spills onto the worktop. 'Well, crazy or not, the cat's gone.' She squeezes the tea bags and drops them into the bin. 'I didn't know who else to ring.'

He steps forward and touches her on the shoulder. 'It's OK,' he says.

Tamsin appears in the doorway, her gaze lingering on Maggie's shoulder.

'Give me the key, Mags. I want to go outside and have a look for myself.'

Carl rattles the key in the lock and goes out into the yard. Maggie's temples pulse like silent drums.

Carl covers every inch of the yard. After that he goes out through the back gate, calling for the cat all the while.

'There's just the bell,' shouts Maggie. 'That's all that's left.'

Tamsin hoists her bag further up her arm. Her gold bracelets clink. 'You can buy bells.'

Maggie turns to her, dumbfounded. 'Why would I buy a bell?'

'For this whole fantasy,' she says. 'To make it more realistic.'

'Fantasy?' asks Maggie. Tamsin nods.

'And I suppose I bought that too,' says Maggie, pointing to the monolith.

Tamsin shrugs and raises an eyebrow. 'It's only a big headstone. They're not that hard to come by.'

'So I dragged one home from the cemetery and scraped the words off did I?' Maggie shakes her head. 'And what's happened to the cat?'

Tamsin pauses and looks at Maggie's stomach again. 'Maybe there wasn't a cat in the first place. Who knows?'

Maggie's hands automatically go to her belly, covering it like a shell made of fingers. 'Carl knows there was a cat. Don't be ridiculous.'

'Well, he doesn't really, does he?' says Tamsin, one nostril and the side of her mouth lifting as if smelling something unpleasant. 'He never saw it. He hasn't got any evidence.'

'Just because he didn't see it didn't mean it didn't exist,' says Maggie.

'Very Zen and very deep,' says Tamsin, tossing her hair over her shoulder. 'Especially if we're still talking about a cat.'

Maggie feels a lump like a rock in her throat, so hard that she has to force herself to breathe.

Tamsin pushes her chest out. 'Anyway, maybe we'll have our own one day. A real one that is. If you know what I mean.'

Maggie notices the lilac semi-circles and heavy lines that lie beneath Tamsin's eyes as if she's lain awake for days on end. She swallows hard. 'Why have you got a problem with me?' she asks gently. 'What have I done to you?'

The lightness of Maggie's voice seems to loosen something in Tamsin and she lifts a hand to her mouth and nibbles her nails, already nipped down to below the tips of her fingers. These two things — the eyes, the nails — make Maggie think of silent alarms, unconsciously triggered.

'You can't have him back,' Tamsin says, so quiet Maggie can hardly hear her.

'What?' asks Maggie.

'You can't have him back.'

Just then Carl calls out from somewhere beyond the yard wall and appears at the gate holding a bundle of grey fur. The cat is bouncing its nose to his chin in a display of feline affection.

'Kip,' says Maggie, her mouth fallen open.

'Is this him?' asks Carl, tugging lightly on the cat's ear. 'He was sitting on a wall a few doors up. He looks fine, perfectly fine.'

156

The cat's eyes are a violet-blue and remind her of the pansies that Carl placed in pots in the yard during their first year of marriage. She gulps at the suddenness of this memory — of Carl bending and moving them to find the best spot; the look of bright joy in his face as he turned to find her watching him do it.

Suddenly the cat leans its head forward. She touches it and the cat responds by pushing its soft face into her hand.

'See?' says Carl. 'He's fine.'

'He seems different,' says Maggie. 'Like a different cat. More peaceful, somehow.'

'Kip,' says Carl, rubbing his head roughly. 'Well, it's nice to meet you, finally.' Maggie waits for the cat to growl or grumble, but it doesn't; it just closes its eyes and lets itself be ravaged by Carl's big hands.

After a while Carl sits Kip on the yard wall, picks the bell up from the floor and fixes it back onto the cat's collar.

Tamsin sighs loudly. 'Can we go now?'

'Hold on,' says Carl, as he watches Kip tiptoe along the wall, turn back to them and then jump down into next door's yard.

Maggie turns to Tamsin, who is now folding her arms and staring at Carl. Her bag looks sunken like a dead weight. 'I didn't imagine it,' Maggie says to her.

Tamsin watches Carl. 'Carl?'

'Well,' says Carl. 'It's back now, that's the main thing.'

'I didn't,' says Maggie, this time to Carl. She notices how, for a few seconds, he stares at her and then Tamsin, a sad tugging at the edge of his mouth. His gaze drops to the ground and he shrugs.

Tamsin turns to go in the house. Maggie follows. But just as she's about to step indoors, she sees that Carl is standing next to the monolith. And then she notices how the surface is rippling and Carl, oblivious, is lifting his hand towards it.

'No!' shouts Maggie.

Tamsin pushes Maggie out of the way and they both watch as Carl is dragged into the monolith without a sound. They gasp.

'Oh my God!' shouts Tamsin. 'Where's he gone?'

Maggie holds a hand to her chest. She can feel her heart pounding throughout her body. For a while she can hear nothing, as if her ears have been filled with water. When it returns Tamsin is still shouting at her.

Inside, Maggie makes tea with shaking hands. She offers a cup to Tamsin, who is standing at the window staring out into the yard, her eyes balls of pink jelly rimmed with smudges of black, like coal dust. When Tamsin refuses to take it from her, she puts it on the windowsill instead.

'He'll be back,' says Maggie, breathing deep to soften the whirlwinds in her stomach. 'Kip came back.'

Tamsin sniffs, then dabs at her nose with a tissue. 'Kip,' she says and tuts. Then she takes the cup and gulps from it, seemingly unaware of its heat. She turns to Maggie. 'This was your plan all along, wasn't it? Get him here, trap him.'

Maggie turns to look at the monolith and sees a streak of white down its front from a passing bird. 'You're giving me too much credit,' she says, her voice low.

'Well, he's not yours,' says Tamsin, her chin trembling like water.

Maggie sips at the tea without tasting it, then puts her cup down. 'He's not anybody's,' she says. 'Least of all mine.'

A gust of wind makes the window frame crack like a bone. Suddenly Tamsin's eyes crease up and she forces the tissue into their corners to try and stem the tears. Maggie touches her on the arm, ready to retract her hand should Tamsin flinch.

'I was like you, always worried about losing him,' says Maggie, taking a shuddering breath in. 'And then I lost him and —' she stops.

Tamsin is still for a time before nodding slowly, the tissue still pushed into her eyes. Maggie rubs Tamsin's arm.

Just then she looks out again and the monolith appears darker, as if it's changed to a deeper shade of black. She squints at it, trying to work out whether she is imagining it or not. As she watches it seems to pulse to an even darker colour and it appears to be smaller than just a few seconds earlier. Maggie runs for the door. As she fiddles with the handle, Tamsin pushes up against her back, desperate to get out.

'What's going on?' says Tamsin, frantic.

'Something's happening.'

They stumble out into the yard. Kip is sitting on the wall again, watching the monolith.

'What is it?' asks Tamsin, a hand to her throat.

The monolith pulses stronger and continues to grow smaller as they watch.

'Oh, God,' says Maggie. 'It's shrinking.'

Tamsin screams and covers her mouth with her hands. 'I thought you said he'd be coming back?'

Maggie doesn't answer but instead steps nearer to the monolith. It is now half the size it was when it first appeared.

'Carl!' shouts Tamsin from behind her. 'Come out!'

Maggie leans forward to try and get a closer look, but all she can see is the throbbing blackness. Then Tamsin is at her side, reaching out.

'For God's sake, Tamsin. Don't touch it.'

Tamsin pulls her hand back. The monolith shrinks further. Kip jumps down into the yard and sits beside them. Maggie looks down at the cat and it meows at her without making a sound. She can see the ribbed roof of its mouth like a small, pink cave.

'We have to get him out,' says Tamsin, sobbing.

'How?' shouts Maggie, the monolith now the size of an upright shoebox. 'We can't.'

The three of them continue to watch as the monolith becomes as small as a pebble on the stone flags.

'It's going to vanish,' says Tamsin, her hands cradling her face. 'It's nearly gone.'

The monolith, now a black dot, winks in and out of existence for a few seconds before finally blinking out for good. Maggie, Tamsin and the cat stare at the ground. Then Kip steps forward, leans its head down and licks at the place where the monolith was, leaving a patch of damp on the flag like a brushstroke. The cat meows silently again and she can see grey dust peppering its tongue.

'Oh, God,' says Tamsin, hugging herself. 'He's gone.'

Maggie crouches down, putting the tips of her fingers against the flags to steady herself. She feels small and frail. Kip crawls up into her lap. She lets the cat nestle into the space between her legs, its violet-blue eyes staring up at her until she feels as if she's swaying.

Tamsin falls to her knees, pale as a candle. Kip's tail twitches against her leg. As Maggie looks into the cat's eyes, she has the sensation of falling into them — swirling around and down until she is no longer sure who or where she is. And then she hears Carl's voice, floating inside her head like smoke, wandering among her atoms and molecules in a sparkling dance of mist.

'I could have come back,' he says, his voice light and free. He makes her think of a mound of shining cloud. 'But I decided not to — at least for a while.' He sounds as if he's smiling. 'I hope you both —' he fades out, but then there's a humming sound and his voice returns. 'You're going to be fine,' he says.

Suddenly Carl's voice is gone and Maggie blinks, aware once more of her surroundings. She turns to Tamsin who, after a few seconds, awakens too.

The cat crawls out from Maggie's legs, runs to the wall and jumps over in one, his tail disappearing out of sight. Maggie feels the coldness of the stone then, chilling her skin.

'I heard him,' says Tamsin, looking about her.

'So did I,' says Maggie.

'He's not coming back.'

Without saying anything more, Maggie rises from the floor and helps to pull Tamsin up. She hears the metallic ping of the cat's bell as he runs away from them. She stops to listen without speaking until the bell can no longer be heard. Becoming aware then of the silent vacuum that surrounds the two of them. And how, after a while, other sounds rush in to fill it.

The Ringing Stone

- John Nicholson -

'Tiree.'

'The Land of Corn' his mother had told him, time and again, her summer-childhood island. 'We took the night train from Glasgow to Oban. Sometimes I slept on the luggage rack.'

From the age of eight he knew what was coming next, the sea-spray on MacBrayne's *Claymore*, the mountain Isle of Mull and another shaped like a hat, passengers rowed ashore to the Isle of Coll, and tying up at Tiree itself. 'We took our bikes. No drive-on drive-off ferry in those days.'

He loved his mother's tales of the flat green island, of the schooner wrecked in Scaranish, of the great Clydesdale horse at Vaul she was allowed to ride bareback, and of adventures with Gaelic-speaking children who knew places their parents had forgotten. Her stories could put off bedtime for an hour.

'Look at these wee shells. Cowries.' She had a sweetie-jar of them, each less than half an inch long, ivory with a blush of pink. She had other shells too, in blues and golds, and white sand she had brought back year after year. 'I just loved the rock pools. The boys would go hitting golf balls across the machair, but I spent my time on the shore. Have I told you how I fed the sea anemones?'

163

'Tell me again,' he would ask when still a boy. 'Not again!' he protested as a teenager. 'Remind me,' he coaxed when she sat huddled in her chair, when the only memories she had left were childhood ones. Her black-and-white snapshots of the girl in a woollen swim suit would bring a rush of reminiscence and her eyes would look up to a horizon beyond him, once again with 'the inner light' her father had so enjoyed in her, blue and clear like a distant sea.

The time came when even those memories failed, when she became as hollow as her cowries. She slipped into her own infinity in the early hours of a still morning, leaving him entirely on his own, an orphan in his forties. All that physically remained of her were her ashes, gritty mineral residues, so impersonal. He felt the need to add something of hers, so he found the sands and shells of Tiree and stirred them in with his fingers. They softened them, added substance, as if each white grain, each pearl-like cowrie was restoring her identity. He would scatter them and her ashes as she had once requested, under a wild rose bush high on the Campsie Fells.

But not all of them. Some would go where he had never been himself, to Tiree. He would throw them to the Atlantic wind and beat a song to her on the boulder she had told him about so often, the Ringing Stone of Balaphetrish.

'Nearly there now, Mum.'

He often talked to her, not so much to her granules in the Pringles box, but to the young woman he imagined walking with him.

'Balaphetrish. What a beach! Did you play here? Did you run down these dunes? Bet you did.' He ran down himself onto the curving silver shore and walked east, onto tar-spattered rocks that for her would have been sand-scoured and clean. His map showed he had just over a mile to go now, across a flat headland of tiny fresh-water lochans, around rocky outcrops and through the flower-filled grasses of the machair.

'The machair,' he said to himself. He loved the word, such a soft word, a whisper that began with his parting lips, brought in a breath from behind his tongue, and curled it near his teeth like a rattle of wind. His feet seemed to spring across it with its mix of daisies, harebells, and buttercups, pink clover, bedstraw and orchids. At first he tried to avoid the orchids, but they outnumbered his efforts. He paused to watch one recover slowly from his step, and then looked up and north to the horizon as if to see what his mother might have been gazing at from her disintegrating past. Across a June sea of greens and grays he could make out darker hills. The Cuillin of Sky? Rhum? He needed a local to tell him, but there was no one anywhere.

He followed a footpath that looked as if it knew where it was going until he found the heritage sign: *Clach a' Choire, The Ringing Stone.* He clambered down a bank, onto a small beach and there it was, laid like some giant egg on a bed of rocks, a wandering stone dumped far from home.

'The Ringing Stone. Is it any different Mum?'

As he approached it he stepped from the coarse white sand he already knew onto a shelf of short turf, a green carpet before an altar. He felt almost deferential, running a hand over its granite flank, feeling the cup-holes he had read about. They were dotted all over its sides, about a hands-width across, in no set pattern. They could not collect rainwater like those on Yorkshire moors. They held no votives, no coins, just traces of powdered rock.

Of course, he thought, these holes are where the Ringing Stone was struck. He found a smooth rock, about the size of his fist, and struck the cup which seemed most used.

The note was musical, unexpectedly high for a boulder ten foot long and as tall as himself. He hammered other holes too, each giving the same bell-like note or a harmonic of the note, sometimes an octave higher. He looked underneath, trying to find out how the Ringing Stone was supported, perhaps like the bars of a xylophone.

He felt a chill, a warning. This was no place for such analysis, for ignoring the instrument in favour of its mechanics. The stone had to be played, not pried for its physics. He now felt he was in a sacred place, an ancient one, with eyes upon him that expected better. He looked round but saw only arctic terns wheeling and swooping, and a movement in the surf that might have been a seal.

He took the Pringles box from the backpack. His mother had loved Pringles, their curved crisp appeal, their taste of the sea. She would

165

have enjoyed the notion that she had possessed the same qualities, and his apparent lack of deference. He held the carton high in his left hand, and wielding the beating-stone in his right began his dedication. An erratic percussion at first, his tribute took form, pattern and momentum as if from the stone itself. He found himself in a rhythm his mother had danced to, <u>da</u> da-da da da, singing a version of a song she had sung:

> *I dal a du vil*
> *I dal a du horo*
> *I dal a du vil*
> *Scattering your ashes here.*

Most of it was Gaelic mouth music, the English his substitute for 'gathering the cockle shells'.

> *I dal a du vil*
> *I dal a du horo*
> *I dal a du vil*
> *Bringing back your ashes here.*

His pounding kept the beat if not the tune, sending a peal into the wind that caught the scattered grains. Cowries tinkled their own melody as they bounced off the boulder, but he did not hear them. He danced around the Ringing Stone, emptying the box, laughing as the last particles found their niche.

'You're back now!' he shouted, 'You are back!'

He heard a woman's laugh as if in response, flute-like and musical, but as before there was no one in sight. His mother would have claimed it was a *bean shìth,* a Gaelic fairy-woman chuckling from the rocks, or a *selkie,* one of the seal-folk lifting her snout from the sea to lure him. He knew it was neither, just an echo from his mother's childhood ringing from the rock-pools on the shore.

He felt composed now. His trysting was done, his mother finally gone. It was time for a new beginning.

He picked his way over blackened boulders towards the sea's edge, as if anticipating an Atlantic cleansing, and found the rock pool he would dream of from then on. It was about ten yards long and four wide, fringed under the water with dark leathery kelp and bladderwrack. Its water was clear and deep above a rippled bed of silver sand. It drew him.

He untied the laces of his walking boots, removed them and his socks, and lowered his feet into the water. It felt as good as a cold beer on the back of his throat, cleansing and demanding more. He stripped, feeling sun on his skin for the first time in the year. He slid off trousers and pants, eased into the water and swam to the centre of the pool. He tried to stand but the water was deeper than it had looked, so he duck-dived, eyes open, to the grainy quartz below.

The sand felt fluid and granular between his fingers, and very cold. The weed at its edges resembled a forest in whose black recesses a threat might lurk. He felt the need to escape and to breathe, so he pushed up hard to break the surface like a fish. He shook his head, flicking salt-spray into the sun, and heard the laughter once again. With his head at sea level, he was now the *selkie*, searching rocky horizons from the surface of the water.

A young woman sat on the rocks smiling at him. She was as naked as he was. The red hair that curled over her shoulders conferred a kind of innocence.

'Sorry,' he said, 'didn't see you. Sorry.' He gasped for breath and composure, and trod water.

She laughed again, the same laugh he had dismissed as a delusion, but now was as real as the pool he was trapped in. She lifted her left hand, pointed behind him, and began to sing.

Was it singing? She made sounds rather than words, high-pitched and pure, a carillon. They came in a rhythm he recognized, the one he had beaten himself, but in a melody he had never heard. He turned to look where she was pointing, and realized, although he could not see it, that it was in the direction of the Ringing Stone. She was mouth-making stone-music back to him. She must have been there all the time.

Despite the chill water, he felt the heat of embarrassment. What an idiot she must think him, although there was nothing in her manner to suggest derision or ridicule. He sensed only warmth in her direct look, that she wanted to communicate, to talk to him perhaps.

'Where are you from? Tiree? Are you a windsurfer? You're a naturist windsurfer!' Repartee might ease his tension.

'I'm from Stirling,' he went on. 'I don't come here often. Do you?'

All she did was smile. The sun highlighted her hair and revealed a scatter of freckles across her face, a feature he had always found attractive in a woman.

'I hope you use sun blocker. With skin like yours.' This was banal, but her response was unchanged, as if his words meant nothing.

'I'm getting cold. Have to get out. 'Scuse me, needs must.' He turned and swam back towards his clothing, and climbed over the seaweed to where he had stripped. He toweled himself with his T-shirt and pulled on his clothes, trying to sound relaxed.

'Tell me about the Ringing Stone.' He raised his head, composed, ready to look her in the eye and nowhere else.

She was not there.

He looked into the pool to see if she had taken his place, but all was still. He scrambled to the highest rocks, looked around and behind them, but she had vanished. 'Hello,' he called, 'are you there? Where are you?'

She had gone.

Throughout the remainder of his stay he sought her, in the hotel, in shops and galleries, in the camps of young surfers on the shore. Sometimes he thought he had spotted her, but the slim figure, freckled face or long red hair always belonged to someone else.

On his last day he returned to the Ringing Stone, but this time there was a group of children hitting it. Any idea of summoning his sprite with stone-music vanished. The pool she had sat beside was whipped by a north wind and showered in spray from an incoming tide. Far from drawing him to its depths it seemed to warn him away. He knew then he would never find her, that his longing for her would have to drain from him, like sand, shells and ashes into the rocks around him.

The Russians

- Philip Langeskov –

IT IS THE DAY after their visit – the Monday – and I am staying on late at work. It is not necessary for me to do this but I am doing it. There are quite a few others here. A tender is due, you see, and, although my role in it is minor, I am eager to hang around, to give the impression of utility, the impression of being here.

On the Internet, I make some investigations into a film I once saw, but can now barely remember. It was about a boy who lived on a beach and befriended a pelican, possibly in New Zealand. I make some notes. My memory is bad.

At a certain point, boredom triumphs and I decide to go home. Enid will be waiting. I look around the office. Those who remain are hunched in front of their screens or huddled in alcoves. As I move to leave, they all turn to watch me. They have grave looks on their faces, as if they think I am about to embark on some absurd voyage from which my return is in doubt.

Outside, the weekend's good weather has passed. The luminous days are gone, as Enid's father said yesterday, after lunch, gesturing to the darkening sky, palms open. He's prone to exaggeration, expansiveness. Perhaps that's why I like him so much. In truth, it is blustery, tepid, a little damp. It's possible – *possible* – there will be a storm later.

171

Across the street, the offices are empty, their photocopiers standing rather forlornly in the flickering light. I stand and look, tracing their reflections in the window. I would normally smoke at this point, but I feel no desire to move for the tobacco in my pocket. Instead, I pull on my coat, cross the road and head down the street.

At the junction, where I would normally turn right towards home, I find that I am turning left. It happens so simply, without fuss, no more than a tug on my shoulder, the briefest pull, and then I know. I do not struggle. This has happened before. It is a question only of how long it will last.

Within five minutes, I have reached the pedestrian precinct. My vision – indeed, all my senses – have become unusually sharp, attuned to the merest detail: the damp patches on the paving stones, the air on my face, the roar of a motorbike. Up above, clouds. On either side of me, the long glassine lines of department stores. Through their high windows, the shapes of mannequins – ranks of them, their arms raised like heralds. These things – the texture of the sky, the gullied walls of the buildings, the posed mannequins – conspire to give me the sense that a procession is under way.

At the end of the precinct, moving rapidly now, I turn – or am turned – to the left. It is curiously pleasurable to move in this way, with no aim, no intention. It as if I am being carried along, held up on a bier.

I go down into the underpass. A woman is coming towards me, breath rising, huddled into a coat, pushing a pram with a squeaky wheel. I hear everything so clearly – her breath, the wheels – that it's as if she has reached me already, when in fact she must be at least forty yards away, more, even. I feel a strong desire to wave my arms at her, to shout – 'Hey! Hey! Look out!' – as if trying to warn her that she is about to come upon some terrible accident. But it's no good: she reaches me, passes me, and then she is gone.

Back on street level, I notice things that are just outside my field of vision – glimmers, glimpses, movements, that kind of thing. A young couple drag themselves up the steps in front of the Forum. Again, I want to put on a show of warning, but I know that it's futile, that I would only appear to them as I am, a man, walking up a hill towards a theatre.

At the theatre, I turn left, into the alley behind the hotel. Its still fascia rises to balconies, lit windows open, the murmur of televisions, talk. I duck my head into the plantation garden, but it is empty, its fountains still. I stop for a moment in the darkness and listen, hearing the roll of the sea, far off, coming against the harbour wall. It's a wonderful sound, perfectly rhythmed.

Presently, across the street, on the corner, I come upon a large house surrounded by railings. It has an air of familiarity, like every house I have ever seen rolled into one. A number of cars are parked outside, black, rain-spotted. In one, a hearse, a man sits in the front seat reading a newspaper and eating an apple. He looks up as I pass, drops the apple from his mouth, and then quickly looks down again, embarrassed, as if I am not supposed to have seen him.

I open the iron gate and enter the garden. Light glows dimly in the large downstairs window, centring on a spot in the middle of the pane, where a kink in the glass marks a sag. I can see no people from this angle, only furniture, of the sort you would expect to see in an entrance hall, the sort that gives nothing away: a grandfather clock, mirrors, a rose table with a lamp.

I go up to the door and knock. Although I have been walking quickly, I feel no tightness in my chest, and my breathing is controlled and assured as I wait.

Soon enough, the door opens and a man appears. He is short, thick like a rope, wearing a black waistcoat, a white shirt. His grey hair is scraped back over his forehead. All in all, he seems a nasty piece of work. Behind him, two ladies in black are taking off their cloaks and heading up a wide staircase. The man and I stand there for a moment, eyeing each other.

'Come in,' he says, finally.

He has a slight accent, but I can't place it. I allow him to lead me across the hall. I think we are going to follow the women up the stairs. One of my feet even begins to rise in preparation, but at the last moment the man stops. It is a very precise, slightly fussy manoeuvre. He turns to me, his hands pressed together.

'No,' he says, indicating a door off to the side. 'You go in here. There are others, but you'll get your turn.'

Sure enough, when I enter, there are others ahead of me: three men, in fact, of forbidding stature, whiskered, well dressed, wearing long coats, ties. Two are seated on a bench that lines the far wall. The other leans against this wall, his legs indolently crossed. He flicks a coin into the air and catches it, showing the result to the two seated men, who tilt their heads in response and exchange smiles. The door closes behind me. They nod as I move to sit alongside them, shifting their coats to make room. In front of me, three candles are ranged on a low table laid with a red velvet cloth.

After a moment of silence, the men resume their conversation. They are speaking a foreign language. Russian, I would say, if pressed. It is hard to identify where one word ends and the next begins. The depth of their voices doesn't help. When they speak they do so with their chins dug in against their necks, and the consequent rumbling resonances of their words hang in my ear a moment too long, causing a tingle.

It is a sensation that I have felt once before, on Saint Martin, that time, when we dashed into the hall out of the rain, dripping wet, eyes closed to stifle our giggles, your heels clicking on the stone until – abruptly – they stopped. A choir was rehearsing the Vespers. At least, you thought it was the Vespers. Once we had regained possession of ourselves – you had to hold me up – we slid into a row and listened, heads bowed, as the conductor took the choir through the opening movements, that astonishing basso profundo seeming to make the whole building shake, and then onto the nunc dimittis - after which we fled, of course, unable to contain ourselves any longer, corpsing up the steps and out into the square.

One of the men coughs and I turn to look at him. There must be a look of complete bafflement on my face, because he leans across. He lifts a fist to his mouth as if he is going to clear his throat. Then, at the precise point at which it seems he is about to speak, there is a creak, a slow one, that elongates its way into the room like a cat. The men all turn a fraction of a second before me and, in the lag, I am able to observe in their eyes the briefest flash of something, some cortex suddenly awake.

Eventually I turn, too. A door is opening. From its shadows, a woman emerges. She is dressed entirely in black and a veil covers her face. She bows curtly to the three other men and walks towards me. I tense as she approaches. Drawing near, she holds her hands out to me. She does it in such a way that I feel compelled to reach up and take them. She smiles when I do this, the faintest movement of her pale lips through the lace, and draws me to my feet.

Joined in this way, we stand for a moment. I look at the men. They are looking at me. Their eyes are fairly wide. With a brief application of pressure to my hands and a tilt of her head, the woman conducts me through into a third room, larger than the second. There, she manoeuvres us until we are standing on a rug in front of an unlit fireplace. The room is cold. There is an icon above the mantel – a dark face surrounded by a halo of gold; on either side, various watercolours, of hunting scenes, ships coming into harbour. The woman begins to speak.

'There is something I wish to discuss with you,' she says. Her voice is calm, composed. 'It is a little delicate.'

I nod.

'Well, then,' she says. 'Is it true that I am being laughed at?' As she says the words, she makes a move with her head, tossing it over her shoulder, almost snorting like a horse, towards the room we recently left.

'The men outside?' I say. 'I don't know that they were laughing. I didn't see that.'

'Perhaps you should look a little closer then. Perhaps you do not know them as I do. At all events, why are they here, tossing their coins and laying their bets and making their jokes? They did not care about my husband while he lived.'

'Perhaps,' I say, 'it is best to believe that they are here simply to pay their respects.'

'Probably you are right,' she says, steering me across the room to where a coffin stands open. The dead man is wearing a dress suit – a white collar, a white tie. He has a flock of unruly black hair, swept back, and a neat moustache and beard, flecked with grey. A silk handkerchief, white, covers his neck and his shoulders seem a little hunched, as if the coffin is just that little bit too small. I find it impossible to read his face. There is no sign of trauma, or despair, or surprise. The mouth has been stitched up and, although his eyes are closed, something twinkles where the lids have been joined, like a run of ice or tiny crystals.

'Here he is. In the final days he gave nothing away. He was as he always was. In the very last hours, we talked in the same way we would had he been about to set off to see a client the country.'

'He certainly looks at peace,' I say, and leave it at that.

For a few moments, we stand in silence. Then the woman crosses herself and steers me back across the room. On the threshold she raises her hands to my lips. 'Thank you for coming. Your visit does my husband a great honour.'

The men look up as I re-enter the room. The door closes behind me. I look hard at them, trying to discern by their actions and habits of dress in what relation they stand to the deceased; which is the colleague, say, which the brother, and so on. I wonder who stands to profit and who to loss. Several times I try to speak, but each time either the first door opens and some other person enters, or the second door opens and the widow emerges to conduct someone else through. In the end, I leave. The doorman bows curtly as I pass.

Back on the street, I look at my watch. It is past midnight. I have missed several calls, all from Enid. The temperature has dropped. The air is crunchy, and the windscreens of the parked cars glitter with dew. I walk a few unsteady paces and then stop. My hands are shaking. I hold them up in front of my face. Beyond them, the sky is completely clear.

That night on Saint Martin, I hailed us a cab, not worrying about the expense. We got out of our sodden clothes and put on bathrobes and t-shirts. Despite the storm, it was still warm, muggy. I opened the doors to the French balcony and we stood for a while, looking at the city, rain-lashed, the last of the sunset buried under cloud. Below us, in the Basin, tracks snaked out from under the station canopy, slick bars of light, the windows of the Saturday evening trains glowing in the gloom.

When the lightning struck, we were on the bed. There was a great sound, like the crack of a whip, or the popping of bulbs. The room exploded into the most intense purplish light. You reared back, then reared back again, I think. It was so bright that for a moment it was as if I could see right through you, see your ribcage, your organs.

'Holy fuck,' you said slowly. 'What the fuck was that?'

The lightning had come all the way into the room, a secondary bolt seeming to dart in through the window, pronging around the iron bedstead. We weren't hit, of course, not in the direct sense. Nonetheless, in that instant, we genuinely felt that we were linked to the sky, singled out in some way, our brains marked. It's part of the mythology, I suppose – a belief that there is more. One hears a lot about lightning strikes, about their deeper, cosmological readings. For instance, there's a story about a man in America, who was struck seven times by lightning and survived. 'Lightning Man,' they called him. He used to tell how, as he became more familiar with the experience, he developed a method of stepping outside himself, keeping a record. He suffered religious conversions, saw visions; railed at the massive sky with his fist. After the third strike, he recalled seeing an 'orphan bolt, a thumb of spark wagging at him.' So much for anger. After the sixth, he believed that he had split in two, and that a thinner, frailer version of himself had stumbled out into the world, to stand, impoverished, on the ground, waiting for the rain to come.

At home, the lights are all off and I climb the stairs without switching them on. In the bedroom, Enid is sleeping. I get undressed by the door. Naked, I open the curtains and look out over the garden, the fresh soil of the terraces like coal in the moonlight. The storm hasn't happened yet. Or, if it has, I missed it. In bed, I draw Enid to me, running my hands up under her nightshirt until I am touching as much of her skin as I can. It is only by doing this that I am reminded finally how cold I am.

The Theory of Circles

- Debz Hobbs-Wyatt -

Unplugged.

It's what you've written in your Blog, dated Wednesday 7th April 5.03 p.m. The very last words. It's all that's left, as if you never existed.

Not really.

Marmalade pissed up the front door of number 6.

A message Tweeted at 4.47 p.m. on the same day. It's ridiculously sublime and yet typical of you. Laced with humour, even to your last Tweet.

At the very edge of the day someone you've never met stares at the pages of the Blog he knows intimately, and waits, the thin white edges of a polo mint dissolving on his tongue. He reloads the page, cusses a dodgy Wi-Fi connection and waits. He waits again until he realises you might just have meant it. You might just be *officially* unplugged.

Facebook status: *Undecided.* That's what you wrote twelve hours before you did it. Before that there was a brief mention that Marmalade had stalked a sock that was in Winifred's garden. In his escapades you said he'd tipped over one of Winfred's ornamental Buddhas which you noted must have been (your spelling) *ahelluva* lot lighter than it looked. You've ended with: *Why do Buddhas look like that Fred Elliot character who used to be in Corrie? I say do why do Buddhas look like that Fred Elliot character? Or perhaps,* you added, *it should be other way round.*

No clues, then an hour later just the word *undecided.* Was *that* it?

And someone called Tracy J had responded with LOL. But it was too late by then -- you'd already unplugged. LOL, POV, IMAO... RIP.

Everything seems so random- but it's not.

Your words. You used to call yourself the Great Chaos Theorist. I remember the post: *Does a polo mint obey the law of entropy when it dissolves. Experiment 1.*

You never did say, or tell us if there was an Experiment 2 or 3.

Sunday April 4th 10.18 a.m: Tweet: *It just goes to show love can blossom anywhere.*

Sunday April 4th, 10.17 a.m: Tweet: *It's official! Mohammad has moved in with Winifred. His moving in present to her: 14 pairs of size 10 slippers.*

Blog posted Monday, April 1st 4.13 a.m. *Big Boobz kissed The Nerd on Winifred's drive. They came home late from school again – boots and coats caked in mud.*

Blog posted Monday April 1st 9.12 a.m: *Last night Mohammad went into Winifred's with a big bunch of purple tulips. He didn't come out for three hours, and when he did his shirt was untucked. By the way this isn't an April Fool.*

That was six days before 'The Great Unplugging.'

That's what they're calling it – but they're still waiting for you, hoping you'll find a way back, tell them all the random *going-ons* on in *The Crescent.* Send them more links to random e-Books like *Social Networking for Dodos* that you said you bought at the same time as: *The Art of Reading Backwards.* But deep down, in that gut place, they all know you've gone. At first they convinced themselves you'd just changed identity, like a snake shedding its skin. They're saying they'd find you, they'd know you anywhere.

But they don't even know your real name.

Nothing is real. Tweet dated Wednesday March 31st, 4.16 p.m.

Facebook, earlier that day: *If you wait long enough everything comes full circle.*

Did this have anything to do with all the geometry references – or was it another random comment to keep them guessing?

The day before that you'd Blogged that you saw Mohammad talking to Marmalade and you even saw his hand hover dangerously close to stroking his chin. You said it was funny how things changed. Like it was another golden rule of the universe. You said *nothing ever stays in the same place.* You added: *except for you.*

Saturday March 13th, 10.20 a.m, Facebook: *Mohammad's visitors finally left- three nephews and The Aunty and at least five times as many bags than they arrived with. A ton of shoeboxes (I might have been wrong about the slipper thing.) Marmalade will miss his secret vindaloos on the front step. The Aunty seems partial to cats (Might have been wrong about her eyeing him up for a curry too).*

Wednesday March 10th, 2.31 a.m. Tweet: *A circle is a special form of ellipse that produces a closed curve.*

Monday March 8th, 4.43p.m. Facebook. *Winifred took Marmalade to the vets in a picnic basket. She told the taxi driver it was on account of him having the runs. She advised him to keep the window open. He mumbled something under his breath and looked really angry.*

Tuesday March 2nd, 4.12 p.m. Blog Post: *The Nerd finally plucked up courage to talk to Big Boobz right outside my window. 'Do you like birds?' he said. 'No! You think I'm a dyke?' 'No, I mean feathered twittery birds.' 'You mean like starlings?' 'Yeah, like starlings.' 'You mean like the one…' 'Yeah, like that one.' 'You mean am I like a Twitcher?' 'Yeah, like a Twitcher. I mean no, not*

183

like a Twitcher, well yeah, like a Twitcher.' 'Fuck off.' The Aunty then appeared in lime-green feathery slippers and shook her head tutting over and over like a stuck budgie. But I did see Big Boobz wink at The Nerd, then she said she was free on Saturday if he wanted to take her to the reserve but he wasn't to tell anyone. 'Wear boots, it gets muddy over there,' he said. Then he added, 'I've got the right gear, you know the right equipment.' She raised her eyebrows, 'I bet you have.' He blushed so hard he turned purple.

Later you Tweeted that *the most predictable thing about people is their unpredictability.*

Sunday March 1st, 4.15 a.m. Tweet: *An ellipse is a smooth closed curve which is symmetric about its centre.*

Friday February 26th, 11.17 p.m. Blog Post: *Mohammad dug a small hole in the dirt in his front garden with a spoon — he did it when he thought no one was watching but Big Boobz would have seen him when she came out to put a black bag in the wheelie bin. And The Nerd would have seen him from his bedroom window when he was star gazing again. They would both have seen Mohammad holding something against the flat of his palm and then placing it gently in the hole. They would have seen him spooning dirt back over it and raking it neat with his fingers. And they would have seen him cry as he read from The Koran.*

Friday February 26th, 5.13 p.m. Blog Post: *Marmalade left a pile of starling feathers a detached head and a line of entrails on Mohammad's front step. It reminded me of a flick painting. Do you know swear words in Urdo sound so poetic? He did a furious kind of dance too, like River dance, only angrier. Or maybe it was a rain dance because it rained for the rest of the afternoon. I know: wrong kind of Indian.*

Before that you'd Tweeted: *Death is the only certainty.*

'Are you sick?' asked @Manic77.
'Are you?' you said.

In early February you said there was a letter, an envelope on a desk that you were afraid to open. You mentioned it in a passing kind of way but it kept us guessing. Some said it was about a new job, others said you were much younger than that, that it was more like about enrolling for college, that it was the right time of year. Then someone said what if it was from the council and you were being re-housed and what would they do without their updates on *The Crescent*. But others said *The Crescent* sounded too posh to be a council estate. Or maybe it wasn't even real. People had plenty to say about that. Then someone said it had to be real and it couldn't be posh if there were foreigners living in the street. That caused a whole lot of posts about racial prejudice. You ended all that by posting: *Winifred used to be Fred.* You never said how you found out or how long you'd known but it started a whole other debate. Good save; if it was deliberate, if it was true. It stopped people talking about the letter anyhow.

Except later you did say something about an appointment, about your *condition.* But no one wanted to speculate about that. It's as if it was said by accident, a lapse, as if you'd slipped into who you really were, for a moment. You never mentioned it again, but it was there, to be sought, like a thread woven between the lines. There was a Tweet that said: *Truth is found not in what's said, but in what's not said.* You said you didn't remember where the quote came from.

Before that you posted about Big Boobz and The Nerd, how they'd been acting weird around each other since the start of the new school year. You said maybe he wasn't gay; maybe he was just shy or scared. It was like you knew something about that.

Sunday January 31ˢᵗ, 4 p.m Facebook: *Big argument in street. Winifred caught Mohammad in her garden. He told her, 'I just trying to watch bird building nest.' 'They all say that,' she said. 'Get out you old dirty man. And stop using your hose on my cat.'*

Wednesday January 20th, 2.22 p.m Facebook: *The nephews have been doing odd jobs for Winifred like repairing the wall in her front garden and The Aunty is making friends with Marmalade. Hope Cat Korma isn't on the menu.*

185

It was around that time you noted an increase in size in the parcels arriving at number six and you treated us to elaborate descriptions of oversize boxes accompanied by eclectic wild guesses. *Far too big to be footwear* you commented once. And you told us about Mohammad's new habit of sitting in wait for the DHL man; how one afternoon in mid January you saw him running into Winifred's garden in khaki combats with the hugest shiny binoculars you'd ever seen. You ended with the comment: *Mystery solved about big box. PERVERT.*

The week before you'd seen the DHL man try to deliver a parcel when Mohammad was out, he'd taken the car you'd remarked which was unusual. You described it as the *poomobile*. You said that's because it was brown and *looked like poo* and you said it *spluttered like a choking kangaroo*. And someone commented on your post by asking *Are you a poet?* You never did say but it led to all sorts of bizarre and wonderful rhymes. This followed the *Three Day Saga of the Missing parcel*. That's what they called it. It followed Blogs that Mohammad had knocked at Winifred's to complain. *'Man from DHL say you took parcel for me,'* he'd said. *'It come when I collecting The Aunty and nephews from airport. They gave to neighbour. You give me please.' 'I have no idea what you're saying you silly man,'* she said. Then added, *'And don't talk to me about DHL!'*

It turned out it was The Nerd who had taken in the parcel. You said you'd seen him at his bedroom, watching the street like a peeping tom. *'Hasn't he anything better to do?'* you'd said.

Wednesday January 1st 3.17 a.m. Tweet: *Circles are simple closed curves which divide the plane into two regions, an interior and an exterior.*

Wednesday January 1st 3.13 a.m. Tweet: *Centripetal force is a force that makes a body follow a curved path. It takes a lot of force to break away.*

Thursday December 31st, 12.13 p.m, Tweet: *Life is too short for New Year's Resolutions.*

What did all this mean? The circle references? About life being too short? Did it have anything to do with a dissolving polo mint? Or your condition? Or about what happened?

I have to decide what I want. This is what you said, three days before in amongst words about Christmas parties on *The Crescent* and Mohammad inviting Winifred in for a tipple, and how they both got extremely drunk and he found out something about her: something you wouldn't say. You said they'd been screaming from the back yard. *'And don't you know NOT to bring a lady lilies? Lilies! Lilies!' she said. 'Tulips, purple tulips are for passion! Don't you foreigners know anything?'* And that's when he stood there and screamed, *'I hate your big ginger pussy!'*

Later you posted: *No one is ever who you think they are.*

Thursday November 19th, 10.40 p.m Facebook: *Watched a TV show on Sky about lions in Africa. They showed a lioness that was rescued from a Russian zoo. It was the saddest thing I ever saw. They were going to move her and take her back to the wild but she died before they gave her freedom. Animals belong in the wild: not in cages.* You wrote the same words in Twitter and on your Blog.

Animals belong in the wild: not in cages.

And the next day you wrote it again.

Animals belong in the wild: not in cages.

In one post you wrote it thirty-eight times, as if it was a punishment.

Animals belong in the wild: not in cages...

For a few days it was like you'd forgotten about them all, as if life on *The Crescent* was passing by unobserved. You did talk about Marmalade. You said he was the only one that was really free. *We make our own traps,* you said. *We look out from the inside and wait for something to happen. But it never does.*

Monday November 2nd, 9.01 a.m. Tweet. *The circumference is the distance around a closed curve. When you stretch out the line, the distance between 2 points is always further than it looks.*

They were words for speculation, for pondering, were you talking about your life? *The Crescent?* But it was quickly forgotten when you followed it up with *Mohammad has a kipper fetish.* Then you Tweeted: *sorry meant slipper not kipper.* It spun the conjecture off in a whole other direction, *centripetal* but it successfully ended the speculation. It produced a lot of interesting posts about kippers.

This of course, followed three months of supposition and detailed accounts of Mohammad's strange deliveries. In one week, you reported twelve parcels. At least you stopped thinking they were ammunition, that he was a conspirator for Al-Qaeda- when in fact he was stockpiling ladies slippers, mostly feathered slingbacks. *Not very effective weapons* you said.

Wednesday August 19th, 10.16 a.m Tweet: *Mohammad is not a terrorist; he's a pervert.* They are specialists in ladies slippers! *slipperytreats.com*

Wednesday August 19th, 10.12 a.m Tweet: *Do flamingos live in Britain?*

Wednesday August 19th, 10.10 a.m Tweet: *There are pink feathers scattered all over Mohammad's front lawn.*

Wednesday August 19th, 10.08 a.m Tweet: *Mohammad shooed Marmalade out of his house with a broom. Not sure cats understand Urdu.*

Wednesday August 19th, 10.05 a.m. Tweet: *Just heard Mohammad screaming!*

Wednesday August 19th, 10.04 a.m Tweet: *Just seen Marmalade go in through Mohammad's front window*

Wednesday August 19th, 09.58: Tweet: *Mohammad just signed for another consignment of boxes stamped SLIPPERY TREATS. Pervert.*

Tuesday August 18th, 2.33 a.m. Tweet: *An arc of a circle is any connected part of the circle's circumference.*

Monday August 17th, 11.02 a.m. Blog: ***WARNING*** Long Post Imminent: *There are people standing outside Mohammad's house and a bright yellow DHL van is blocking the road. A car has been blaring its horn on and off for three minutes. That's what brought Big Boobz out of her house and now she's standing in the street in cerise spotted pyjamas with her hands on her hips, exposing her midriff, her belly button glinting where the sun catches. She keeps looking at the DHL man, who looks kind of Italian and handsome, if you squint.*

The Nerd is at his window also watching the Italian man, with a squint. Winifred is still inspecting her wall, or what there is left of it, and the DHL man keeps shaking his head and tutting. 'It's all your fault,' Winifred tells Mohammad. 'How it my fault?' he says. 'I not driving lorry.' 'Well he wouldn't be here if wasn't for your parcels now would it?' The driver of the car now gets out (Blond, kind of handsome without having to squint). He says, 'Look I need to get to mine-number twenty-seven, can you move that thing?' 'Thing? This is a state of the art, Ford F-450 Super Duty E...' starts M. DHL and now Winifred looks up from her close examining of the wall and gives him one of her hard super stares, like she's beaming lasers at him. 'It's a yellow bus,' she says, 'a big clumsy yellow bus. You'll have to pay for my wall.' Then she looks at Mohammad who is smiling in satisfaction, 'It's still your fault,' she says. 'Look, can you just move the van so I can get to number twenty-seven please?' the man now says. 'Can't you go the other way round?' says Winifred, 'We're busy here.' 'There's a bin lorry blocking that end.' As he speaks she struts towards him towering above him; she's an enormous woman with bristly whiskers and the man seems to cower in her shadow. 'Did you hear me?' she says. 'We have business to sort out here.' 'When how long are you going to be?' 'How long? How long? How long is a piece of string?' 'I just really need to get back to number twenty-seven.' 'Patience,' she says, 'is a virtue.' And she turns with a majestic sweep of her hand and walks back towards her front door. 'Where you go now?' Mohammad says, not noticing Mr DHL man wink at Big Boobz and climb back into his van. 'I'm going in for a pen and paper,' she says. 'Insurance.' 'But--' Mohammad starts to speak when he sees Mr DHL is now back behind the wheel and has started the engine. 'Winifred!' But she's gone and the van is already pulling away. 'Winifred!' At the same time the blond man now jumps back in his car. So now the van and the car leave and that's when I see The Nerd is watching from his bedroom window with his mouth gaped open. Maybe he has a thing for Mr DHL or maybe it's Big Boobz? Maybe he's bisexual, not gay. 'I suppose this is exciting as it gets around here,' Big Boobz says to Mohammad and starts to walk back towards her house. Mohammad starts mumbling something about the youth of today when Winifred appears on her doorstep clutching a notebook. 'They gone,' Mohammad says. 'I try to warn you but you go in house.' She does her stare and Mohammad doesn't wait any longer but bolts his front door and slams it shut behind him. Marmalade appears suddenly and starts weaving around Winifred's legs. 'Go away,' she says. 'Look at my poor wall.' Marmalade, as if on cue, jumps the pile of bricks and walks, bold as brass, up to Mohammad's front door where I

189

see his tail quiver and a steaming arc of yellow piss hits the door. Winifred folds her arms across her chest and laughs. Then she rolls her head back and laughs some more. She laughs so hard she gets the hiccups. Loud belching hiccups and even Marmalade stops mid flow to look at her. She hiccups again and holds her breath, puffs out her cheeks, goes cross-eyed. She breaths out, hiccups again, cusses and goes back inside.

Now all is quiet again on The Crescent. I see Winifred at the kitchen window drinking backwards out of a glass.

I wonder about the man at number twenty-seven.

PS. Told you it was a long post.

You should write plays NottherealPeterAndre25 wrote in comments.
Maybe you do? added GobScoffer1.
You never replied. You hardly ever replied.

Friday July 31st, 1.11 a.m. Tweet: *Do Crescents have corners?*
Friday July 31st, 1.10 a.m. Tweet: *Someone has moved in around the corner. Rumours say a doctor.*

You didn't say a whole lot in June, it was as if you'd *unplugged* then, maybe it was a practice run. Most thought you were on holiday, others thought you were ill. The posts you did write were nonsensical, more random than usual. You talked a lot about circles. Someone said you were a mathematical genius, that you were full of answers. Others said *Yes but what is the question?* That spun us into philosophical folly until someone finally said: *Does it matter?*

Apparently the answer to that was: it did.

Sunday June 14th, 1.33 a.m Tweet: *A crescent is the shape produced when a circular disk has a segment of another circle removed from its edge*

Wednesday May 20th, 10.45 a.m. Tweet: *His name is Mohammad.*
Wednesday May 20th, 9.31 a.m Tweet: *Word of the day- Ethnophaulism- it means ethnic slurs http://www.answers.com/topic/paki*

Wednesday May 20th, 9.28 a.m Tweet: *Not all Indians are from Pakistan.*

Wednesday May 20th, 9.21 a.m. Tweet: *Is Paki an offensive word?*

Wednesday May 20th, 9.15 a.m. Tweet: *A Paki has moved in to number 6.*

Wednesday May 20th, 9.11 a.m. Tweet: *NOISE! NOISE! NOISE! Trucks!*

Before the Mohammad *moving in tales* you'd talked mostly about Winifred and her Buddhas. You said you thought they were breeding, multiplying at night and were now outnumbering the gnomes at number 5. You called it *The Great Gnomic Wars*. People started Blogging about pixies and fairies and it started a whole other debate. Someone even ran a PVA, which is a *Population Viability Analysis* that biologists use to predict the stability and the fate of fragile populations like the Cheetah. Then someone else said you could not negate the impact of migrations on Leprechaun populations following the increase in frequency of Irish Sea crossings. By this time they'd all forgotten it had anything to do with Buddhas. But you didn't. You said *Buddhas were a sign of enlightenment.* You said to achieve this *Buddhists required abstraction from normal life* – that you said was called *ascetic practice.* You said it like it was something you envied.

There were also posts about Marmalade who you said had taken up residency in the back yard of number 6 since there was a starling's nest, guarded by a golden Buddha. And around the same time you posted about The Nerd who you said was bent. *A fruit loop* you called him and that started you on fruit Polos which you said you detested, you said the mint ones were the best. But you did point out the fruit ones took longer to dissolve. Several people put it to the test. Most commented you were right.

If you don't like fruit Polos don't suck them DavidCassidyrocks had commented.

Monday May 11th, 3.07 a.m. Tweet: *What happens to all the holes?*

Monday May 11th, 3.05 a.m. Tweet: *When you crush Polo mints they glow in the dark.*

Monday May 11th, 3.03 a.m. Tweet: *140 polo mints are eaten very second.*

Monday May 11th, 3.01 a.m. Tweet: *An annulus (Latin 'little ring') is a ring-shaped geometric shape. It is the area between two concentric circles.*

Everything runs its course.

It's something else you said, like it was another law of the universe.

Is that what happened? To *The Crescent*? To the Polo mints? Maybe that's what will happen to the speculation; eyes will shift to Blogs and Tweets and Facebook pages of other strangers. But they'll keep on checking, once in a while, seeking the randomness, hoping to find out what happened to Mohammad and Winifred – if love still blossoms, in spite of the odds. If someone else has moved into number six or if Big Boobz and The Nerd are still enjoying the antics of avian behaviour seen through Mohammad's missing binoculars. And maybe some will even ask what happened to Marmalade.

Of course I will know.

But I didn't always.

Monday May 4th, 8.01 a.m. Blog: *Just smashed my fifty-two minute record for dissolving a polo mint on my tongue.*

It was the first time I found you, the first thing I read, almost a year before you unplugged. An absconding mouse, a time slip into a cyber universe as if Google had plummeted me unknowingly into randomness. I was sure I'd typed 'Pogo Champions'- something just as random, in one of those nothing-better-to-do-Google- moments. And there you were, just like that, one line that made me laugh between claims that Big Boobz Dad was having secret midnight rendezvous' with the woman who used to live at number six and speculation that's why she had to move out and about The Nerd giving his phone number to the postman. Oh and something about there now being four gnomes in the front garden of number five when there used to be one and did gnomes reproduce sexually or asexually? Or were they like worms if you cut them in half?

So there I was, suddenly a part of it all.

I often wondered how the others found you. If it was by the same serendipity, all of us being sucked into it like a spinning vortex of polo mints and mad neighbours and killer cats. Did you ever *not* accept a Facebook Friend Request?

What I didn't know then was that I was one day to become more than just a part of it. I was to be in it.

It's funny the way it happened, a cameo, a walk-on part in a play I'd stumbled into unwittingly. And there I was, a few months later, reading about myself. I never knew that our Crescent was *The Crescent*. And I still remember how you called me *kind of handsome without having to squint*. Maybe it was providence; another act of serendipity that I happened to forget my clinic appointments book that day and came back like that. And that I had to go the wrong way round around the loop, or perhaps, in hindsight the right way, if such a concept of right or wrong exists. Perhaps I had slipped into some fantastical parallel universe, the direct consequence of a refuse vehicle obstructing one end of a closed loop. *Funny how things work out*: your words, not mine. As if we'd always been there, two points on a curve, waiting to bisect.

You tell me the world is bigger than you thought it was; like a circumference stretched out. You say it as if you've just discovered the world is round, not flat, the road curved, not straight. You say you have a different view of everything. And you say that's because of me. But it took me five months to finally admit I knew who you were, as if I was trying to keep ahold of something. As if there was a bird on my palm and I was afraid to let it go. But then one day I did. I opened my hand.

It was one comment on a Blog: *I live at number 27.*

The beginning of the end. 'Like a new moon,' you said. 'Everything comes full circle.'

So tonight I go right back to the beginning, to where it all started, even before I found you. Seems that book on the *Art of Reading Backwards* came in quite handy in the end.

It all started, naturally, with a Tweet:

Marmalade pissed up the front door of number 6.

The Latin word for Crescent is *crescere*, which means 'to grow.' It's what you said. Words spoken, not Blogged or Tweeted or in a Facebook status. Just spoken. You said it when you told me your real name.

Just before you typed the word: *Unplugged.*

My Oldest and Dearest Friend

- Charles Wilkinson -

The woman he could scarcely believe was still his wife got into the back of the car as though he were a chauffeur. They had been driving since early morning and now Herefordshire, still broken-rivered and sodden after the previous week's floods, lay behind them. She had suggested stopping for coffee in a little border town, the last place with an English name that they would pass through on their journey. Although it wasn't raining at the time, the grey-black streets glistened fitfully in the scurrying sunlight, and, to the west, banks of rain gathered above the hills. Patrick Hopton noticed that many of the small shops were empty, their windows graced only by notices in quivering capitals apologising to former customers; in one he could see unopened manila envelopes curling on the window sill. At the top of the main street was an Italianate red-brick town hall. There were three fish and chips shops, all of them closed. In her high heels and dress from Aquascutum, Monica had looked as though she had got lost on her way to Ludlow, the absence of half-timbered teashops of a recognizable type being a particular source of irritation. The only hotel was shut for refurbishment. While he went to buy a newspaper, Patrick had left her staring at an unpromising establishment called the Coffee Corner. Three of the four tables were occupied by bikers

197

eating full English breakfasts; the fourth had been commandeered by a yellow plastic bag and an ancient woman in a mauve skirt who was smoking and knitting with an intensity that suggested that she would be there for the whole morning.

'What was wrong with the coffee shop?' he said, after she had slammed the car door for the second time.

'There is no point in deliberately trying to annoy me.'

'I'm merely pointing out that now we are in the country it is unreasonable to expect everyone to dress as if they were in Knightsbridge.'

'Do you imagine,' she said, 'that my lawyers have become less competent simply because we have crossed the border into Wales?'

*

She had been threatening to leave him for five years, but Patrick never had to remind himself that there was no good reason why she should not keep her word. He glanced in the rear mirror and then turned the key in the ignition. Within minutes they were in the wind-blurred foothills: the fields fractured with dry stone walls; a white farm or two chalkmarked onto the middle distance; and, placed on what was almost a mountain, rows of mature conifers, those nearest the road in a ragged line, like a blue hand with the fingers close together.

Patrick had been surprised when Moira agreed to accept the Russells' invitation. None of the previous three visits could be accounted a success. It was, he thought, partly something to do with the house. Tony Russell had bought the land cheaply from a bankrupt farmer and somehow obtained permission to demolish the existing structure - a dilapidated byre that had apparently been a dwelling at some point in the eighteenth century - before commissioning an architect, whom he described as the Frank Lloyd Wright of Llandrindod Wells, to build their new home. A charmless structure of glass and concrete clad with white tiles, it had been inserted in the hillside like a false tooth. Patrick was willing to concede that in, for example, Mallorca, it might have been just about habitable, but in Wales, no matter what the season, its walls had an uncanny pallor and its wide windows admitted a sinister grey light the colour of amalgam. All attempts to landscape the small, steep garden in a way that would soften its surroundings had failed.

From the back of the car came the sound of his wife expressing an opinion. He concurred audibly and immediately in the hope that this would solve the problem; indeed, after a minute or two, she ground to a halt in mid-sentence and began some inoffensive rummaging in her shoulder bag. In the last few years, Patrick had noticed amongst his family, friends and acquaintances an increasing propensity to express opinions, some of which were already unnecessarily colourful, with a vigour and disregard for the conventions of polite conversation that would once have been thought unacceptable. Tony Russell had always been a man of strongly held views, but in his retirement some of these had been embellished to the point of oddity. The first dinner party that Monica and Patrick had attended at the Russells' new home, an occasion on which old friends from Birmingham were to be introduced to new friends from Wales, had broken up prematurely as a result of Tony's opinions on celibacy. From the very start Patrick had been ill at ease. Although all of the male guests were formally dressed in collar and tie, the Welsh in dark suits, old friends and English incomers in blazers or tweed jackets, Tony was attired as if he had hopes of playing a round of golf at Augusta, Georgia: bottle green 'pants', and a v neck Pringle over a purple roll neck sweater. The conversation during the first course had been uncontroversial enough; possibly because the obligations of a host were a sufficient distraction: Tony had appeared especially worried about the wine, a Bolivian red that a man in Beguildy had assured him would go down well. And it wasn't until the lamb casserole had been served that he had begun to get into his stride.

'Now I certainly wouldn't disagree with you there,' he'd said, responding to a young Welsh farmer's assertion that nurses were badly underpaid. 'Yet it seems to me that, in return for greater economic security, members of what one might call the 'essential' professions must be prepared to make certain sacrifices'.

'What do you mean by that?' replied the farmer. Even in winter his bony face was raw, red and shiny.

'Well, if you were to say to me that nurses shouldn't be allowed to join a union.'

'I wouldn't say that!'

'And neither,' Tony had replied calmly, 'would I. And yet it is surely right to expect that those who provide essential services should forgo the right to strike.'

'I'm not so ...'

'I regard myself,' Tony had interrupted firmly,' as a moderate on this issue. I would not, for example, go along with those who maintain that nurses should be celibate.'

'Who an earth is suggesting that nurses should be celibate, for god's sake?' Let me remind you that the celibacy of firemen is a principle that has already gained widespread acceptance amongst those of us who given some thought to this issue. Legislation is surely only a matter of time.'

Even now Patrick found it impossible to decide whether Tony had been being serious. The guests had started shift uneasily. No one had drunk enough of the sour Bolivian wine to have the confidence to laugh.

'Widespread acceptance from whom?' said a local solicitor.

'Well, of course, if you *want* your house to be burnt to the ground,' Tony snorted incredulously, 'because the people who should be dealing with the problem are too busy indulging their carnal appetites to come to your assistance then you must be a man of unusual tolerance. That's all I can say.'

Perhaps Tony Russell really had developed pyrophobia. That he was overstating his case was nothing new, and it was certainly a fact that his house was a long way from the nearest fire station. The Welsh farmers, however, beginning to suspect that they were being made fun of, left before coffee was served.

*

Mercifully, there had been no sign of him so far that morning and Anthea Russell had been left to prepare lunch in peace. Although she

200

was a naturally bad cook, and didn't have to try very hard in order to fall well short of accepted standards of hospitality, she wondered if there was any way, without poisoning Patrick in the process, she could finally bring home to Monica Hopton that her journey had been unnecessary. Leaving the chicken to continue drying out in the oven, she went into the dining room. The enormous plate glass windows overlooked a foreground of mist and stone. On the opposite side of the valley, and sensed rather than seen behind the low lying cloud, was the dark, brooding presence of mountain that kept the valley in shadow for the best part of every morning. She took the cutlery out of the drawer and began to lay four places. The table, which was the only piece of furniture of modern design that they possessed, had a glass top so when food was spilt it was possible to intervene if any of the guests should try to grind it into the carpet. Andrea toyed with the idea of putting some fresh flowers in a vase and then thought better of it. In the industrial blue light of mid-morning, a blue that seemed to belong to subterranean basements and operating theatres, everything looked artificial. As she mitred the napkins, it occurred to her that it was odd that after the move Tony had insisted on keeping all of their furniture and paintings. The walnut chest of drawers and the Windsor chairs, which had looked so comfortable in their home in Birmingham, stood diminished and awkward in acres of unfilled space; the careful little watercolours in gilt frames seemed somehow less significant than the emptiness that surrounded them. Andrea looked at her watch. The Hoptons would be probably in Wales by now and she hadn't even thought about the starter. There were two large tins of tomato soup in the garage. If she added a little double cream and some basil that would probably do. It was simply not worth going to a great deal of trouble when the only person who deserved to eat even so much as adequately was Patrick. From upstairs came footsteps followed by the sound of a lavatory being flushed. Tony had arrived back late the previous evening from the Llantyrn Arms; he was sober but apparently puzzled that someone should have taken objection to his description of the Royal Society for the Protection of Birds as 'a front organization for neo-fascists and other known criminals.'

Now that Tony had finally succeeded in offending all the locals, and fewer and fewer of their friends from Birmingham were prepared to make the journey to visit them, Patrick and Monica had some claim to be regarded as not only their oldest but also their only friends. Not that Tony would ever have admitted this. As he never tired of saying 'I have my friends and Anthea doesn't have hers.' He seemed to regard the various threats by Rhodri, the landlord of the Llantyrn Arms, to have him barred as mere affectionate banter. 'They like a man who speaks his mind. They respect you for that.' Three times in the last month Andrea had said that they should sell the house and move back to Birmingham. Tony had responded to this by dressing up in a navy blue yachting blazer and well-pressed white trousers; it was just possible that this was intended to convey subliminally that he was still the captain of his ship.

Thirty years ago the Hoptons and the Russells had been neighbours. Both couples had young boys of about the same age who had got on so well together that a wicket gate had been built in the laurel hedge separating the two gardens. That way the children would not create a disturbance by knocking on each other's doors whenever they wished to meet. After a while, however, the adults got into the habit of using the gate as well, and one summer the gentle click that it made when it was being closed became one of the sounds of the garden, inevitable as the soft hiss of the water-sprinkler and the crunch of the wheelbarrow on gravel. It was a summer that was unusually hot. A summer when the days seemed blurred and the bright colours in the garden would run one into another. There was the smell of sweet peas, she remembered, and the cabbage whites, crests of silver riding on invisible currents. And at nights they slept with the windows open and the sounds came in from the garden and joined them. Then Tony had to go to a conference in Scarborough, and on the first night he was away she lay awake, naked under a single sheet. And it was no surprise when she heard the click of the wicket gate, the faint creak of the door she had left ajar as it was slowly opened wider, his footsteps only just audible on the stair, the susurration of that single sheet as he drew it aside.

She positioned the napkins so that they faced one another across the cutlery as though they were in conclave. As she stepped back to assess her handiwork, she became aware of the fact that Tony was standing in the hall and staring in at her. He was wearing a black silk dressing gown embroidered with a motif of golden dragons.

His face was a little redder than usual and what was left of his sparse grey hair stood up awkwardly as though he had gone to sleep shortly after having washed it. Encouragingly, he looked very ill.

*

There was no traffic on the road, but an irritating rattle that he had noticed when they were on the Droitwich by-pass returned. He slowed down as they passed through a hamlet that seemed to consist of little more than a grim chapel with a corrugated iron roof, a few bungalows with gnarled gardens and an unwelcoming pub: cloud-grey stucco, an empty car park and a blackboard with a rain-smudged menu. From the back came the slither and rustle of cellophane as Monica opened a packet of cigarettes.

A faint patch of sunlight glimmered for a moment on a distant mountain, ripening grey to ochre, giving a false promise of harvests to come. The hamlets with their chapels and grocery stores, the farmhouses, the bungalows with their dwarf gardens, even the grey dribble of dry stone walls - all had gone. Now it was just the bare hills: rock, heather, bracken, a few white dots that might be sheep. It occurred to Patrick that it would be an entertaining place in which to break down. He could imagine Monica's squeals of dismay turning to outright horror when she discovered the mobile phone wouldn't work. There would be no point in hurrying off to try to get help from the nearest farm. He had a feeling that a place he'd seen in the distance some miles back had long since been abandoned. No doubt they would just be forced to sit in the car until a friendly Landrover came along. He glanced in the mirror. As she gazed out of the window her expression was a mixture of boredom and impatience, but he now knew why she thought her journey was worth it: she was determined to make sure that he wouldn't experience even the faintest flicker of enjoyment throughout the weekend. Not that a weekend with the Russells would have been a sybaritic occasion even in her absence. On their last visit, Andrea's cooking had been so awful that it was no longer possible to pretend that its badness could be thought of as somehow pioneering, an interesting way of extending the boundaries of what was permissible in English cuisine. Tony, who for reasons that were not immediately discernible, was dressed as a Japanese Emperor, had been taciturn to the point of rudeness. Patrick found it almost impossible to remember him as he had once been: jovial, kind to the children and always ready to join in their games; his hospitality well meant, in spite of the aridities of Andrea's cooking and his uncertain opinions, which had always had an idiosyncratic flavour, had been more or less acceptable, because although sincerely held, they were rarely expressed, and seemed more the products of momentary irritation than a well-oiled engine of social embarrassment.

The road was wider and smoother than Patrick remembered. It was just possible that they would arrive early. Perhaps they should stop after all, but there was nothing to stop for. And then as he glanced at the mountainside on his left he seemed to catch sight of a figure struggling underneath a heavy burden. A man carrying a sack - or was it a body? They were past it before his mind began to edit the scene. There had been no perceptible movement. Slowly a stunted tree, twisted by the wind, replaced the melancholy image. It occurred to Patrick that, although undeniably remote, such a spot would not have been an ideal place to commit a murder. The ground was most probably stony, and there was little or no cover. Traffic was certainly infrequent, but should a tractor or a van pass slowly by there was no obvious place to hide. As he rounded the corner, he saw the forest, row upon row of conifers. Those lower down the slope were small and leafless, their neat regimental alignment was clearly visible, but above them lay an impenetrable dark green wilderness.

*

When he described his symptoms, she knew at once that he was having a heart attack. She told him where to find the Rennies and then went back to the kitchen. It would all be a question of timing. If it happened quickly - and there was no doubting that he looked as if he couldn't possibly last much longer - then everything would be very straightforward. She'd simply tuck him up in bed, tell the Hoptons that he was ill and not to be disturbed and then phone the doctor afterwards. But should he manage to hold out until their guests arrived, the picture would become much more complicated. There was a serious possibility that Patrick or Monica would insist on sending for an ambulance immediately. The chances of his surviving the journey to Llandrindod Wells were slim, but it was a risk that she would rather not take.

She could hear him banging about upstairs and shouting incoherently. It sounded as if he were hurling the medicine cabinet around the bathroom. Although she had not intended to make a sweet course, she emptied the contents of the fruit bowl into the Magimix and waited for the comforting whirr to steady her nerves. Then she remembered that since the Hoptons had been invited to stay for the whole weekend it was inevitable that Tony's absence would have to be explained. The best that she could hope for was to postpone the discovery of the body until after lunch. After the fruit had been reduced to a grey-green fluid, she walked over to the fridge and found a pot of sour cream that she had been meaning to use for some time. There was still noise coming from above; it sounded like a mixture of prayer and complaint. She turned on the radio.

Twenty minutes later she went upstairs. The house had never been so quiet before. His silk dressing gown, a present that she had given him shortly after his retirement, was lying crumpled on the floor outside his bedroom. For the first time she realized that she would have to ring her children. Mark was in Hong Kong and Peter was in Amsterdam. She hadn't seen them for over three years. Would they come to the funeral? Although it wouldn't be an easy journey for either of them they would probably both feel obliged to attend, knowing that there wasn't someone at hand to help. The long years at the boarding schools that Tony had insisted they should attend had bred a sense of duty that was equal to special occasions. As she picked up the dressing gown, its mythical creatures shimmered in the cold light.

*

It was with considerable satisfaction that he was able to look into the mirror and not see her pale, disdainful features staring out of the window. The whole business had been so very much easier than one could possibly have imagined. In fiction, he noticed, it was customary to stress how difficult it was to commit a murder, as if this somehow added verisimilitude. His experience showed that this was very far from being the case, even when no forethought or planning had been involved; although clearly this was not an insight that he would ever be able to share.

As soon as he saw how conveniently the lay-by had been positioned, he had decided to pull over. There was no point in trying to entice her into woods. The one aspect of her behaviour that he knew he could count on was her steadfast opposition to even the most reasonable of his requests. Although the traffic was still very light, it was just possible that a car might go past. It was a risk he was happy to take. If he pushed her down onto the backseat and then strangled her, the precise nature of his ministrations would be less evident from the road. Even if her flailing arms were visible, no motorist would have wanted to interrupt what could easily have been lovemaking or a praiseworthy attempt to discipline a difficult child. Once he was certain that she was dead it would be a simple matter to get her into the woods. He would put her arm round his shoulders and hold her as upright as possible until they were safely under cover.

She had proved heavier than anticipated, and the way that her head rolled uncontrollably and in a manner that was hardly consistent with a mere indisposition had made his progress less dignified than he would have liked. As soon as he was satisfied that he could not be seen, he had propped her up against the nearest tree and paused for breath. He would not feel entirely comfortable until he had manoeuvred her somewhat deeper into the forest. There was a disheartening absence of undergrowth and he had no spade with which to dig a suitable grave; moreover, the neat rows in which the conifers had been planted ensured the forest was much less dense than it appeared from the outside. He must press on until he reached the mature trees that he knew were higher up the slope; there a suitable spot was bound to present itself.

As he had made his way back, it occurred to him that leaving his car unoccupied in the lay-by for such a long time had been regrettable. It was just possible that some officious nobody would have made a note of his number; on balance, however, he had to admit that this was unlikely, and he was very pleased with the resting place he found for Monica. With any luck they wouldn't find her until they started logging, and, judging from the general lack of activity in the area, that wouldn't be for another twenty or thirty years. He got into the car and turned the ignition key. What was a little more worrying was that he was now almost certain to be late arriving at the Russells. And without Monica. Involuntarily, he almost took his foot off the clutch. Saying that she was ill was out of the question. Tony would be almost certain to insist on ringing her up. A holiday abroad? A dying relative? None of it would sound in the least plausible to anyone who knew them as well as Tony and Andrea. And had anyone seen her getting into the car when they had left Birmingham? Then there was the little town where they'd stopped a couple of hours ago. Would anyone in the Coffee Corner, or whatever the place was called, remember Monica peering contemptuously at them while they tried to digest their bacon and eggs?

Half expecting to see her, he glanced in the mirror and although there was nothing there he seemed to hear her voice complaining. The whole thing was absolutely typical of him, she was saying. He couldn't even organise a simple murder. No wonder they'd had to go on living in a poky little semi in Selly Oak long after all their friends had moved into five-bedroomed houses in Sutton Coldfield. Sheer lack of foresight and proper planning. Her father would have murdered her properly. Even her brother would have made a better job of it than he had. And there was another thing. He had no manners. He hadn't said anything to her at all just before he killed her. He'd offered no explanation whatsoever. Didn't she deserve better than that after forty years of married life? Well, he mustn't think that she was going to put up with treatment like that for very much longer. Did he seriously imagine that her lawyers were any less competent just because she was dead? He looked at his hands. There was not a scratch on them, and there was no dirt, he knew, on his trousers - or even on the soles of his shoes.

*

The white wine was very pale and had a faint greenish tinge; she noted ruefully, it still tasted metallic. Andrea put the bottle back in the fridge and went into the dining room. It had been unreasonable to expect any improvement since the previous occasion when she had tried it two weeks ago. The table was still set for four places. On the sideboard three more bottles of the same vintage as the one in the fridge reclined in an ice bucket. They came from a small vineyard in Lincolnshire, believed to be the most northerly in Britain, and represented, or so Tony had told her, terrific value. Several more cases were maturing in the garage along with a decade's supply of the Bolivian red and a Jeroboam of homemade elderflower champagne. An interest in wine was one of the many enthusiasms that had afflicted Tony since his retirement; enthusiasms which she sometimes believed had eroded all traces of their old life together. Although in the past neither of them had been great wine drinkers, and she had insisted on leaving the selection to Tony, on the rare occasions when they had dined in a restaurant on the Hagley Road, he had always succeeded in choosing something palatable. Now there was this beverage from just outside Louth which should only have been sold with an accompanying packet of indigestion tablets.

A great grey streak of rain clattered across the speckled window. She watched it slide down jaggedly, blurring even the mist and spray beyond. There had been fine days, days when she could almost understand what had made him decide that they should live where they did, but whenever they had guests it would always rain, and she would be left nodding fatuously while Tony described the wonderful view, the view that their visitors might have seen if only they'd had the sense to come on another day. But there always a hint of triumphalism in his tone, a sense that such a sight was something very special, a privilege that had to be earned by living in the place and was certainly not something that could be summoned up to satisfy the whims of those who had merely dropped by. She recalled a visit from Ted and Marjorie Johnson-Smith, their last as it happened. A cold damp March with scudding grey skies and winds that rattled the plate glass windows. The boiler was malfunctioning again and the tiny radiators in the living room emitted a warmth that was barely detectable. Anthea had worn woollen stockings and a skirt of the thickest tweed that she could find. Huddled in the waxed jackets that they had refused to take off, the Johnson-Smiths had glared balefully at Tony - his garish cotton shirt, short trousers and flip-flops suggested that he had dressed for the beach - as he extolled the virtues of Welsh country living. Plainly impervious to the emotional and actual weather around him, he had somehow succeeded in creating his own microclimate. It was hard now to remember the shared moments of the early days of their marriage: the visits to the Town Hall to hear the CBSO, the trips to the Walker Gallery, and the strolls through the Botanical Gardens. She put down her wine glass and walked over to the window. A car was parked at a slightly odd angle at the bottom of the hill. There was something vaguely familiar about it, and it occurred to her that the Hoptons had arrived early. But why should Patrick leave the car the down there when he must have known perfectly well that there would be no problem in getting up the drive unless there had been an unusually heavy snowfall. After a few minutes, a man got out of the car and began to stare up at the house. He was too far away for her to be sure that it was Patrick. How odd, she thought, not to recognise someone she had slept with - even at that distance.

*

At the foot of the hill he braked and pulled the car over onto a grass verge. Although he knew that he was visible from the house, he could not quite bring himself to go on up the drive and park outside the front door. He told himself that this was because he had expected to arrive late and now found that he was ten minutes early. He was on a slight incline, his seat tilted backwards as if he were visiting the dentist. If she was watching, she must be wondering what he was doing. A half-memory floated to the surface of his mind. A seaside town. The flap of gulls. The beach at low tide tarnished in the evening light. Had she been there? No. Surely it was a childhood recollection. And now it was raining, and the windscreen wipers dissolved the delicate grey watercolours again and again.

He got out of the car and looked up at the house. It appeared smaller than he had remembered it, but somehow more a part of the landscape, an old tooth rotting in a grey gum. Andrea had told him that they had had trouble with the roof. It was so flat that the rainwater wouldn't run away into the gutters and little lakes had formed. He heard Tony say that the house looked at its best in bad winters when it was barely distinguishable from the ice and snow around it. All of Tony's life had been spent in an office working for a firm that never gave him the promotion he felt he deserved. Quietly spoken, conservatively dressed and diligent at work, he had kept his occasional flourishes - the tie that was too loud, the opinion that produced a moment's awkward silence - for his family and friends. And now, in his retirement, something had emerged from its hiding place, something that could only exist in a cold high place. As Patrick stared at the house, he noticed a shape at the corner of the window. He was not sure whether it had been there when he had got out of the car. For a moment he thought that it was a figure looking down at him, and wondered whether he should wave. But there was no sign of movement and it could so easily have been a dark fold in a curtain or a trick of the light.

*

The clatter of cutlery and the rain beating against the window. With her left hand, she picked up the wine bottle and began to pour. When his glass was only half full, he raised his right hand and smiled, and then he picked up his knife and fork and pushed a piece of dry chicken towards a mound of potato. At the other end of the table, a third pair of hands, hands with delicate wrists and well-manicured fingernails, began to search a shoulder bag. After a brief interval a cigarette was produced. He heard the dry rasp of her thumb on the lighter. A flame at the second attempt. Why did she have to smoke in between courses? The remorse and tenderness that he had felt when he had seen her asleep, curled up like a child on the back seat of the car, had died with her first question. Why had he stopped there? Did he expect her to walk up the hill?

And now a fourth pair of hands was opening a bottle of gooseberry wine which, a voice was assuring them, had just the right amount of acidity to complement the sweet course. Patrick looked at Anthea. How often did she think about the one night that they had spent together? It had been so warm that he hadn't even bothered to put on a dressing gown. He still remembered the feel of the grass on his bare feet, and the click of the wicket gate, so unexpectedly loud in the still night air that he had waited for a moment, fearing to see lights turned on in neighbouring houses, before hurrying to the door that he knew would be open.

'I've told Rhodri that he should give his customers some of this instead of the awful German muck he serves them. This is the nearest thing to Welsh wine that you'll ever find, I told him. And the elderflower is even better.'

Tony had used their early arrival as an excuse for an expedition to the Llantyrn Arms. Although the fact that they had to drop in at the Post Office and General Stores for a supply of indigestion tablets had suggested a fairly brief session, they had stayed for an hour and a half. Patrick would never forget the way that the locals stared into their beer when Tony walked in; some of them seemed to shrink, as if they were trying to disappear into the bar stools.

'Do you know what those stupid bastards in the pub were talking about? The Common Agricultural Policy. 'War against France,' I said, 'that's the only policy worth even thinking about. Show no mercy until they cede the Aquitaine.''

In the Llantyrn Arms they would have forgiven Tony if he had been drunk, but he only sipped a half of bitter. And as he talked he watched them very carefully, his eyes searching their down-turned faces for the least sign of dissent.

Andrea brought in the sweet course and Tony poured the wine into

211

four small glasses. There was something decidedly nautical about the way that he was dressed. In his blue blazer, well-pressed white trousers, crisp white shirt and cravat, he could have been at Cowes. Not that there was any immediate chance of a little yachting after lunch. Although it was hard to be sure without consulting a map, Patrick suspected that there must be few parts of Wales that were further from the sea.

'To Patrick and Monica,' said Tony, raising a glass of the bubbling gooseberry, 'our oldest and dearest friends.'

Monica lit another cigarette. She glanced at Patrick for a moment and then turned away and shuddered, as if she could still see the forest in his eyes.

'Yes, yes,' said Patrick, half-rising from his seat and then sitting down again. 'To our oldest and dearest friends, Tony and Anthea.' He raised his glass. Who were their oldest and dearest friends? David and Millicent were dead; Giles and Joanna were in Portugal; Ted and Marjorie had gone to Malta. So perhaps it was true.

Anthea went over to the side-table and picked up the cheese-knife. She was wearing a huge shapeless sweater that made it impossible to tell whether she had lost or put on weight. He could still recall her body, pale in the summer moonlight. It had been there every night, fixed in his dreams for forty years.

They had all stopped speaking and the only noise inside the house was the click of the knife on the cheeseboard. Then the rain pressed its white hands against the window panes as though begging to come inside, as though jealous of the wind that had insinuated itself down an empty chimney, sneaked across the carpet and pushed the door with such unnatural gentleness that it swung to like a gate that was being closed behind him.

Terms and Conditions

– Sarah Evans –

'Are you sure?' Kara asked, her eyes switching rapidly between David and the baby.

'We'll be fine,' David said. 'Won't we now?' He leaned down to tickle the baby's tummy, which immediately made Sean gurgle and curl his limbs inwards, reminding David of a Venus flytrap.

Kara continued hovering by the door. But *she* had been the one to bemoan the fact that she never got to the gym. Now it came to actually leaving the baby, even for a couple of hours, she seemed mired in reluctance. Maternal guilt? Or just guilt? He wasn't sure.

'I don't know. Perhaps...'

'Perhaps what?' Irritability flared. If she wasn't going, he wouldn't mind a workout himself. He looked at her. She was wearing an ancient sweatshirt of his, her hands twisting and stretching the cuffs of the sleeves, the washed out cotton bagging over her body. She'd gained weight with the baby. *You could do with the exercise*, he thought. And then he said it, watching her flinch, her teeth biting her lips, holding back her response.

'We'll be fine,' he repeated.

'OK. OK then.'

She crouched right down to kiss the baby, her bottom in the air, even more lumpish now she was on the floor. She clambered up to her knees and pressed her lips damply against David's cheek. She smelt of milk and talcum powder. Close up, he could see the threads of grey in her hair. Her face was lined and drawn. Starting over again with a baby at forty was a strain, a strain on both of them.

'You're an angel,' she said as she stood to go.

David listened for the crash of the front door then returned his gaze to Sean.

Sean was still curled up, lying on his multi-coloured, multi-textured play-mat. His hands had captured a foot and he was attempting to manoeuvre his toes into his drooling mouth. 'Who's a clever boy then?' David said, tickling the baby's tummy again, and being rewarded with a gummy smile. 'And whose clever boy are you, eh? Eh?' David maintained his *talking to a baby* voice; he kept his smile. Sean carried on smiling, gurgling, squirming, stretching those tiny toes. He wouldn't see the calculation in Daddy's gaze as David scrutinised the miniature features, seeking traces of himself.

The colour of the eyes perhaps; but then blue was hardly unusual. Button noses all looked the same and it would be a while before the adult form emerged. The shape of the face? Chubby cheeks were another baby feature that Sean would grow out of.

When it came to babies, David had always been sceptical of the resemblances thing. A lot of the time it was wishful thinking, he considered. A claim of ownership and a bid for immortality. With Richie, the whole clan of relations had endlessly commented. Doesn't he look like his dad? But a bit of his mum as well. Doesn't he look like Granddad, like Aunty Doreen, like Cousin Pete? It was incessant. But he let himself be drawn into it; he remembered the swell of paternal pride.

The memory of that pride hurt; where had it got him? Searching Sean's face and expecting answers wasn't getting him anywhere either.

He stood up brusquely, severing eye contact; coffee might help kickstart him out of his sour mood. Sean emitted a low whimper. 'It's all right,' he said. 'I'm just making coffee. I'll be right back.' His voice reverted to a normal adult tone. He wasn't sure he saw the need for the cooing and ga-ga-ing anyway.

From the kitchen he could hear the whimper build into an intermittent cry. *For Christ's sake.* He'd only been gone two seconds. The baby's shifts in mood were disconcerting, the finger-click transition from burbling contentment to consuming misery. He ought to go and pick him up immediately; that way he might halt the escalation. His hand stirred the mud of grains and water in the cafetiere, releasing the complex aroma and the promise of caffeine. He kicked the door shut to muffle the noise.

Returning minutes later, he found Sean at full throttle, his back arched and twisted, his face all blotched and scrunched. David watched. He sipped his coffee and watched. Then he placed his mug down and picked Sean up. Sean's body was rigid with resistance as he emitted great hiccuping sobs. 'There, there,' David said, his voice not at all soothing. 'There, there.' He hoisted the baby over one shoulder. Dribble glooped down in a translucent thread, down to and over David's clean shirt and he looked round for something to wipe the baby's mouth with. A heap of baby chaos covered the top of the plastic changing table in the corner. Baby wipes. Nappies. Cotton buds. He picked out a facecloth.

His hand patted Sean's back as he paced up and down, gently jogging the baby's weight. He felt Sean relax a little, his mass beginning to slump like a sack of beans. He felt himself soften and the creep of remorse. Sean might after all be his.

'I've something to tell you,' Kara had said, her eyes averted, talking low and fast. It was late one evening; they'd just got back from dinner out with friends during which she had been uncharacteristically quiet. 'I'm pregnant; I can't be certain that it's yours.' The second landmine followed the first in such rapid succession that they existed side by side in a mangle of incomprehension and gut-churning dismay.

The baby's cries subsided into soft snuffles and David was just thinking about putting him down and getting on with something. He heard the soft ploop-ploop.

Shit! Well yes, exactly.

217

Sean was starting to twist and squirm. David soothed his back under the soft T-shirt and with the tip of his fingers eased the nappy away from his skin, just enough to catch the unmistakable whiff.

Christ!

He hated this.

With Richie, he'd done his stint of nappies. He'd been working of course so Kara had dealt with most of them, but he made a point of doing his share in the evenings and at weekends. Hardly an aspect of parenting anyone enjoyed, but he'd been keen to prove his full involvement. This time, Kara had not asked him to change nappies and he hadn't offered. It was part of the tilt in balance between them, he thought. The remnants of her guilt and her gratitude for his forgiveness.

But forgiveness wasn't a simple thing. It wasn't enough to reason it out and hope it might be true. The flames of hurt and jealousy had dampened over the last year. But they still flared up strong and bright at unexpected moments. They had shifted more from hurt to righteous fury. He breathed in slowly. He knew that to end a twenty-year marriage on the basis of a single drunken act would be unreasonable. And he'd be harming himself as much as punishing her. Infidelity was easily done. Not as if *he* hadn't been tempted from time to time over the years.

His arguments were familiar and pat, and failed to mollify his mood.

He swept aside the paraphernalia littering the changing table and laid Sean down on a towel. The baby's cries were at maximum volume now, his misery out of proportion to the discomfort.

'I don't like this any more than you do,' David said, his voice adult and cross, which didn't help of course.

He forced himself to switch to autopilot. Over the last year he'd grown practised at that. Sometimes he wondered if all that was left of his and Kara's marriage was a semi-civil veneer with nothing underneath. They had been happy, he reminded himself. Hadn't they? Her admission had switched him to an alternate reality in which all his certainties lost substance.

'It was just one of those stupid things,' she had said. 'It really didn't mean anything.' She'd been flattered by the attention. 'At my age.' Her smile was wistful.

'Was he younger than me?' David had demanded.

'Does it matter?'

'It matters to me.'

She shrugged. 'I guess so.'

'He either was or wasn't.'

'Yes.'

'Better looking? More successful?'

'It wasn't like that.'

'Well what was it like?'

But she insisted there wasn't more to tell. He wondered sometimes if it would have been easier if she had kept quiet; her confession felt self-indulgent, transferring the burden of knowledge from her to him.

He took a fresh nappy; he placed the baby wipes to hand; he undid the soiled nappy and braced himself.

He hated this. He hated dealing with the stench and smear of shit. Sean's legs were kicking every which way, determined to make the process as difficult and messy as possible. The stinking gunge was everywhere: Sean's mottled bottom, his legs, smudging over the towel, onto the plastic of the table and David's fingers. 'Stay still.' He captured both Sean's ankles in one of his hands, feeling the surprising vigour of the kick and holding on a bit more firmly than he ought to.

Here he was, cleaning up after some other guy's shit. Some younger guy. The thoughts were fast and furious. Putting up with sleepless nights. Forget meals out and art galleries and cinema trips. Disremember holidays. Forgo all thoughts of sex. And all for someone else's baby?

Not that he particularly wanted sex just at the moment; watching the birth had been a turn off in that regard – all that blood and tearing flesh and (as it happened) shit. With Richie, he'd felt such dew-eyed awe and wonder; with Sean the whole thing had turned him queasy. He'd nearly fainted like some bloodless wimp.

219

He bundled Sean back up, placed him in the cot and dealt with the foul nappy and wipes. As he scrubbed his hands and fingernails under a scalding tap, he felt himself cave in with exhaustion. He was getting on for fifty for Christ's sake; all that energy he'd had first time round seemed impossibly remote.

The coffee he'd made earlier had gone cold, but he drank it anyway. It tasted foul.

At least Sean was quiet. David went and sat down at the computer and thought of all the practical things that needed doing. Checking online bank accounts and bills. Googling for a local plumber to fix their leaking toilet. Managing their rental DVDs so they got sent something other than award-winning foreign films in which the minutiae of people's loves and losses would depress him. He was too restlessly tired to organise himself to action.

He looked across at Sean, his head turned to one side, his mouth sucking on a diminutive fist, looking every square-inch the Michelangelo cherub.

The line of the brow: perhaps he detected something of himself in that. Kara had been very precise. She and David had made love on the Saturday night (*as usual,* because after twenty years they'd developed these routines). Her conference with its overnight stay in a posh hotel had been the following Wednesday. That was too close to know with any certainty when she had conceived.

'I'm sorry,' she said. 'I guess it's fifty-fifty.'

Fifty-fifty. Toss a coin and hope it's heads.

Except…

His fingers tapped the table as the PC booted up, chugging and churning away, filling the screen with indecipherable lines of code.

Except, after Richie, after a suitable gap, they had tried for another baby. He remembered lunar cycles of temperature charts, urine tests and targeted, vigorous sex. And the bleeding which seemed more and more inevitable with time. Tests failed to pinpoint anything obviously wrong with either of them. It could be like that sometimes, the doctor had said.

So Sean coming along seemed too much of a coincidence. This other guy's sperm had managed what his own had not.

220

Bastard! The flame flashed up hot and bright.

As for Kara, surely she could at least have taken precautions. He remembered her insistence that he have exactly that type of excruciating father-son chat with Richie. Never mind pregnancy, she had knowingly exposed herself – and David too – to God knows what.

He brought up Google and typed in: *paternity test.* He started clicking on the most promising looking links as he tried to remember why he wasn't supposed to do this.

'If you don't want another baby, not at our age, I'll understand,' Kara had said finally, her arms hugging her body in, as if to protect what was growing inside. 'I mean…' She faltered. 'I don't want our marriage to end over this. We can talk about our options.'

Kara saying this, when she had so badly wanted a second child.

She stared ahead, her gaze fixed on the floor. 'But I'm not prepared to undergo an amniocentesis to determine paternity.' Her eyes flick-knifed up to his, her voice acquiring an edge of steel. 'I won't take the test and decide to terminate because the baby doesn't have the right genes,' she said.

He understood her terms; he hardly wanted to play a Nazi game of selection himself, setting conditions on life and death.

'So if I – if we – have the baby it means both of us have to accept it, whatever the paternity,' she continued, her voice low and determined. 'In which case there's no point testing after the event.'

But did a bit of DNA matter, really, she had said, her voice and eyes pleading with him. Compared to the day-to-day commitment of being a parent. Was biological paternity that big a deal?

He'd allowed himself to be persuaded; he'd promised to love the baby whatever. But like forgiveness, love could not be delivered on a promise. He looked over at Sean who was sniffling in his sleep, dreaming baby dreams. What did it mean to love a baby anyway? He'd never had to ask himself with Richie.

His fingers kept clicking and his eyes kept roaming over the details. In terms of chemistry, a paternity test was straightforward. In practice, rules and regulations made it needlessly complex. Full consent needed from both parents. A DNA sample needed from all three of them.

If he asked Kara, she would say no.

He pictured himself forging her signature and sneaking her passport out of her bedside drawer to take a copy at work. Neither of those was difficult. Getting a sample was a little trickier. Would a mint scented smear from her toothbrush do the trick? An image formed, himself a dark shadow looming over her while she slept, judging the moment to swoop in with a swab the second her mouth opened. What if she woke? How would he possibly explain himself?

Not that Kara was in a position to lecture him on bad behaviour. What business was it of hers anyway?

She didn't need to know, he thought. She knew bloody well the baby was hers. What right did she have to lecture him about what being a parent meant, to leave him always questioning and searching for clues?

He clicked on the link for a US site. This one was refreshingly different to the UK nanny-state, providing a caress of reassurance for an unsettled mind. *Are you a might-be Dad?* it asked in soothing green. *You have a right to know!*

He looked over at Sean, who, as ever, was drooling; he looked over at the carton of cotton buds, which had drifted halfway across the floor.

It was day seven. Seven working days that is. The Royal Mail online tracking facility had confirmed his package had arrived on day four. The lab guaranteed a three-day turn around for the result to be handily delivered by email. It was due today. All through the last week and a half, David's thoughts had kept thrusting, enamel sharp, through the soft routines of day to day. He had been even more irritable than usual with Kara and Sean.

He looked at his onscreen clock. With five hours time difference, there was no point logging on till two pm.

Ten minutes to go.

His eyes skimmed the internal report he was supposed to be drafting; his mind refused to be remotely engaged by the question of economic activity and opportunities in the Middle East.

He highlighted some text that was pure waffle. *On the one hand X, on the other hand Y.* He failed to think of anything more definitive.

Five minutes to.

He thought of the yes/no of the result and of it flicking a switch in his mind. One state of the world versus another. A real dad or not. Like contemplating the theoretical possibility of infidelity, until it actually happened, it was impossible to predict how it would feel.

Three minutes to.

He ran a spell and grammar check which kept offering errant solutions to things he knew were perfectly OK. He tried to remember the difference between *that* and *which*.

One minute to.

His hands tightened as he brought up *hotmail*. He managed to mistype his password and had to enter it again. Two new messages. The listings for his local cinema. Pizza Express had a Valentine special coming up. He checked his spam filter just in case. *Say no to loneliness.* If only his mess of a love life could be solved by a beautiful girl from Russia.

'D'you have a minute, David?'

He turned abruptly at the sound of Simon Barnes' voice. *Shit!* What sort of sad-fuck loser would Simon think he was, with that girls-from-Russia email decorating his screen? Closing it now would just draw attention to it.

He tried to focus on what Simon Barnes was saying. 'Yes,' he said. 'Sure.' Sure he had to time to look at the tender Simon was holding out and produce a draft by end of day. Simon had only been with the consultancy a year, but he'd recently been promoted to Partner, while David still languished as Associate. At least a decade younger than him too.

Simon. Under pressure, Kara had provided a name for her shag-mate. Pure coincidence of course. But somehow he pictured the slick bastard as a Simon-clone. An energetic go-getter with full head of hair, his gym-sculpted body sweating confidence from every pore.

'Have you heard from your Richie recently?' Simon asked, overly chummy. His management training showed. David's eyes skidded to the photo of Richie at eleven attracting dust at the back of his desk; he'd never added one of Sean. At the edge of his vision he caught the flash of a green envelope. *New mail.*

He heard himself adopt an upbeat, indulgent tone as he gave an account of Richie's latest phone call. 'Chile at the moment.' His heart sank as he forced his lips to smile and offer basic details. He had so badly wanted for Richie the things that he'd achieved. 'A' levels in quantitative subjects. A degree from a respectable Uni. A lucrative career. But Richie wanted none of it. Dropping out of sixth form, he'd set off backpacking for a year, working bars and farms as he went. It hadn't helped of course the fast-fire arguments and fist-tight tension between David and Kara.

Sean's arrival – the disruptive havoc of a baby – had been the final tipping point. Though Kara refused to think so. She remained convinced it was all somehow David's fault: 'You never let him be himself, always suffocating him with *your* expectations.'

'First thing tomorrow then,' Simon reiterated as he retreated.

Finally!

David turned to look at his screen. His hand hovered over the mouse.

Results the header of his email said.

Having not been busy, now he was. Having been unable to concentrate, his thoughts were laser sharp. From a corner of his mind came the bleat that he ought to ring Kara and warn her he'd be late. The intention never quite translated into action. Not as if he was accountable to her for every second.

He stayed in the office until gone eight. Later than he needed to really, producing not so much an outline as a pretty full draft, explaining with great enthusiasm why *R&B Economics* were ideally suited for the consultancy job in Melbourne and picturing himself escaping out there for a month or more.

Afterwards, he headed to the pub; he'd not done that for years, sitting at a table on his own, watching the groups of joshing colleagues and the hand-holding couples while slowly sipping his way through a cold, clear pint. He bought a second pint. And then a third.

He gazed round at the wood and bare-brick décor and waited for the alcohol to bring clarity to his thoughts. He'd wanted to know and now he did. With 99.9% accuracy. Which was enough certainty for anyone.

But one certainty did not lead to another.

His eyes lingered on an all female group in the corner; he listened to their eruptions of laughter. He tried to imagine being back in the dating game, of an attractive female being gratified by the attentions of a middle-aged, mid-management type. A woman with dramatically black hair swept her gaze his way, then leant in conspiratorially towards her companions, prompting more laughter. He thought about the sheer effort required for seduction.

It was nearly ten when he got back. Kara had every right to be angry: he'd not rung her; he'd kept his phone switched off; his breath was sour with booze. Mentally he listed the complaints that she failed to voice.

'Sorry,' he said. Aware he sounded anything but. 'Got held up at work.'

'It's OK.' Her smile was tight.

He noticed that she'd dressed up a bit more than usual. Her sleek black top clung closely to her breasts; she'd applied make-up. 'I can heat you up something to eat.'

'OK. Thanks.'

She brought him lasagne. Homemade. But it had turned dry and hard at the edges.

She sat beside him while he ate and asked dutiful questions about his day. When he'd finished, she reached to clear away his plate, then hesitated.

Her head was inclined away and in profile he caught a glimpse of the lovely girl he'd fallen in love with and married. All her youthful passions and hesitations. The woman he'd promised to cherish. The woman who had failed to keep her own promises.

It was just a crazy thing, she'd said. She got carried away on champagne and flattery.

'David,' she said now. It overlapped with him: 'I'm tired. I'm going up.'

'I'll join you,' she said.

They undressed wordlessly, faces averted from one another, pulling on thick nightclothes. In bed he lay on his side, his body faced away from her. She shuffled close until her breasts pressed against his back;

he felt her arm reach round his waist and her hand coming to rest on his thigh. Perhaps he might have tried to stir himself if he'd thought this was an expression of her own desire. Rather than yet another weary effort.

Her caressing fingers began to irritate him and his hand reached down and took hold of hers and moved it. 'I'm tired,' he repeated.

She shifted back a little, breaking body contact, and both of them lay very still.

'David,' she said again. The radiators clunked a final goodnight call. 'This isn't really working is it?' Her voice was slow and sad.

'I don't know.'

'I can't change it. I wish I could. I wish I could go back and for it not to happen.'

'Even if it meant not having Sean?'

'Yes.' She said it too quickly.

She was lying, he knew that. He thought of the way her face melted and the lines faded as she exchanged caramel smiles with Sean. 'But it needn't mean that,' she continued. 'We can do the test, if you want.' She sounded flat and defeated. 'I mean if it will make a difference. We can find out for certain.' It was her last hope, he thought, trying to believe in the fifty-fifty and willing it to be heads, not knowing he'd already seen the way the coin fell.

His impulse to tell her was only momentary. 'I don't know. I need to sleep.'

But he lay there, not sleeping. Her breath was shallow and he thought she might be crying, but he wasn't sure. And then her breathing deepened to a slumbering wheeze. The hours passed slowly; he was worn out, but he couldn't sleep.

She'd never been cross enough to blame him for what had happened, but perhaps he had been partly at fault. Too distracted by his own disappointments to notice their growing distance. *Champagne and flattery.* It had been a long time since he had offered her either of those things. He had stopped paying proper attention, thinking once-a-week perfunctory sex counted as intimacy.

He heard the first faint cry from the nursery next door. With Richie he had got up in the night sometimes, bringing him back to Kara to be

226

fed, walking him back and forth in the dark to settle him. Doing his bit. He'd not done that with Sean.

Kara didn't stir.

At the next faint cry, he slid out of bed. Not as if he could sleep anyway. He headed for the small room which until recently had been a study and still contained tall bookcases, their shelves bowed down with folders. The tins of duckling-yellow paint he'd bought were still sitting in the shed. Another unfulfilled promise. Sean was lying on his back, crying only intermittently, warning signals for what would come if no one came running to satisfy his needs. But he stopped, his eyes big and wide when he saw David; he lifted up an arm, his fingers stretching out like a starfish. David picked him up, placed him over one shoulder and walked cautiously down the stairs. He remembered the time he'd slipped carrying Richie, and the bouncing, bruising descent, in which his reflex was to hug the baby safe, with no attempt to break his own fall.

Everything was neatly laid out on the kitchen counter. Kara had tried breast-feeding, but it had all been harder than with Richie and she'd recently relented and given in to formula-milk. The bottle was already washed and sterilised, but needed ninety seconds in the microwave to be sure. He'd watched the routine often enough. He stopped the timer just before the ping. The cartons were more expensive than the powder, but worth it to simplify the night routine. The milk didn't even need heating because Sean was happy with it at room temperature. He was a happy, easy baby generally.

But he wasn't David's happy, easy baby. To an accuracy of 99.9% the baby was not his. He tried to access his just sense of rancour and betrayal. Sean had twisted his head round and was watching as David poured the milk one-handed into the bottle. With his big eyes and rounded cheeks he was an appealing baby. His dark fluff of hair and olive skin had a look of Kara, mixed up, of course, with something of the Simon-bastard clone.

David tilted the bottle, making sure the teat was free of air. He started feeding Sean, watching the small cheeks suck in and out in needy spurts. *I wish I could go back and for it not to happen.* Kara's words replayed. He felt the solid reality of flesh-and-blood-and-bones

227

weighing down his arms and tried to imagine the baby dissolving, ceasing to be. The teat slipped out of Sean's puckered lips as he paused. His eyes were wide with trust as he offered a guileless, gummy smile to David.

It mattered, David thought; it was much better to know. It mattered, yet nothing had really changed. Not as if a baby truly belonged to anyone anyway.

With one finger he stroked the petal-soft cheek. 'I will try,' he said, his voice sounding loud in the nocturnal quiet. It felt a feeble type of promise. But he would try to be there to help Sean grow into himself. At least any shortcomings wouldn't be down to David's faulty genes. He felt an unexpected lightness at the thought.

Sean's body bucked as he transferred his gaze; David's eyes followed to where Kara had appeared in the doorway, her features blurred with sleep, her hair a soft halo.

'He looks very content,' she said, her eyes focussed on the baby. 'He does have a look of you.'

'Yeah,' David said. 'Perhaps.' He would try harder with Kara too. But he didn't see the need to start confessing.

Night Nine

- Tim Mitchell -

Night Seven

It's getting closer, doc. Whatever it is. It wakes me in the small hours – between two and three. It's happened every night for a week, but now the times are synchronising. Three nights in a row between 2.30 and 2.35. And last night less than thirty seconds after the night before. Once I'm awake now, I don't sleep again. I don't know what it wants. I just lie there in the silence, eyes open in the dark. Brain fizzing and crackling, terrified.

'Write about it,' was your advice yesterday, wasn't it, doc? 'Put it down on paper and stare at it. Work towards a conclusion.' Well, that's what I'm doing. But it's not getting me anywhere. I won't stop, though. You told me how important it is to persevere, didn't you?

I'm up here at the top of the house now, up in the attic room, pinned under the roof. I moved here when it started. It's not just the nights I spend here, either, I'm here during the daytime, too. I've got the TV, computer games, movies, comics. Trying to keep my mind filled with junk. An old habit, as you know. One, though, I'm having trouble keeping up.

After I came back from the clinic, doc, after they'd 'cured' me – I think it was six years ago now, but I have so many problems with time – I used to live my life down on the ground floor. Drinking and smoking with the guys. They were still hanging on then, hoping to get the band together again. Once they'd all drifted away, though, I moved up a couple of floors, up to the bedrooms, and hung out there, smoking and sleeping. On my own, mostly – there was the odd girl. I spent years like that. And now I'm up here, alone all the time, not smoking and hardly sleeping.

There are rats behind the boarding in the attic. Yesterday morning at four I heard a scurrying and a rush and a surge of claws up there, like a dog after a rabbit. At midday I went and looked through the storage door. Grey and brown feathers, a wing and a foot.

Behind me here, in the cupboards, invisible and silent, my old guitars are lined up – eternally patient.

Sometimes when I'm lying awake, I hear pissed-up kids running and screaming down below. Their feet echo and their voices float up and scratch at the air outside my window.

I want it to rain. I want a downpour, a wall of sound.

I'm telling myself that I need to stay awake. It can't come if I'm awake. I tell myself that if I can just keep my eyes open until 2.45 – that's the time I've settled on, doc – then I'll be safe. But I know that's not the way it's going to be. Because I need it to come.

Night Eight

The gap's down to fifteen seconds now. Last night I thought I saw a fur-clad creature squatting on my stomach – incubus, funny man. 'Sleep!' it laughed through teeth gritted from the effort of grinding its buttocks into my pelvis. Behind it I saw William Blake's giant Flea, motionless, with its gold scales and blood bowl. The straight man.

On the table by my bed now, I have a kitchen knife. Russell took my gun away years ago, back in the bad times. I'd been firing it up into the clouds, shooting at the hairy, fallen angels up there, grinning at me. There's also a big pile of your useless foil-wrapped pills on the table, doc, along with that pale-blue, fragrant candle you gave me – was that your idea of a joke?

A few months ago I was out in the neighbourhood, doc. Shuffling along the streets. I do go out occasionally, you know.

Leaning against a shop window, I stopped to watch the world go by. I was holding two fingers up to it from behind a cigarette, one leg drawn up on to the glass. You'll be aware that my balance, even on two legs, is not great. I lost it. My hands and arms wouldn't co-ordinate and I fell and hit my head on the ground. I lay there, dazed. People staring and laughing.

While I was down there, sprawled on the pavement, frowning and squinting, I saw a guy over the road, standing in a doorway. He was looking at me with his head on one side – like a monkey checking out a grub. He was laughing, too – but not like the others. He recognised me. Nobody knows me, doc, not the way I look now – but this guy did. Not only did he know *who* I was, though – he knew *what* I was. What I've become.

Was it then that that all this started, doc? That would make sense. Did he come and find you, that monkey? Did he chatter to you? And did you like what you heard?

Hey, doc, guess what? You won't believe it, I may have been wrong yesterday – about this writing business. I think it may be beginning to work. Perhaps you *were* right after all, you son of a bitch! (How does that make you feel?) Yeah, I tell you, Russell knew what he was doing when he took you on. 'Hey, get a load of this,' he told me the day he brought you round, 'this guy's a doctor, a psychiatrist *and* a hypnotherapist!' He couldn't believe his luck. Three quacks for the price of one.

Russell did all right by you, didn't he, bringing you to me? And how did you reward him? By making me get rid of him. I miss Russell. I know he was past his best by then. I know he had gone soft. But he was my friend. What do you think he's up to now? Do you know where he is? Is he far enough away for you, doc?

I don't like the new guy you found. I hardly *see* him. He just sends me things to sign. Russell used to come round on his bicycle. He'd bring a bottle of red and a couple of joints. Russell kept it all together for me, doc, from breakthrough to breakdown. And then on again, through all the days of my half-life.

He was the one who took the flak when I cancelled the US tour – when everything kicked off. Russell just soaked it all up. I couldn't have climbed into a plane and gone over there, doc – I couldn't even leave my room. I was falling into a hole inside my head. Russell pulled me back from the edge. Helped me fill that hole with rubble and rubbish.

Russell was good back then. It's amazing what he managed to build out of two albums, a few outtakes and a handful of demos – my 'life's work'. Re-releases, remastering, repackaging. Getting my stuff into commercials and onto soundtracks. Persuading people to cover the songs. What a cult I was. I know that things are harder now. I know that something needs to change. I do realise that, doc. I hear you and the new guy talking: 'We need a strategy to energise the market. We've got to stop the drain of resources. We have to free-up some capital.' Well, thanks to your writing therapy, doc, something is changing. I'm starting to think about the rubble in my mind. And what would happen if it were removed. Would I be back on the edge then – with you two watching and waiting for me to fall? Is that the new strategy, doc?

Nothing moves in this room now. I can't even hear the rats any more. They've smelt danger and they've gone. They don't want to die. But hey, get this, doc – I don't want to die, either. And I'm not going to. I can't just get up and leave, though, like them. All this – the waking and the stillness and the quiet – it's a preparation for something. Something I need to confront. And I'm not scared of it any more

Night Nine

It's ten o'clock. I'm waiting.

I sat in the conservatory this morning. The sun was pouring through the glass. I was dozing. Suddenly there was a bang on the roof. I opened my eyes. Through the windows I saw a flurry of feathers – a sparrowhawk was wheeling in the air, six feet away from me. It fell to the ground, gathered itself, eyed me and then flew, flat, down the garden, and up into the apple tree. For a second it sat on one of the branches. Then it shot up into the sky. I went out of the conservatory. Outside there was a handful of tiny, brown feathers scattered on the ground. I gathered them up and brought them upstairs. I put them in a jar on top of the TV. Neatly patterned, pretty feathers.

Then I climbed up here to the top of the house and opened the cupboards. And there they were, my beautiful guitars – shimmering in the light, under their gauze of dust. A long line of them. An infinity of guitars. I hauled out the old Gretsch acoustic for the first time in years, rubbed it down, leant it against the wall and stared at it.

Then I picked it up and held its body against my chest. The fingers of my left hand began to move along its neck. The fingers of my right began to stroke the strings. Can you believe what happened then, doc? A melody came into my head. And words began to form. I wrote a song, doc! Just like that. My first song for nearly *ten years*. See, I remember how long it's been since I did *that*. Do you want to know what it's about? OK, I'll tell you. It's about a doctor and a monkey.

Yes, something's happening all right, doc – but not what you expected.

So, I'm sorry I didn't answer the door when you came round this morning, but I was busy.

This will be the final night. The end to all this.

I know now what it's been doing. It's been using time to find a place in my mind, to zero in on the rubbish and the rubble and choose the right spot to dig. It's going to clear that hole.

I stare wide-eyed at the clock.

It's 2.43. I snap upright in my bed and look at the wall. All is quiet here underneath the roof.

But something has happened – inside my head. The rubble has gone, doc. But that doesn't mean I'm going to fall through that hole – sorry. Because there's light pouring up through it and it's projecting images on to the roof of my skull.

Images of the dressing room before the final gig of the last British

235

tour.

The guys getting ready – beating drumsticks, punching shoulders, slapping walls.

Russell comes in, grinning. He says the touts and the kids are scrapping outside in the rain, and we laugh. He digs out a French roll from the landslide of food on the table and begins to tear at it. We grab our guitars.

When we hit the stage, there's a wall of sound from the punters – and they leap and shove as they scream. We give them a sixty-minute sonic onslaught, and they're in ecstasy. They want more, of course – but it's not going to happen. This tour's over for us. The next time we play will be in America. It's the world we want now.

But first it's back to the dressing room and those other tables, piled high with booze.

I leave the after-show party after an hour. I need to walk around on my own. My head's bursting.

I'm out wandering through the city, a cool breeze aerating my mind.

A backstreet. The entrance to a club. Girls are coming out, clattering on high heels and jangling at the wrists as they clutch at each other's arms. Difficult, you'd think, doc, to prise one apart from her friends? To pick her off and carry her away? Not for me. She doesn't quite know who I am – actually, she's in a bit of a state – but she's sure I'm somebody. A few words are all I need. I take her elbow and we're away, the streetlights turning her skin dark gold.

Back at her place, clothes are spread across her bed and draped over the chairs – little skirts and coloured tights, wool jumpers. On the floor, I get busy with the spoon and the needle. And then she stands up, swaying slightly – and shakes her head. And then she says, 'No'. I look at her in disbelief. I tell her there are people who would kill to get their hands on this. She's wearing – hang on, doc, it's coming back to me – yes, she's wearing a pink ruched top and pale blue jeans. She has brown hair over tiny ears, blue eyes. I talk to her quietly. I stroke her arm. I brush her cheek. Finally she says, 'OK'. Maybe I say, 'Good girl'.

Afterwards she leans back on the bed. There's a sly smile on her face.

I've seen those smiles before. I've seen smiles like that in the *mirror*.

Later I turn my head and I look at her. She's very still. Her eyes are closed. I crawl over, and I shake her shoulder. I pinch her cheek. Then I pick her up – she's very light. Is her name Julie? Judy? I lay her on the floor and breathe into her. Yes – Judy. Doesn't get on with her mother. Left home at sixteen. Her doll-like breasts swell once. Her eyes open. Then her chest subsides and her eyes stay wide and round and empty. The digital display on her pink plastic alarm clock says 2.33.

I slip out of the door, close it slowly and take the stairs down. It's quiet outside. Peaceful. Outside her block I walk quickly across the concrete. The moon is right above. Up near her room the trees shiver. From a balcony somewhere, a laugh floats out.

You really should leave here, doc. Quick. You and the new guy. And you should take the monkey with you. But thanks for your help with the rubble. The hole's closing up now. Things are knitting back together.

What does that mean for you, do you think? Maybe you're not sure. Well, perhaps you could put something down on paper and stare at it – work towards a conclusion? But will you have the time? Can you get far enough away?

Yes, you really should leave now, doc. Put your scales and blood bowl in your bag and run.

Eleanor: The End Notes

– David Rose –

I am, at last, only too ready to confess. It has been, over the years since her death, a bigger burden than I had hitherto realized. I am happy to relinquish it.

Hard to know how or where to begin. Perhaps obviously, with the Delius, which is also where it ended.

An unseasonal frost, thick as snow until the sun's arrest. A municipal hall with quite atrocious acoustics, agonizing decay. And very hard seats. But heaven.

It's a strange work, isn't it? the Delius, one I had never cared for really. But with a wayward Nordic beauty that suited Eleanor perfectly. Right from the serenely passionate opening, she 'had' the work. Even that normally rather clumping accompanied cadenza was fleet and light.

I knew even before the concert it was hers. I arrived early, as was my practice, slipped round the side of the hall to listen through the windows to the final run-through. Always the test of an artist's mettle, as the adrenalin is just beginning to flow and the nerves are still in abeyance, before sight of the audience. I couldn't see her through the high windows, curtained against the dazing light. Nonetheless, I fell in love, impossible suitor though I would have made.

241

And then, when she strode into the hall, pale faced, bare armed, brown hair tossed back, and stood, and I looked at her feet below the velvet skirt, I knew. You can tell so much, can't you, from a musician's stance, a violinist's especially.

Then the attack. Despite the orchestra, largely amateur, the insecure pulse from the semipro conductor, she just...floated through. The Scotch snap was perfection, the cadenza, as I said, and the ending, when the music dissolves into Northern light - I had to cover my ears from the crassness of the applause. But she was there, still half caught in reverie, half radiant against that applause, face lifted, violin at her side.

I had to leave. There was Holst to follow. Mercifully not The Planets. I think it was the overture to The Perfect Fool, so, though a dedicated Holstian, I had to leave.

I didn't want to meet Eleanor that evening. I had instructed the friend who had tipped me off not to tell her I was to be present, to protect both parties from disappointment.

I decided instead to write, suggest as drily as I could the recording contract, only later to tell her what it meant to me. I was afraid, above all of gushing. God knows, I'm gauche enough without that.

I didn't, when I wrote, specify the work to be recorded, and on meeting her, we were both agreed it wouldn't be the Delius. We were both afraid the essential spontaneity would be lost in the studio. We decided instead on the Walton. But the decision at least enabled me to tell her how much the performance meant to me. I suggested we went back to it in a few years' time.

I also suggested, as a sort of emotional seal to the contract, taking her to meet May Harrison.

May had known Delius, indeed he'd written the Double Concerto for her and her sister Beatrice, and completed, with Fenby's help, the third violin sonata for May. She had by then been long retired and was being cared for by her younger sisters. There was a childlike Bohemianism about all of them - all sharing a bedroom and speaking only French to each other - that I thought would appeal to Eleanor.

So the following Sunday, after a set-to with the starter, we motored down. I sat in the garden with the sisters and the dogs (they bred them) while May and Eleanor talked and laughed and dipped into scores.

On the way home I determined that when funds permitted, in lieu of a proposal, I would commission a work for Eleanor herself.

It seemed feasible at the time. My little label wasn't doing badly. In those days, to the public at large classical music meant Mantovani, while to classical lovers 'pop' music also meant Mantovani, so one could find one's niche, and recordings of light music subsidized the serious side, the 'hobby' side, as my friends liked to say.

At the time, I had just signed a pianist to rival Russ Conway, and was anticipating a modest return.

Alas, a few contre-temps developed over the contract, an agent appeared out of the blue, and I barely broke even. So the commission - and the Walton - had to be filed under Action Later.

Fortunately I hadn't mentioned the commission to Eleanor, so it didn't affect our friendship. I accompanied her when I could (not musically, that is), mostly the chamber music/church hall haul, but she loved it, every recital a hurdle.

I helped too with her repertoire, made suggestions. I introduced her to the Finzi Introit - do you know it? A lovely work, well within the scope of amateur orchestras.

She had also taken in the Delius sonatas; they were to be her first recording. They weren't easy to squeeze onto one LP, so I had reason to be proud as well. They attracted perceptive reviews and sold moderately well through the Delius Society.

But I was anxious, more than she, for a full-blooded concerto, a real hit. So I succumbed, brought out a record of old standbys - Parry, Elgar miniatures, Gardiner, and of course Eric Coates. OverCoates, as we called him in the trade, as his music helped more than one label to keep out the draughts. Thankfully it sold well on account of his wireless theme tunes, and at last the Walton could go ahead.

There was an instant set-back - a mix-up over the orchestral parts, the publishers sending those of the Viola concerto, later justifying themselves by blaming my writing (I was, not uncommonly, between secretaries at the time) but after that it went swimmingly. Eleanor, bless her, worked so hard. She was even more of a perfectionist than I realized. She had a fierce frailty that made me worry. She was never satisfied.

Her opening was superb, the wistful sognando beautifully caught. But she had some difficulty with the lilting theme halfway in, due, I guessed, to nerves, poor love. I suggested we redo the passage. She wanted to replay the whole movement. I had to gently explain that although that was a luxury we could afford in the sonatas, with just a pianist to pay, orchestral time cost money.

Foolishly I told her of Klemperer's remark to his daughter when asked to put down some patching for a live recording - Lotte, ein schwindel. She often thereafter used that against me, laughingly mostly. But I explained that we were all after perfection, engineers too. She took the point.

We did some more patching in the fiendishly hard second movement, but by the last movement she had relaxed, and I decided to allow the first take to stand.

I had thought of her doing the Walton sonata as coupling, but I decided to wind her down gently, like a racehorse, so I kept on the orchestra and we did Portsmouth Point and Scapino, Eleanor playing on the first desk.

After I had finished the master tape I asked her to listen to it with me. She refused. She said she was afraid of all the mistakes she'd pick out. She always preferred live performances where the mistakes would be carried by the inspiration of the moment, forgotten.

She asked if the patches were discernible. I answered that they weren't, that I was as much a perfectionist as she, and, dare I say it, as talented in my own field. She then said simply,

'Are you satisfied, Cecil?'

I said I was. That was enough for her. She never, to the end, played her recordings.

She trusted me, do you see? And that trust made my betrayal possible.

When I think back, remember her talent, the frailty of her talent, of all talent...

To celebrate the release of the recording I took her to Fortnum and
Mason's for tea. Eleanor, bless her, insisted on buying me a new tie, as
the one I was wearing somehow got wet as I poured the tea. I still have
both ties in my rack.

The record had some gratifying reviews, and sold over the months.
Our only sadness was that May was now long dead; Eleanor could no
longer repay her encouragement with her own success.

But she had friends aplenty, all pleased with her. We began to plan
further recordings, plan her career, as they'd say today, although in
those days it was just a case of getting on with the next job. And there
were plenty of them now, on the strength of her acclaim.

She was widening her repertoire all the time - the Szymanowski First,
his Mythes for violin and piano (new to me), the Fauré sonatas. And I
was introducing her to some of the overlooked English works I felt it
my vocation to champion.

Then came one of those serendipities that change everything.

I mentioned, apropos Delius' The First Cuckoo in Spring,' the story
of May's sister Beatrice and her nightingale.

Beatrice used to invite friends and organize weekends for deprived
children at her Surrey cottage, and give outdoor cello recitals in the
evenings. At one such, a nightingale responded and a duet ensued.

This happened again and again, in fact became a reliable occurrence.
Word got to the BBC, who sent a van and recording engineer to tape
it. It was the first outside broadcast, and later relayed round the world,
at popular request.

Eleanor was utterly enchanted. She wanted to do likewise. She
obtained a score of Messiaen's Catalogue d'Oiseaux, and transcribed
some of them for violin.

With some misgiving, I loaded a recorder and spare battery into the
car boot, with a hamper, and we trundled down to Windsor Great
Park.

A lovely hazy summer evening. She played and played but no bird
sang.

Just as we were going to call it a day, a robin flew down and perched
on her bow. She was childlike in her delight. Alas no song, then it flew
away. But she was happy.

We had a half bottle of wine and sandwiches on the grass, in the setting sun.

We got back to the car only to find that with the weight of the recorder and the unmade road, we had had a puncture. I set to changing the wheel.

It took longer than I expected. I explained to Eleanor that being a recording engineer is not the same as repairing a car or designing the Forth Bridge. Luckily she seemed to have a knack with spanners, so, despite a little oil on her dress, it didn't spoil the trip.

On the way home I hit on the idea of getting hold of some bird identification recordings, overlaying them with Eleanor's playing in call and response duets, and issuing them on EP.

But I felt a record needed something substantial, so I decided to have her do Vaughan Williams' Lark Ascending and issue it with the bird duets on a ten inch LP.

She was wonderful in the VW, strong and agile in the soaring notes, fragile in the climb.

In preparing the recording, I had the inspired idea of adding some snatches of actual larksong after the closing bars. I worried about complaints from the VW Society, but in the event they seemed happy. Unfortunately I did have complaints, from Messiaen's publishers over the transcriptions. The whole situation became - if I may risk a pun in a mea culpa - a messy'un, but we eventually came to an agreement on royalties. Messiaen himself, I later heard, was charmed.

In the meantime, the record sold, sold like hot cakes, as you may remember, sold to all sorts and across the board. Apart from the money, it also made Eleanor's name, and meant she could record more substantial fare.

With the proceeds from that and an LP of a negro choir doing arrangements from My Fair Lady I decided to treat Eleanor to a new violin.

I had heard through contacts of one going, by William Robinson of Plumstead, an admired name in the trade. I telephoned the dealer and motored down to Guildford.

Nothing has ever given me greater pleasure than presenting her with that violin. A beautiful thing, pure-toned, crackle-free varnish. It's the

instrument you hear on all her recordings from then on: the
Szymanowski First, the Bax, the Elgar/Walton sonatas...

But that is to anticipate. Before those records came that silvered
cloud that changed my life. Our life.

I had promised to attend a recital she was giving in Dorking, and
arrived a little disheveled. I had contrived to lock myself out some days
before, and as the landlord was away, was reduced to sleeping in my
mixing studio. My chequebook being with my keys, I had sufficient
readies for a pair of clean socks and a vest. My shirt I had washed in
the basin and hung on a cable (it was still damp round the collar).

That was the occasion, and probably the reason, for Eleanor's
proposing. What she proposed was not so much marriage as 'taking
me in hand' but who was I to argue semantics?

You can imagine perhaps, though I doubt it, how I felt.

We planned the quietest of register office weddings, but somehow her
friends found out and as we left the office they were waiting, armed
with confetti they had made from an old orchestral score. We were
showered with minims, crochets and quavers.

They told us later the score was Bluebeard's Castle. I said I had never
been married before.

Then they dragged us to a makeshift reception in a scout hall; cold
buffet with white wine and cider and impromptu performances of
Mendelssohn and Bach, culminating in improvised csardas in which
Eleanor, after several ciders, proved astonishingly uninhibited.

I know all this sounds too jolly, too joyous, for a confession, but it's
important that you understand, understand what came later.

From then on we were inseparable. I was there at every concert, every
curtain call, awaiting every flushed return. That year we recorded the
Szymanowski, coupled with Wienawski to follow the Polish theme.
Then she started learning the Bax, by way of tribute to May Harrison.
But I still cherished my original ambition, and decided to fulfil it for
our first anniversary.

By then Beatlemania was in full spate, but there were still sufficient middle-aged music lovers to appeal to. I managed to secure the Joe Loss Orchestra for an album of arrangements from Bandwagon. I called it Losst In Transit, which I like to think helped it strike a chord, and it sold steadily for some months.

With weeks to spare I popped the surprise to Eleanor - a commissioned work of her own - and asked her for suggestions.

We deliberated for some time. Neither of us had any idea whom to approach. We had recently heard a concerto on the wireless by Malcom Williamson, liltingly elegiac, indeed written as an elegy to Edith Sitwell.

We duly wrote to him care of the BBC. Unfortunately he had by then embarked on an operatic follow-up to his Covent Garden success the previous year, didn't want the distraction.

Then Eleanor was told of a Polish composer living in England, living in fact on a houseboat at Twickenham, who had in his Polish past won the Szymanowski Prize. It seemed an omen.

We motored down to Richmond and walked along the towpath to Twickenham, hoping to locate him. Eleanor seemed to think if we could see a houseboat with a piano we had found him. I was dubious.

Eventually we gave up, visited Marble Hill House, and walked the twilit towpath to Twickenham Bridge.

Luckily a friend of Eleanor's who had played under him in Birmingham gave us the name of his publisher and we wrote.

His reply was charming but a little evasive. Could we specify what we had in mind? He had several works he needed to finish or revise, and didn't wish to stray far from their sound worlds.

We specified only that the violin be prominent and the forces small, a chamber work, ideally, but otherwise he had carte blanche.

What resulted was 'Peripeteia' for violin, bassoon and triangle.

I must admit my heart sank when I first saw the score, but from such unpromising materials a masterpiece had been written, poignantly exploiting the contrasting timbres. In the first movement (there were only two) the contrast was between the violin's kaleidoscopically changing three-note motif and the almost static, tethered range of the bassoon's four notes; between the stridently lyrical, mercurial violin and the bassoon's phlegmatic gruffness, punctuated by the triangle's rills. I liked to liken it to Cassius Clay versus Sonny Liston, the triangle acting as timekeeper-cum-referee. But at least one of Eleanor's friends saw in it a portrait of our marriage, which rather upset her.

In the second movement (I take it you haven't heard the work), a palindromic reversal of the first also reverses the roles, the bassoon gaining a dour, conciliatory eloquence, the violin now muted, wistful, the triangle chiming metronomically throughout. And this, this - premonitory though we did not know it - proved the more accurate portrait. But that again is to anticipate.

Eleanor, poor angel, set to and learnt her part. How hard she struggled at first, the idiom being so outside her usual range. But she mastered it. And we had found an excellent bassoonist, not the least phlegmatic himself, in fact most rehearsals ended in hi-jinks over a bottle of wine. (It was the triangle player who was somewhat dour, dry at least - a Euclidean temperament, Eleanor said.)

They premiered the work in Windsor and we recorded it the following day with, I'm glad to say, very little patching - 'quilting' as Eleanor called it.

We coupled it, for contrast, with Malcolm Arnold's Sea Shanties for Violin and Accordion. It didn't sell as well as we hoped, but it brought her heightened respect as an adventurous artist. I felt immensely proud, of her and of myself.

Perhaps that pride was hubris? For soon after, tragedy, as they say, struck. Actually less of a strike, more a gradual attrition.

We were trying to decide on a follow-up to the Szymanowski. Eleanor at length chose the Prokofiev First, for its similar fairy-tale quality, and I booked the orchestra and venue.

No problems showed up in the rehearsals, but the recording...

She was exquisite in the hushed, magical opening, agile in the pizzicato. But when the first theme returns softly on solo flute (you know the passage, I'm sure) her accompanying ornamentation was marred by a succession of sharp intakes of breath. I put it down to nerves or indigestion, or the fact that she was more closely miked than usual, and we were able, after several attempts, to patch it.

I detected it again in the scherzo, but as that is more raucous, it didn't intrude. The last movement gave me a few problems, and Eleanor seemed unusually tense, but determined to come up with a perfect take. Eventually we succeeded.

I was then taken up with the usual post-recording work, and Eleanor always made a point of practising alone, so we made no mention of it all.

But at her next concert a few months later - she was doing the Bax - I thought I heard, from the front row, the same wince. The audience hadn't seemed to notice so I shrugged it off.

A week later she gave a chamber recital of Fauré and Grieg. Then it was unmistakable.

They say every marriage is a secret to those outside it. But to one inside it too, especially one as ill-prepared for marriage as I.

And that tragedy brings you closer. The closeness was an embrace across barbed wire. I became more solicitous, but had to work hard to hide it. Eleanor had perhaps the harder part, of pretending not to know that I knew, although in point of fact I knew very little. I tried to put it down as my over-reaction to an undeserved happiness.

Eleanor carried on her fiercely independent self-hood, practising alone behind locked doors. So we kept up that embrace. Until the day I noticed the door unlocked.

I listened outside for a while to her playing, then peeped inside to catch unawares her hair being tossed in concentration.

The room was empty.

Full, rather, of her presence, emanating from a tape recorder. From the spool I could tell she hadn't been gone long, but could afford to be away for an hour or so. I closed the door and leant against the wall.

Driven after several drinks to the despicable, I found her diary. For that day, just a time. I traced back, those similar bald entries over several months, back to the first, of both name and time. Appointments with her doctor.

I cried in both relief and worry.

That was when the strain began in earnest. Unable to confront her
with my compromised knowledge, yet not knowing exactly what that
knowledge was, save from a glimpsed bottle of painkillers in her
handbag, I was forced to second-guess her decisions, make tactful
suggestions...

It was clear from her whimpers and grimaces, clear to me at least,
that concerts were proving a trial, that she couldn't keep them up.
How to tell her, or rather, enable her to tell me?

I put it to her that I still had so much repertoire I wanted her to 'put
in the can' for me that perhaps, for my sake, she could forego live
performances for a while. She finally agreed.

I knew it wouldn't be easy. Those whimpers of pain, of which I think
she was quite unaware, would necessitate endless takes, tactful
patching. Her views on that hardened. Needing the recording sessions
as surrogate concerts, she craved whole, unblemished takes, the sweep
of perfection. I had to defend the endless fiddle, the stop-and-start, the
cumulative piecemeal perfection. I realized how unsatisfying that type
of perfection is for an artist.

I had to argue that she was being selfish, that there is the subjective
perfection of the artist, but also that of the listener, that there is the
need to create, sustain, a momentary perfection to redeem the
ramshackle, humdrum life of contingency that most of us live. That,
ultimately, it is the achieved artefact that is important to the world,
whatever that means.

We were recording the Lennox Berkeley at the time. The endless
battles with the cantus firmus in the Lento, the tears of frustration as I
rejected what to her were perfect takes, wore us both down. Eventually
I cobbled together a reasonable tape and we called it a day.

I insisted on her taking a break for a while, but she soon fretted to get
back to work, so we started on the Prokofiev Second, to complete the
set.

On the second night she went straight to bed, taking a painkiller, for
a headache, she said. I went in later, watched over her bed. One hand
under her cheek, the other arm thrown back, her hair floating on the
pillow, she was sleeping fitfully, her lips shaping little soundless cries.

That was when I thought the unthinkable.

251

Next morning I stopped her a few times in the run-through of the Andante, then gave her her head in the take.

At the end she looked up, waiting for the retakes. No, it's fine, I said, 'in the can'. Let's press on.

On the way home I said quietly, I've capitulated.

That evening I got out the Schwann catalogue.

It's a bit like horsebreeding, a question of pedigree.

Tracing the lineage, the stables, who had studied with whom. Eleanor had studied with Warburg who had studied under Enescu who also taught Menuhin ... And so forth.

It was, I suppose you would say today, like getting a DNA match. Not exact, but near enough to tweak.

So I obtained a recording of the work (I won't tell you whose) and, with some judicious adjustment of the balance, I spliced in the necessary passages, altered the speed a little so the graft 'took'. I would always be aware of the grafts, but I was confident that the results were no more artificial than the usual patching. It was the nearest to perfection I could achieve under the circumstances.

But what next?

Our original intention had been to record neglected works of the English repertoire - the Havergal Brian, the Britten, Holst's Double Concerto, Rubbra's sonatas. That was no longer possible. For where would I obtain the grafting stock?

I had to tactfully steer Eleanor away from that idea, persuade her of the need to prove her mettle in the standard repertoire.

Thus we did the Mendelssohn, the Brahms, two of the Mozarts. The patches, the grafts, were getting longer, but by careful choice of stock, and care in sending out the review copies, I got away with it. But for how long? Her stamina was depleting, though the resolve was still there.

Then came the moment I had been dreading. She brought up my promise to record her in the Delius. Perhaps sentimentally as well as artistically, she was determined to hold me to it.

What the hell to do? There were so few recordings to draw on. The Pougnet/Beecham of 1946 was too well known, too distinctive.

What else was there?

Then, almost in despair, I came across a reference to yours. I wrote to your company's distributor in Sweden for a copy.

It was - is - a wonderful performance. You may suspect flattery in that, but to counterfeit a phrase, plagiarism is the sincerest form of flattery.

I found it pure-toned, coolly lyrical, so similar to my memories of Eleanor's performance. And, luckily from my view, unknown outside Scandinavia.

I arranged the venue and orchestra and we began recording. I took the precaution of setting Eleanor well forward from the orchestra - the close-miking now would hardly matter.

In spirit she was inspired. But as I feared, I was able to use hardly any of it. I got her to repeat a few passages for form's sake. But the finished record was, I have to confess, almost entirely yours.

Not the opening bars, though. Those were hers, and are sublime, as I hope you'll agree. If only she'd been able to maintain...

None of this is meant in mitigation. I just want you to understand.

I delayed the release as long as I could, but Eleanor became increasingly impatient as she declined. I gave in, coupled it with the still unreleased Berkeley and brought it out. I sent out only limited review copies. Ironically, they were very well received, you will be pleased to hear.

It sold moderately well for a while, then went the way of most recordings - n.l.a. in the catalogues.

So it would, should, have remained, had I not been foolishly persuaded to re-release it on compact disc in her memory. That decision, and the boy's own sleuthing in the musical press - but no! It's as well it was found out. I have opportunity to make amends, to you at least. And I'll be with Eleanor the sooner.

I hope this letter reaches you still alive.

-O-

Brockleby-Barr my dear sir,

How gratifying your package, I found. My eyes give trouble in these late days, so I played first the disc before reading your letter. Thankfully. For I was entranced.

Yes, they are not my opening bars, and this threw me off the scent, as you say. But how assured, how beautifully judged. And later too, the yearning, infinity pitied passages of the slow movement, so sadly lovely. The arpeggios in the cadenza, the 4/4 dance rhythms of the scherzo, so hard to make lyrical - these I admired.

Then my attention snagged (is this correct?) on the clarinet's second figure in the closing bars. He plays an A. It should have been A flat. I was reminded of a similar mistake in our recording. A coincidence? An error in the score?

And the violin's fading close - not as whispering as I would have liked.

Then I summoned my attention to your letter, to discover this was indeed my own performance. What strange elation I felt at first.

Your Scottish poet tells of the gift to see ourselves through other's eyes, or ears. This, my dear sir, is what you gave me. And how proud it made me for a time. For the praise of others is a poor substitute for one's own self-worth. And that is in normal life denied the artists. We know only the frustration, the failures, the wasted attempts.

My defence lay in giving only public concerts, in giving up recording altogether. My recording company pressed to record my concerts live, but no. I had no wish to preserve my errors with the coughs of auditors on plastic for posterity.

I have not even played your disc again, for the same reason, in fear of all the old dissatisfactions flooding in. Within minutes of the realization it was mine, I was remembering the difficulties of those 4/4 passages, the number of takes, the final abandonment. Also the second, and third, thoughts on the tempi of the cadenza, the linger of the close... All the elation rubbed away.

But for those minutes I was happy, a happiness I had not expected. I had glimpsed of freedom, a moment perfection. I was grateful.

I hope you read my clumsy hand, and that in my turn, this letter finds you still alive.

Unthologists

David Rose was born in 1949 and spent his working life in the Post Office. His debut story was published in the *Literary Review* (1989), since when he's been widely published in magazines, including *Main Street Journal*, for which he became Fiction Editor. His first novel, *Vault: An Anti-Novel* was published by Salt last year, with a short story collection to follow next year.

Sandra Jensen's work has been published in *Word Riot, AGNI, Unthology No. 1, Fleeting, The Irish Times* and others. In 2011 she won the J.G. Farrell award for best novel-in-progress for her first novel, a literary adventure set in Sri Lanka during the 80's. In 2012, the Arts Council of Ireland awarded her a literature bursary to complete this work. She avoids staring at the blank page by educating YouTube commenters about the plight of the slow loris. Contact information is on her website at www.sandrajensen.net.

Sarah Dobbs is a lecturer in Creative Writing whose work has been published, broadcast and performed by *Flax*, the BBC, Bolton Octagon and *SWAMP* Journal. She is currently co-writing a textbook on English and Creative Writing scheduled for publication in 2013. Her first novel *Killing Daniel* is being published by Unthank Books simultaneously with this collection and she is also at work on her third book, *Project Violet*. Follow her @sarahjanedobbs.

Mischa Hiller is the award-winning author of *Sabra Zoo* (Telegram 2010), *Shake Off* (Telegram 2011) and several published short stories.

Gordon Collins has been a market risk analyst in London, a maths lecturer, an English teacher in Japan and a computer graphics researcher specialising in virtual humans. He has three different degrees in mathematics as well as an MA in Creative Writing from the University of East Anglia. He has been published in *Riptide Vol 3*, *Danse Macabre*, *Infinity's Kitchen*, *Liar's League* and the *UEA Creative Writing Anthology 2010*. His first novel, *Extremely Normal*, is about Russell's quest for normality in the face of the imaginary friends that his doctor controls his life with.

Ian Chung is a graduate of the Warwick Writing Programme, soon to begin teacher training. More of his work can be found in *Dr. Hurley's Snake-Oil Cure*, *Foundling Review*, *Ink Sweat & Tears*, *Quarterly Literary Review Singapore*, and *The Cadaverine*, among others. *Camroc Press Review* nominated him for Sundress Publications' *Best of the Net* in 2010. He reviews for various publications, including *Sabotage Reviews*, *The Conium Review* and *The Cadaverine*. He is the founder of *Eunoia Review*, and is also on the editorial teams of *Epicentre Magazine* and *The Cadaverine*. When not editing/reading/writing, he watches more TV than is reasonable for one person and harbours dreams of writing a multi-volume science fiction saga.

Sharon Zink is a former academic of German-Brazilian extraction. Her first poetry collection, *Rain in the Upper Floor Café* was published when she received the title of Shell Young Poet of the Year at the age of seventeen. She has also been named as Writers Inc. Writer of the Year and shortlisted for the Raymond Carver Prize and in *The New Writer* short story competition four times running (including being named as Editor's Choice). Her fiction has appeared in anthologies and journals in the U.K., U.S. and in translation in Mexico and a production of her work at Edinburgh Festival received an award from

The Scotsman. Her first novel, *Sharonville*, is currently under submission while she completes her new book, a NASA-researched literary thriller called *Emptiness*, a chapter from which was published in *The New Writer* in April 2011. You can find more about her writing and work as a literary consultant at www.sharonzink.com.

Ashley Stokes' first novel *Touching the Starfish* was published by Unthank Books in 2010 and his first collection *The Syllabus of Errors, or Twelve Stories about Obsession, Loss and Getting in a State* will be published in February 2013, also by Unthank. Contact information is on his website: www.ashleystokes.net, or follow him on twitter: @AshleyJStokes.

Angela Readman's stories have been published in *Pank, Metazen, Burner, Southword* and *Crannog*, amongst others. In 2011 she won *Inkspill Magazine's* short story Competition and was placed second in The Short Story Competition. In 2012, she won the National Flash Fiction Day Competition. She enjoys telling market researchers she's a taxidermist and looking at pictures of people's desks. She can be found, and lost, on twitter @angelreadman

CD Rose has left a trail of short stories on the web and in books (including *Unthology No 1*). He currently edits *The Biographical Dictionary of Literary Failure* (bdlf.wordpress.com).

AJ Ashworth is from Lancashire and has an MA in Writing from Sheffield Hallam University. She won Salt Publishing's Scott Prize in 2011 and her short story collection *Somewhere Else, or Even Here* was published by them in November of that year. The book has since been longlisted for the Frank O'Connor International Short Story Award and shortlisted for the Edge Hill Short Story Prize.

John Nicholson was born in Scotland and has a degree in chemistry from Edinburgh University. His career in science education took him to Uganda, Cyprus and to UEA. This is where he discovered the delights and freedoms of writing fiction, being inspired and formed by tutors on its Creative Writing Diploma courses. Two of his short stories were published in *Summer Times in the Algarve* (Ed. Lisa Selvidge) and a very short story, *Compost*, in *Staple*. The *Ringing Stone* was written for his wife Ailsa who first told him, fifty years ago, of magical family holidays in Tiree and who took him there recently to see if it was still as lovely. It was.

Philip Langeskov was born in Copenhagen in 1976. He has an MA in Creative Writing from UEA. A recipient of the David Higham Award in 2008, his writing has appeared in various places, including *The Decadent Handbook, Five Dials, The Best British Short Stories 2011* and *The Warwick Review*.

Debz Hobbs-Wyatt is a full time writer/editor/publisher working from her home in the mountains of Snowdonia where she lives with her cats, Cagney and Lacey, and her cocker spaniel, Rosie. She has an MA in Creative Writing and has had several short stories published. She is also seeking an agent for her fourth novel. Debz is a partner and the publicist for Bridge House Publishing, Editor for CaféLit – an online short story site, and the Director of her new venture Paws n Claws Publishing and the PAWS workshops scheme. She edits and critiques for writers and writes a daily Blog all about writing and publishing.

Charles Wilkinson: born Birmingham 1950. Educated at the universities of Lancaster, East Anglia and Trinity College, Dublin. Publications: *The Snowman and Other Poems* (Iron Press, 1978) and *The Pain Tree and Other Stories* (London Magazine Editions, 2000). His stories have appeared in *Best Short Stories 1990* (Heinemann), *Best English Short Stories* (Norton), *Midwinter Mysteries* (Little, Brown) and *Unthology 2* (Unthank Books). His recent work has appeared in *Poetry Wales, Poetry Salzburg, Earthlines, Other Poetry, The Warwick Review, Tears in the Fence, Shearsman, The SHOP* and other literary magazines and anthologies. He lives in Presteigne, Powys.

Sarah Evans has had dozens of stories published in magazines and competition anthologies. In 2011, *The Tipping point* won the Rubery Short Story Competition, *Loving Someone Else* was the winner of the tenth Glass Woman Prize and her story *Stuck* appeared in *Unthology no. 2*. Other stories have been published by Bridport, Earlyworks Press, Bridge House, Writers' Forum and Sentinel Champions Magazine. She lives in Welwyn Garden City with her husband and non-writing interests include walking, opera and dancing.

Tim Mitchell is the author of a novel, *Truth and Lies in Murder Park: A Book About Mr Luke Haines (Benben Press, 2009)*. He has also written books on Jonathan Richman, John Cale and Television. As a musician he has performed and recorded with the poet Jeremy Reed. He has recently completed a novel about spying and is now working on another, based on the life and work of a 17th-century Flemish painter.

Lightning Source UK Ltd.
Milton Keynes UK
UKOW040603190912

199255UK00001B/15/P